MARIGOLDS, MISCHIEF, AND MURDER

a Camelot Flowers mystery

Erica Wynters

D1519905

Acknowledgements

I decided to try my hand at writing a cozy mystery many years ago because of my deep love for the genre. Cozy mysteries were there for me while I was balancing a demanding job in mental health while going to graduate school to become a licensed marriage and family therapist. Cozy mysteries were there for me while I was raising small children and all I could manage was grabbing a few minutes of uninterrupted reading at a time. Cozy mysteries were the escape from stress I needed. They soothed me, entertained me, and kept me going. I hope I captured a portion of that in Gwen's story.

My first go around with writing this book ended with a cozy mystery that read more like a suspenseful rom-com. The basic elements of the cozy mystery were there, but I'd been drawn back to my romance writer roots to such a degree that it looked much more like a romance novel than a mystery. I let the book sit for a couple years while I wrote other romantic suspense novels before picking it up one day almost two years ago and giving it another go. This book looks nothing like the original. The main character doesn't have the same name or the same occupation, but the building blocks of the mystery remained the same.

There are so many people I want to thank. Nichole Evans, who was my critique partner while I wrote the original iteration of this book, and cheered me on through the long writing and editing process. My original beta-readers, Emily, Shelly, Marissa, Tara, and Kristina, who all took the time to read the original version and give me such helpful feedback. I hope you love this version as much as you loved the original. Bethany Stedman, who was my critique partner when I decided to give this a rewrite a try and submit it to my agent. Bethany has spent countless hours on Marco Polo talking me through the rewrite, supporting me when I got emotional about how hard it was, and cheering me on by loving my books and my characters as much as I do.

I'm so grateful for my literary agent, Dawn Dowdle, from Blue Ridge Literary Agency, who saw potential in this book, and worked with me to get it cleaned up in record time to submit for publication. I've heard horror stories from other authors about agents who never get back to them, are hard to reach, and clearly spend the most time on their already established authors. From the very beginning, Dawn has been miraculously speedy at replying, worked hard to create a community among her authors, and has been a champion for my books, including this one.

Dawn and I submitted this book to exactly one publisher, a dream publisher for me, Gemma Halliday Publishing. I discovered Gemma's books years ago, and was so excited to find a mystery series that threaded romance and humor with hunting down murderers. She writes books I love to read and aspire to in my own writing. Gemma and her editor, Susie, saw potential in this book and gave me the chance to edit it to rise to that potential. I'm a better mystery writer because of them, and hope to continue to hone those skills so we can see more adventures with Gwen, Finn, Chris, and Penny. Besides, we need to find out who Gwen will end up with? Team Finn or Team Chris?

And finally, but most importantly my family. My mom read an original version of this book, and helped me get it ready to submit to agents with her detailed eye. She caught a lot of spelling mistakes I'd missed. Both my parents and my sister ask about my writing and show they care. My amazing husband, Ben, who has sacrificed countless hours to me sitting at my computer, supported me going on weekends away to write and edit, and listened to me both when I've been excited and frustrated with the process. My kids, Micah and Savannah, are so excited this book is coming out. They helped me brainstorm titles and are thrilled that something they helped create made it into the book.

Last but certainly not least, I want to thank everyone joined me in the charming, rural and completely fictitious town of Star Junction. While Star Junction, Illinois doesn't exist, I grew up in a small town in Wisconsin that served as a model for Star Junction. I hope you had fun escaping with Gwen and her friends and will be excited to visit again in the future.

MARIGOLDS, MISCHIEF, AND MURDER

CHAPTER ONE

———

"How deep is it? I can't look," Chris said as he squeezed his eyes shut, his palm bloody.

"I can't tell," I said tightly. "You have to hold still." I fought a wave of dizziness as I dabbed at the wound on his hand. "It's not deep. Just long."

"That hurts," Chris complained. He tried to pull his hand away, but I tightened my grip.

"Hold still," I said. I dabbed the cut with a disinfecting wipe. "You're lucky you're not on your way to the hospital for a tetanus shot."

The future youth center looked more like a construction zone. Jagged ends of two-by-fours had been discarded beneath the rusty scaffolding that barely propped up the sagging ceiling. Sawdust floated through the air, filtering the weak winter sunlight as it worked its way through grime-covered windows.

As I shifted my feet, my toe bumped against the wrench that had caused Chris's injury. This place was going to be the death of me. Or the death of Chris. I might kill him for dragging me into this mess. "Maybe you do need a shot," I muttered.

"Believe me, I don't need a shot, Nurse Ratched," Chris said sourly, although his lips twitched in a barely contained smile. That was Chris, finding the humor in every situation.

I opened a bandage and pressed it to the wound. At least he had a first aid kit. "Why am I always taking care of you?" I asked, trying to remain stern but recognizing the way Chris's charm always worked its way under any annoyance I might feel.

The boyish grin that always made my stomach drop like I was riding a roller coaster spread across his face. "Because you love me," he said confidently.

I wrapped gauze around his hand. "Who said anything about love?" I teased.

"Ouch!" Chris clutched his chest as if I'd dealt him a fatal blow. "You really know how to hit a guy where it hurt, Guinevere Stevens."

"No way," I protested. "No pulling out the Guinevere. That's fighting dirty."

Chris's eyes twinkled mischievously. He knew I hated my full name, given to me courtesy of my wonderful father, who also happened to be obsessed with all things King Arthur and the Knights of the Round Table. It was no accident our family business was named Camelot Flowers. At least he hadn't used my middle name too. Then the cut on his hand would be the least of his worries.

"Fine, *Gwen*," he said, relenting. "We both know you love me."

I scooped up the debris from my makeshift nurse's station. "Oh, please," I countered. "What about what's-her-name? Bambi, Tiffany, Crystal? I'm sure she's already in love with you."

Chris chuckled as he scooted off the counter and said, "So, all the women I date have stripper names?"

"What would your mother say if she heard you talking like that?" My words were scolding, but I couldn't keep the grin off my face. I'd walked right into that one.

Chris draped his arm over my shoulder. "It's a good thing she's not here." He scanned the open space, his smile tightening. "Thanks for all your work today. Not many people would spend their day off in this dump."

I could already envision the groups of teens hanging out, having fun, knowing Chris was there to talk them through the most difficult parts of adolescence. I'd given him the same pep talk a dozen times over the past year, but it was clear he needed it again. "This place is exactly what the town needs," I started. "We know what it was like growing up here. It's easy to get into trouble with nothing to do."

"Are you saying I got into a lot of trouble growing up?" Chris teased.

"We both know exactly what you were like in high school," I said with a grin.

Chris picked up the wrench and tossed it into the overflowing toolbox on the counter. "So does everyone else in Star Junction," he said, his tone bitter.

"Forget about everyone else. The people who matter

recognize how much you've changed."

Chris huffed out a breath, as if releasing the weight of everyone else's expectations. His boyish good looks, blond hair, and perpetually sun-kissed skin, even in the middle of an Illinois winter, only amplified his wide grin and cornflower blue eyes.

"You're right," he said. He leaned against the counter, the doubt gone, replaced by the patented Chris Crawford charm. "As usual."

"Don't you forget it," I joked as I brushed at a strand of hair that had fallen out of my ponytail. I caught my reflection in the small mirror Chris had hung above the sink and almost fell over from fright. "Why didn't you tell me I looked like this?" I said in horror.

Chris glanced over from where he was collecting paintbrushes to rinse off. "Looked like what?" he said absently.

I bugged my eyes out at him in disbelief and gestured at my hair, my face, and then my whole body. A fine layer of dust covered my normally honey-brown hair until it looked like I'd prematurely aged in the five hours I'd been helping Chris.

I'd walked in a woman six months away from turning thirty and was leaving looking eighty. There was a streak of what I was praying was dirt but could be some kind of toxic mold under my right eye. My light-blue sweatshirt and black yoga tights were streaked with dust. A mysterious wet patch on the middle of my sweatshirt was concerning since it wasn't wet to the touch. Gross.

Chris shrugged and said, "You look like you worked hard today."

"I have dinner with Penny in…" I glanced at my Apple Watch. "Twenty minutes. I'm probably going to have to wash my hair a dozen times to get all the plaster dust out."

Chris paused in his cleaning and really looked at me. "Where're you guys going for dinner?" he asked.

"Bucky's," I said, not sure where he was going with this line of questioning.

Chris smirked, and I knew some kind of joke was coming. "I guess even that place has standards."

I picked up a shop towel and threw it at him playfully. "That wasn't nice," I said.

"I'm kidding. I'm kidding." He walked over and wrapped me in a hug. "You look like my best friend," he said as he wiped at the smudge under my eye with this thumb. "Dirty hair and all." While his smile was still charming, it was also genuine. "What would I do without you?" he asked.

I melted into his embrace, momentarily forgetting I looked more like a zombie out for brains than a florist helping her friend realize his dream. "Probably die of tetanus," I said into his solid chest.

Chris chuckled, sending a tendril of warmth through my body. He pulled back and patted my arm before moving to gather up the tools lying around the room. "What've you got planned for the rest of the weekend? You know, besides girls' night at Bucky's." Chris grabbed a large screwdriver off the scaffolding and pointed it at me for emphasis. "And why Bucky's? That place is a pit," he added.

"Bucky's might be a little rough around the edges, but we've been going there since high school. It's tradition," I said defensively.

"Some traditions are meant to be broken," Chris said as he set the screwdriver into the toolbox.

"Not this one," I insisted. I tucked my water bottle into my purse.

"Say hi to Penny for me," Chris said as I prepared to leave.

"Sure thing," I said. *Or not. She doesn't need to know I spent all day with you.*

I skirted past a set of sawhorses to reach my jacket and scarf hanging on hooks near the door. As I wrapped the scarf around my neck, the door jerked open, a blast of icy air slapping me in the face.

Justin Hunt barreled into the room, his jeans and work boots dusty, his thick black brows pulled down over dark-brown eyes that flashed with anger. Black hair curled at the nape of his neck, and he sported the olive skin tone of his Italian heritage. "Crawford!" Justin shouted at Chris. "You lying, cheating—" Justin skidded to a stop, annoyance flashing across his face as his gaze met mine. "Gwen," he greeted me, the acknowledgment anything but friendly.

That was fine with me because I wasn't feeling particularly friendly either. Justin may have been a six-foot-three-inch pile of muscle, but I'd known him since we were both toddling around the sandbox in diapers. I didn't care how angry he was. He wasn't going to get away with almost running me over.

"What on earth is wrong with you?" I snapped. "You scared me half to death."

Justin's eyes narrowed into slits. His gaze was fixed on Chris, although he spoke to me. "Sorry," he said, sounding anything but sorry.

I'd never seen Justin and Chris fight. Not like this. "What's going on? Why are you charging in here like a man intent on causing trouble?" I asked.

"Nothing you need to worry about," Justin said. His words sounded reassuring, but the anger rolling off him in waves had me on edge.

Chris stopped in his efforts to clean up the space, gripping the hammer he was holding a little too tightly. "Go get ready for dinner," Chris said to me. "Just a little misunderstanding. Nothing that can't be worked out." Chris's reassuring smile never faltered, but the tension in his eyes betrayed him.

The growing pit in my stomach warned I should stay. "I don't need to rush off," I said hesitantly.

Chris slipped the hammer into the toolbox and said, "It's okay, Gwen. Really."

I would've felt better if Justin had also assured me everything was fine, but if Chris wanted me to go, I'd go. I glanced between the two men one last time before walking past Justin into the cold winter air.

The wind cut through my sweatshirt as I hurried to my green Jetta. Justin's cherry red truck was parked next to it. I glanced at the closed door. Should I go back in? I'd left them standing like two gunslingers facing off at high noon.

I climbed into my car and got the heat going. The dirty windows of the building reflected back the late-afternoon sunlight, preventing me from seeing inside. I waited a beat longer before pulling out of the parking spot and pointing my car toward home.

The guys would work it out. They'd been friends since elementary school. Played football together in high school. Gotten into enough trouble around town to irritate the adults in their lives but kept it innocent enough to never experience any real consequences. Chris had matured in the years since high school. Justin not as much. Despite all of that, they'd remained friends. Whatever Justin was upset about would blow over. It had to.

Thirty minutes later, I pushed my way through the scarred wooden door of Bucky's with wet hair and an apology ready for being late to dinner. The greasy smells wafting from the kitchen transported me to Friday nights as a teenager spent gossiping over who was going to ask whom to prom and whether or not our American Government teacher was wearing a toupee. My gaze traveled the room, searching for Penny. I found her waiting at a booth in the back, reading something on her phone.

"Gwen!" The shout came from the direction of the bar, and I turned. Mitch Alcomb was sitting with some of his buddies. His flannel shirt tucked into faded Wranglers fit right into the Friday night crowd at Bucky's. As always, he was wearing a beat-up baseball cap that said *Texaco* on it. His bushy brown eyebrows danced on his forehead like two fuzzy caterpillars. "I heard you spent the day helping Crawford clean up that old heap down on Lincoln," he called across the room.

I glanced in Penny's direction to see if she'd heard him. Ugh. Of course she had. I caught Penny's gaze and held up one finger before crossing the room to Mitch. "Yep. Making some real progress over there," I said.

"He better watch it," Mitch said as he chuckled. "That dump is an accident waiting to happen."

"That's what I told him," I said, finally feeling justified in all the lectures I'd given Chris about the safety of the building and doing the work to fix it up himself.

Mitch tipped his beer in my direction and said, "Maybe I'll see you on the dance floor later."

"Maybe," I hedged.

Dancing and I weren't exactly friends. It started the moment I'd gotten paired up with Charlie Green for the square dancing section of PE class in middle school. The embarrassment of having to dance with a boy who clearly never showered had translated into two left feet. I'd never recovered.

"Hey Gwen, long time no see," a voice said from behind me.

I turned at the greeting. "Tony? What are you doing in town?" I asked in shock.

Tony Reagan grinned, brushing a lock of his dark hair back out of his eyes. "Just visiting my folks for the weekend. Ran into Mitch at the Piggly Wiggly, and he invited me out for drinks with the old gang," he explained.

Mitch slapped Tony on the shoulder and said, "Needed to make sure Mr. Investment Banker from the big city hadn't gotten too big for his britches."

Tony snorted out a laugh, but on closer inspection, I could see the changes from the small-town Tony I'd grown up with. While Mitch and the other guys at the bar wore faded jeans, T-shirts, flannel shirts, or the occasional sweatshirt, Tony wore dark jeans, a little too fitted to his body to be at home in Star Junction. His sweater was black with a slight V-neck, and also fitted. The whole look was stylish without being fussy. Tony might be comfortable at Bucky's drinking beer with the boys, but moving to Chicago two hours to the northeast had definitely changed him, or at least his style.

"How are things in Chicago?" I asked. "Do you love living in the city?"

Tony shrugged and said, "It's fine. Building investment portfolios pays well, but it's not what I wanted to be doing with my life."

"Damn right it pays well," Mitch chimed in. "That's why this round is on Tony." Mitch tapped the bar, getting the bartender's attention. "Another round on Tony," he said loudly enough for everyone sitting at the bar to hear.

Tony grinned and held up a finger as he said, "One round. One round is on me."

I'd often wondered what it would be like to live in Chicago. A few field trips as a child to Shedd Aquarium or the Field Museum combined with family vacations over a long weekend had been fun, but I was well aware that visiting a place and living there were two very different things.

I'd left Star Junction for college, getting my business degree from University of Wisconsin Whitewater before moving home after graduation. Whitewater, Wisconsin was small by Chicago standards, but with a population around fifteen thousand, it was three times the size of Star Junction. That was all the "big city" experience I needed.

My phone buzzed, and I glanced at it to see a text from Penny. *If the food comes and you're still talking to the boys, I can't be responsible for what happens to your fries.*

I shot a look in Penny's direction. She quirked an eyebrow before bending her head back over her phone. My phone buzzed again. *I'm starving.*

I got the hint. I turned to Tony and Mitch, who were deep in conversation about the Chicago Bears' chances in the playoffs. "It was nice to see you, Tony. When do you head back?" I asked.

"Tomorrow. Bright and early. Got to beat the weekend traffic," he said. While he'd been animated in his conversation about football, he sounded suddenly weary at the thought of heading back to the city.

"Say hi to your folks for me," I said before turning to Mitch to include him in my goodbyes. "Have fun tonight, boys. But not too much fun."

"I'm going to check in on that dance later," Mitch said, reminding me I'd need to come up with an excuse for that.

"No promises," I teased right back.

I weaved through the tables that would be moved to the side later once the live band started and slid into the other side of the booth across from Penny. "You already ordered?" I asked, not bothering to pick up the laminated one-page menu.

Silence.

Everything about Penny was bold, from her jet-black hair cut into a sharp bob at her shoulders to large, hazel eyes rimmed with expertly applied eyeliner. Tonight, her wide mouth, which was pulled into a tight, disapproving line, sported hot-pink lipstick. As the silence stretched, I fought the urge to squirm in my seat.

"I'm sorry I was late," I finally said. "Believe me, you're glad I took the time to shower." If the lecture was coming, I'd just as soon get it over with so we could enjoy the rest of the evening.

But she didn't mention my tardiness. What she was upset about was much worse. "You spent the day with Chris? Again?"

I dropped my gaze to the menu. They'd added a salad, although the only dressing option was full-fat ranch. I guess even Bucky's could change. Slightly. "I helped him with some painting at the new building," I explained.

"Do you think that's wise?" Penny said. Her tone was in full-on teacher mode. It was a tone that had been known to make the high school football players in her English class quake in their Nikes.

I played with the straw sitting next to a stack of napkins. "Chris is my friend. I help my friends with things."

"But that's the problem," Penny said as she leaned forward, her voice filled with concern. "I've tried not to say anything. I've tried to let this thing run its course, but it's been almost eighteen years and nothing seems to be changing."

"What are you talking about?" I said, playing innocent, but part of me knew what she was about to say.

"You need to face reality. You and Chris are friends. You're probably his best friend. But you don't want to just be friends, and that's the problem."

Our server, Nancy, approached. Her thick blonde hair was streaked with gray and pulled up in a high ponytail. Her glittery blue eye shadow belonged to the 80s more than in the present day, but Nancy had been rocking some kind of glittery eye shadow ever since my first memories of her sitting across the aisle from us in church when I was a child. I could only hope I was willing to embrace what I loved when I was her age, no matter what anyone else thought.

We spent a minute engaging in the obligatory chitchat that came with living in a small town like Star Junction. This time it was about the weather and the upcoming pie social. I played my part in the conversation, but my heart wasn't in it. Penny's tight smile hinted that our conversation about Chris and my nonexistent relationship with him wasn't over.

Nancy segued from discussing the upcoming pie social to talking about the task at hand. "Your food should be out any minute. Do you need anything? Refills?"

We both had waters, but Penny also had a glass of what I expected was Dr. Pepper. "Can I get a Diet Coke?"

"Sure thing, hun," Nancy said. She tucked her pencil behind her ear before heading back to the kitchen.

Penny nailed me with a pointed look and said, "I don't like seeing you get hurt."

I smoothed my napkin over my lap. "I won't," I said quietly.

Penny's hazel eyes softened. "There's a pattern with you and Chris Crawford. You're important to him. I'll admit that. But because of that, he does things that seem flirty." She threw her hands up in the air. "Heck, flirty is who he is. You've been in love with him since sixth grade—"

"I wouldn't say—" I interrupted, but she interrupted me right back.

"You've been in love with him since sixth grade," Penny said pointedly. "And so you start seeing something that's not there. You get your hopes up, and when it becomes clear he sees you as just a friend, you're crushed."

Penny had made comments about how much time I spent with Chris before, but she'd never laid it out so plainly. Her words stung. "That's what you think happens?" I asked.

"That's what I *know* happens," she said.

I watched a couple slow dancing to a country song on the jukebox, not bothering to wait for the live music.

Penny's tone softened as she said, "I'm worried about you. Chris has had eighteen years to fall in love with you. I don't want you to waste your life following him around like a lost puppy."

This just kept getting worse. "You think I follow him around like a lost puppy?" I asked in horror.

Penny backpedaled, her face stricken. "I didn't mean that. Not like a puppy. Not really."

Was that what everyone thought? I glanced around the room at people I'd known all my life. Friends of my parents. Former teachers, coaches, and neighbors. My friends from high school. Did they all pity me?

My phone buzzed, and I pulled it from my purse to see a text from Chris. *Thanks again for helping today. Sorry you had to see that with Justin. It's no big deal. We'll work it out. You're the best. I'll buy you dinner this week as a thank-you. Anywhere but Bucky's.*

My smile came automatically, but just as quickly, it slipped off my face. This was what Penny was talking about. I shoved my phone back into my purse. I could do this. I'd never succeeded before, but this time would be different. "Then I'm done with Chris Crawford," I said emphatically.

"Let's not be overly dramatic," Penny said, rolling her eyes. "No one said you had to be done with him. Just find some balance. There are plenty of guys who would love to sweep you off your feet."

Penny had clearly been out of the dating scene too long. "We've known everyone in this town our whole lives. Believe me, there's no one to date. You got lucky Jack was willing to move back here with you after college. You married a great guy and managed to stay close to family."

Nancy set our food on the table and wiped her hand across her brow, pushing her graying bangs to the side. "Can I get you anything else?"

"More ketchup?" Penny asked as she shook the nearly empty bottle.

"Coming right up," Nancy said with a smile.

I pulled apart my chicken tenders, letting the hot steam escape. "There's no one for me to date in this town, but I hear what you're saying about Chris. I can't help it. Those broad shoulders, the way his hair falls over his forehead just so, and when he touches me…" I shook myself back to reality. "Plus, what we went through all those years ago was traumatic. Everyone knows shared trauma bonds people together. It's science."

Penny snorted, almost choking on her Dr. Pepper. "Trauma?

I don't think both of you being forgotten by your parents after school and having to walk home together counts as trauma."

"Getting chased into the woods by Mr. Kowoski's giant, evil dog and then getting lost and having to wait until a search party found us huddled in the dark was traumatic," I challenged.

"I guess you're right," Penny conceded. "The whole town was pretty scared that day. Your mom must have called my mom a dozen times, checking to see if you'd turned up at my house."

"Chris and I have needed each other ever since," I said before popping a piece of the chicken into my mouth, savoring the greasy goodness you could only get at a dive like Bucky's.

Penny grimaced and said, "That's what worries me. Chris needs you, but he doesn't *want* you. You deserve to be wanted."

I waved my hand around at the room. "Then help a girl out, because it seems that all the good guys are taken."

Penny glanced around the room at the groups of people enjoying a night out after a long week of work. The corners of her mouth pulled down. "You might be right," she said, sounding defeated.

"Maybe Chris will come around," I said. "He did hug me today, and it was perfection." I fanned myself and pretended to swoon, earning a laugh from Penny.

"I refuse to let you waste any more time waiting for Chris to figure out how amazing you are. I'll think of something." Penny stared off into space, absently chewing on a french fry. She straightened up and slammed her hand down on the table. "I've got it," she practically shouted.

I bit down on the inside of my cheek and yelped as pain shot through my mouth. "Seriously, was that necessary?" I said as I cradled the side of my face.

"Sorry," she said, but she didn't look sorry. "What about the new guy?"

I carefully chewed the rest of my bite. "What new guy?" I asked.

"The new guy," Penny said. Her hazel eyes sparkled with excitement. "The new detective at the police department. Baxter or Butler or something."

It wasn't like me to miss out on town gossip like this. "Uncle Stan mentioned they were hiring someone from out of town, but I didn't know he'd started already. How did I not know this?" I asked.

"Maybe because you've been too busy helping hunky Chris

make his decrepit dream a reality," Penny teased.

"Shut up." I tossed a fry at her. "You can't criticize my crush and tease me about it at the same time."

"I'm pretty sure I just did," Penny said as she tucked her dark hair behind her ears. Then her smile softened. "I worry about you."

"I know," I said with a sigh. "And you're right. Chris has never shown any interest in being anything but my friend. My head knows it, but my heart can't seem to catch up."

Penny laid her hand over mine and said, "His loss."

The front door banged open, interrupting our sentimental moment. Cold air snaked through the room, sending a chill up my spine.

"Hey! Shut the door!" someone yelled from near the bar.

I twisted in my seat. Justin stood in the open doorway, his hands balled into fists and his nostrils flared. "Where's Chris!" he shouted.

CHAPTER TWO

———

Mitch rose from his seat at the bar and started toward Justin like a man approaching a skittish horse. "Hey, man, what's going on?" he asked Justin.

Justin looked around the room wildly, stopping when his gaze met mine. "Where is he?" he snarled.

Dinners and drinks forgotten, everyone's attention bounced between Justin, Mitch, and me like they were watching a soap opera unfolding before them in real time.

Mitch reached Justin and laid a hand on his shoulder. "Take it easy," he said.

Justin was tall and strong, muscles honed from days of manual labor, but Mitch matched him in both height and strength. Old football buddies with a friendship that had only strengthened since high school, if anyone could defuse the situation, it would be Mitch.

Justin pushed him away, his attention still focused on me. "Where's Chris?" he asked me again. "That lying bastard said he'd be here tonight so we could settle this thing once and for all."

I sat frozen, unsure how to answer without making Justin angrier. I had no idea where Chris was.

Mitch clamped his hand on Justin's shoulder and said, "Leave Gwen out of this. No one's seen him all night. Come on. I'll buy you a drink."

"If he's staying, I'm leaving," Tony said sharply. He sat with his back to Justin and Mitch, but his words had clearly been directed at them.

Justin flexed his hands as if preparing for a fight. Andy Fox, the owner of Bucky's, flicked the bar towel over his shoulder and stepped out from behind the bar.

While not overly large or covered in tattoos like the stereotypical owner of a dive bar like Bucky's, Andy's presence loomed large. As a former Marine, he commanded attention. His gray hair was still styled in a military buzz cut. He'd owned Bucky's longer than any of us had been alive. No one messed with him. "We're not going to have any trouble tonight, boys," he said in a low, gravelly voice.

"Then I'd get him out of here," Tony said, waving his beer bottle in Justin's direction, his words a little too loud. His speech wasn't slurred, but he'd definitely drunk more than that one beer.

"If anyone's leaving, it's you," Justin shot back.

Mitch leaned in and whispered something to Justin.

The expression on Justin's face shifted from murderous to annoyed to…fear? His gaze darted around the room as if suddenly aware of the attention he'd drawn to himself.

Justin shook off Mitch's hand and growled, "I won't let Chris get away with this." He pushed through the door and disappeared into the night.

I knew it. I should've stayed. Instead of things calming down between the friends, they'd only escalated. I shot off a text to Chris. *Justin just showed up at Bucky's looking for you, and he was super mad. What's going on?*

The room was silent for a moment, as if everyone was collectively holding their breath before it filled with the sound of excited whispers. Nothing very newsworthy ever happened in Star Junction. The gossip mill would be grinding away by morning with speculations about what had caused the rift between Justin and Chris.

"What was that about?" Penny asked. "And how are you messed up in it?"

"I don't know what's going on between them, but Justin got to the center as I was leaving today, and he wasn't happy. I've never seen him like this," I said.

"Those guys have been friends forever," Penny said in confusion.

If it was a guy thing, Chris might not want to talk to me about it. Another guy might know, though. Maybe even Penny's husband, Jack. "Would Jack know?" I asked, hoping someone could shed some light on this.

Penny shook her head and picked up a french fry. "Nah, even though we've been back for years, most people still treat Jack like an outsider. I don't think he'd know anything."

"Welcome to life in a small town," I deadpanned.

Penny snorted out a laugh. "You said it." She glanced toward the bar. "And Tony? What's everyone so uptight about tonight?" she asked.

I looked up as if searching for answers from the heavens, although all I could see was the stained seventies-era drop ceiling. "Maybe it's a full moon thing?"

Penny chewed her bottom lip. "Something's sure stirring everyone up," she said.

* * *

Two hours later, I shrugged into my wool coat and braced to face the cold. A quick check of my weather app revealed the temperature had dropped close to zero while we'd been at dinner. "Remind me why we live here again?" I asked Penny.

Penny grimaced and said, "Because *there's no place like home* seems like the right answer. This time of year, though? I think it's because we're nuts."

"We're definitely nuts," I agreed.

We stepped outside, and I pulled in a deep breath, letting the cold sear into my lungs. *Don't show the cold you're afraid of it*, my dad always said on bitter winter mornings. Scientifically, his statement didn't carry any weight, but as a child I'd felt warmer every time we engaged the ritual.

"Helping Chris again tomorrow?" Penny asked. Her tone was light, but clearly there was a right answer here.

Thankfully, I didn't have to lie. "I'm spending the whole day in my pajamas in front of the fireplace," I said.

We said goodbye, and I hurried across the parking lot to my own car. Ten minutes later, I was in my flannel pajamas and fuzzy slippers. There were some benefits to small-town living. A short commute from my house to anywhere else in town was definitely one of them.

As I went through my nightly routine of double checking the locks, filling the electric tea kettle for tomorrow morning, and slathering on all manner of creams that promised to keep me looking young forever, I thought about Penny's assessment of my relationship with Chris.

I couldn't deny the truthfulness of her words. I'd been in love with Chris ever since he used his silly stories and impressions to keep me calm in the woods all those years ago. We fit together like two puzzle pieces. Our connection seemed like fate.

Justin was important to Chris too. Heck, they'd been friends longer than we had. I couldn't figure out what they could be fighting about. And what was the deal with Justin and Tony? No one was getting along, and none of it made any sense.

Crawling under the covers, I checked my phone, ensuring the ringer was on. With my parents in the Florida Keys for their annual escape-the-worst-of-winter trip, I should have been able to sleep soundly, but my dad had been in and out of the hospital lately with a series of infections related to his diabetes. There was nothing I could do from thousands of miles away, but the thought of my mom not being able to get ahold of me in the middle of the night was unbearable.

I plugged the phone in and snuggled deeper under the covers. First thing tomorrow, I'd hunt Chris down and find out how to repair his relationship with Justin. If the boys could've fixed it themselves, they would've succeeded before Justin barreled into Bucky's tonight ruining everyone's good time with his outburst. That had settled it. I was going to have to be the one to fix whatever was broken.

* * *

Ding, ding, ding.

I sat up, jerked out of the warm, sandy beach of my dream and back to my cold, dark bedroom. Chris had been in the middle of declaring his love for me as waves lapped against our feet.

I collapsed back on my pillow. I should not have been dreaming about that. Operation Get-Over-Chris was being undermined by my own subconscious. I rubbed the sleep from my eyes and squinted into the darkness. How could it be morning already?

My sleep-fogged brain took a moment to catch up to the reality of what was happening. It was still dark. Not morning. I scrambled for my phone and checked the time. Two. Who was texting me at two in the morning? My mom? I shook the last vestiges of sleep from my mind and opened my text messages, but the text wasn't from my parents. It was from Chris. *Emergency! I need you. I'm at the center.*

Emergency?

I jumped out of bed and searched the floor for the jeans I'd worn yesterday. My hand finally closed around them near the foot of my bed, but I stopped. I wasn't supposed to be at Chris's beck and call anymore. I looked back and forth between my bed and the jeans.

I dropped the jeans and climbed back under the covers. Chris would have to figure this one out on his own. Besides, what kind of emergency could there be in a nearly empty building in the middle of the night?

I stared at the ceiling in the dark. Why was Chris at the work site at two in the morning? What was the emergency? As much as I tried to go back to sleep, my mind flipped through worst-case scenarios. The building was structurally sound, but it was filled with tools and equipment, much of it dangerous.

I flopped onto my side. If Penny needed me at two in the morning, I'd be there in a heartbeat. How was this any different? A friend needed my help. I was just doing for Chris what I'd do for anyone. I groaned as I climbed out of bed. Maybe I was just making excuses.

This time, I didn't stop long enough to put on the jeans. I yanked my arms through an oversized-cardigan sweater that served as a makeshift bathrobe in the winter, shoved my feet into my boots, and crammed a wool hat over my hair. The legs of my red-and-black-plaid pajama pants pooled over the tops of my boots, flopping against my legs as I headed for the stairs and out the door.

"This better really be an emergency," I muttered as my car sputtered to life. Even the car was upset about being up this early.

As I drove down the quiet streets, anxiety gnawed at me. I paused at a stop sign and texted Chris. *On my way. Are you okay?*

No response.

I turned the corner onto Lincoln. One more block. Chris was probably dead, and it was my petty decision to ignore his text that cost him his life. "Calm down," I said to my empty car. "He probably couldn't sleep, got caught up in finishing the kitchen, needed advice, and didn't realize what time it was."

I turned into the parking lot. The building was dark. No work lights. No cars in the parking lot. Still no reply from Chris.

Scenes from every horror movie I'd ever seen invaded my mind—a woman walking toward the creepy sound coming from the basement, slowly opening the door as it creaked on its rusted hinges. Was this one of those situations? Was I turning into the stupid woman who got herself killed by the middle of the movie because she didn't run away?

I put the car in *Park* and stared at the building. Stupid or not, I had to make sure Chris was okay. I'd just check the door. It would be locked. Chris would text me back and let me know everything had been fine and he'd already gone home. He'd probably reopened the cut on his hand. That would definitely count as an emergency to him. Especially with what a baby he'd been about the blood.

I climbed out of my car and made it to the front door still alive. No monsters jumped out of the shadows. This wasn't a horror movie. I was overreacting to everything. I pushed on the handle, testing the lock. The door swung open at my touch, and my breath caught in my throat. Not a good sign.

I peered through the window next to the door, but the room was lost in shadows. I cracked the door open and stuck my head inside. "Chris?" No response. I stepped into the room, the door falling closed behind me. My breath puffed into the cold air.

I pulled my phone from the pocket of my baggy sweater and turned on the flashlight, panning the beam around the room. My gaze traveled over the sawhorses and tools in the corner. The light played off the stainless-steel sink at the back of the room. I ran the light up and down the scaffolding.

Sawdust from projects half-finished filtered through the beam of light from my phone and tickled my nose. "Chris? This isn't funny. If you're messing around, I'm going to kill you."

The beam of light reached the floor, centering on a pair of boots attached to a pair of legs. My breath caught. Panic flared through my body. I ran and skidded around the corner. It wasn't Chris. I choked back a sob as the harsh light from my phone bounced off the vacant eyes of Justin Hunt.

CHAPTER THREE

———

A flash at the edge of my vision caught my eye, and I scanned the light down Justin's body. The red handle of a large screwdriver jutted out of his chest. The phone dropped from my hand, bouncing on the cement floor and throwing grotesque shadows around the horrific scene.

What if I'm not alone in here?

My hand clamped across my mouth as I swallowed back a scream. My gaze darted around the room. If someone wanted to kill me, wouldn't they have done it by now? But what did I know? I wasn't a criminal mastermind.

I scrambled to my phone and held it up, using the light like a shield between myself and whatever lurked in the shadows. "Don't try any funny business," I shouted into the darkness, my voice cracking. "I'm a black belt in taekwondo." It was a lie, but a lie that made me feel marginally better.

Still the room was silent. I inched closer to Justin. His dark-brown eyes stared back at me, the look on his face one of surprise. My stomach churned. Where was Chris? Why would he ask me to meet him here? Was he hurt too? I needed help. I needed the police. I dialed 9-1-1 through my shattered screen protector.

"9-1-1, what's your emergency?" a woman's voice said.

"I found a body. A dead one. At least, I think he's dead. He's got a big screwdriver in his chest. Maybe he's just hurt?" I prayed I was wrong about Justin being dead as another wave of panic squeezed the air from my lungs and tears burned the backs of my eyes. "His eyes are open. I need—"

"Ma'am," the operator interrupted, "I need you to slow down and take a deep breath. Are you safe?"

"I don't know." My voice came out a strangled whisper as I backed toward the nearest wall.

"I'm sending the police and an ambulance to your location. I need you to stay on the line with me," she said firmly but calmly.

"Okay," I said as I pressed my back against the wall, wishing it would swallow me up.

"Are you hurt, ma'am?" the operator asked, her voice calm.

"No, Justin's hurt!" My voice was anything but calm.

"Someone there is injured?" she asked.

My gaze cut to where Justin lay on his back, staring sightlessly up at the ceiling. "I don't know. I think he's dead." Sirens sounded in the distance. "I can hear the police," I said.

"That's good. Can you meet them at the door?" she asked.

"I'm scared to move. What if someone's in here with me?" I asked, the fear threatening to undo me.

"Is the door unlocked?" she asked.

"Yes," I squeaked out.

"Okay, then just stay right where you are," she said soothingly.

Red and blue lights danced across the room as a police cruiser pulled into the parking lot. I peered through the window next to me. An officer climbed out of the driver's seat, paused, and spoke into the radio on his shoulder. A few seconds later, another siren.

"The police are here," I told the operator. I couldn't stop shaking. I couldn't feel my hands. I fumbled the phone, almost dropping it again.

I raised it back to my ear in time to hear the operator say, "I'm going to hang up. The police will help you."

"Thanks. Thank you so much," I said, my voice wobbly with unshed tears.

The officer advanced on the building, his hand resting on the gun at his side. He glanced behind him as an ambulance pulled into the lot but continued forward. I squinted through the grimy glass as the officer passed through a pool of light cast by the streetlight overhead.

Tommy Palmer Jr., another high school friend—although he'd been one year behind Justin, Chris, and me—reached the door. He disappeared from view as the door eased opened. "Police! Anyone here?" he called out.

"Tommy?" I asked.

Tommy swung his flashlight in my direction, and I raised my hand to shield my face, blinking rapidly.

"Gwen?" he asked, sounding shocked. He lowered the

flashlight, pointing it at my feet. "The dispatcher said there was someone on the scene but didn't give any identifying information."

Tommy stopped by Camelot Flowers, our family's flower shop, every Friday to buy flowers for his wife. They'd just had their first baby. Seeing him now flooded my body with relief.

"What's going on?" he asked as he moved toward me.

"I got a text from Chris asking me to meet him here. He said there was an emergency. When I got here, I found Justin." I pointed to the corner where Justin lay. Tommy swung the beam of light toward Justin and froze. Uncertainty played across his face, but he gave his head a slight shake and moved toward the body.

"Have you touched him?" he asked.

"No, I—I couldn't," I said.

"Where's Crawford?" Tommy asked as he bent down and placed his fingers on Justin's neck. The stricken look on Tommy's face told me everything I needed to know.

The door banged open, and two paramedics marched in carrying bags of equipment.

"Over here, guys," Tommy called out.

They wove their way through the minefield of construction debris and knelt to examine the body. Tommy pushed himself to standing and repeated his question. "Gwen, where's Crawford?"

"What?" I rubbed my hand across my eyes, trying to blot out the image of Justin lying dead on the floor, but it was seared into my memory.

The paramedics went to work on Justin, attaching all sorts of equipment I didn't recognize and using terms I didn't understand.

Tommy moved to stand next to me. "You said Chris asked you to come here. Where is he?" he asked again.

I tore my gaze from Justin's body as I pulled the edges of my sweater closed across my chest. "I don't know. When I got here, the door was unlocked. Once I found Justin, I called 9-1-1. I was too scared to move," I explained.

Tommy looked over his shoulder at the paramedics and said, "Wilson, we gotta check the building for anyone else who might be injured."

My gut twisted, and I sagged against the wall behind me. Tommy reached out and grabbed my arm. "You okay?" he asked.

My worst fears came to life as my mind digested Tommy's words. "You think Chris is here? That's he's hurt? Or worse?" I said, my voice trembling.

"Let's get you settled in my car where it's warmer. Chris is probably fine, but we need to check just in case. Can you show me where the light switches are?" Tommy asked.

I led him to a panel of switches across the room. This didn't make sense. Justin was dead. Not just dead. Murdered. Things like this didn't happen in Star Junction. Things like this didn't happen to people I knew. I flipped three of the switches, and the ancient florescent lights sputtered to life. I winced as my eyes adjusted to the suddenly bright space.

I looked back at Justin's body and shuddered. The scene was even more horrific under the harsh lights. Tommy took my elbow and steered me toward the door. "Come on. Let's get you settled," he said. "I'll let you know as soon as we've cleared the building. You're going to need to stay until Detective Butler gets here. He's going to want to ask you some questions." Tommy led me toward the car, my movements on autopilot.

Tears pricked the back of my eyes as I thought about Justin's parents sleeping peacefully in their house across town. Tommy leaned across me and turned the heat up. "I've gotta go back in and help. You sit tight. We'll get this sorted out and get you home in no time," he said.

I wasn't an expert on murder, but I didn't think it could be sorted out in no time. I leaned my head back against the cold, hard vinyl of the seat. How had I ended up here? *That's easy. You jumped when Chris called.*

I slid lower in the seat and pulled my hands up into the sleeves of my sweater. Where was Chris? Why would he do this to me? What would I tell my parents? As the car warmed, I blinked, fighting sleep. Maybe I'd close my eyes for a minute, gather my thoughts. Maybe then I could figure out how Justin ended up dead in my best friend's building.

* * *

A sharp rap on the window yanked me into consciousness. I yelped and tried to scramble away from the face staring at me through the fogged window. The man opened the door and extended his hand. "Hey, hey, hey. It's okay," he said soothingly.

His brown eyes, the color of golden whiskey, glowed under the lights in the parking lot. He scanned my face and then my body as if taking some sort of inventory. "I'm Detective Butler. I understand you found the victim?" he said.

"Yeah, I found Justin," I said weakly. My eyes stung with unshed tears. I sniffed and rubbed my hands over my face.

A murder.

In Chris's building.

I sprang out of the car, causing the detective to take a step back. "Where's Chris?" I demanded. "Did they find him? Is he okay?"

Detective Butler folded his arms across his chest and looked down at me. He was at least a foot taller than me, towering over me in his crisp blue suit covered by a dark-gray overcoat. Appearing to be in his early thirties, his dark-brown hair, short on the sides but longer on top, was gelled to perfection, despite the early morning hour. He had a short beard that he ran his hand over as he regarded me silently. He smelled expensive, like cologne from a high-end department store.

Wearing expensive cologne and what looked like an expensive suit. Meanwhile, I looked exactly like someone who'd rushed out of bed in the middle of the night, mismatched pajamas and all. My hair? Who knew what was happening up there?

I'd decided to grow my hair out two years ago, and to say I'd been successful would've been an understatement. It nearly reached my waist, which meant I wore it up more often than not. My hair could look sleek under the best of circumstances, but give it even ten minutes in bed, and it was more likely to resemble a demented form of bed head. Not the sexy kind. I wasn't that lucky.

"There's no sign of Chris Crawford in the building," Detective Butler said, pulling me away from the nightmare of my appearance back to the real nightmare.

I sagged against the car with relief. Chris wasn't here. My mind wrapped itself around this new information as I stared at the patchy white paint covering the front of the building, the front of Chris's dream. "Then why would he ask me to come here?"

I hadn't realized I'd asked the question out loud until Detective Butler responded, "That's a very good question, ma'am."

The implication of his words pushed through my confusion. "What do you mean, that's a very good question. You can't think that Chris…" I trailed off and gestured toward the building.

"I'd like to ask you a few questions," Detective Butler said, all business. "Let's go inside."

I took a step back, my pulse quickening. I shook my head, and my breath snagged in my throat.

Detective Butler looked perturbed by my hesitation. "The paramedics have already left with the body," he said.

"I can't go back in there. I won't," I whispered.

"It's too cold to stand out here and talk," Detective Butler reasoned.

"We can talk in the car," I said as I gestured toward the car that was still running, the heat warming my back through the open car door.

Detective Butler pulled a slow breath in through his nose, letting it out just as slowly. "We're not going to have this conversation in the cruiser. I'd rather not have to take you down to the station." He took a step toward me. "Is that what we need to do? Have a formal interview at the station?" he asked.

The shift from concern to hostility wasn't lost on me. I planted my hands on my hips as I said, "Are you saying if I don't go back in there, you're going to arrest me?"

He huffed out an irritated breath. "I'm not going to arrest you." He quirked an eyebrow. "Unless I find reason to," he said.

I pulled myself up to my full five-foot-four-inch height. "There's no reason you should arrest me. I'm the one who called the police," I snapped.

"The first thing they teach you in detective training—the person who called it in is suspect number one," he said. Did I detect the hint of a threat in his tone?

"You've...I mean...what?" I tucked my hands up under my armpits but resisted the urge to stomp my feet against the cold. I wouldn't give him the satisfaction. "You've got to be kidding me. I'm trying to help. Justin was a friend. We weren't close, but we went to high school together. I care about what happened to him. I certainly didn't murder him. I don't have any reason to murder him. I don't have any reason to murder anyone." I scuffed my boot into a chunk of dirty snow. "Except maybe you," I muttered.

"Are you done?" He sounded annoyed, but when I looked up, a hint of a smile played at the corner of his lips before his face reset into a mask of professionalism.

"I'm done," I said reluctantly. I didn't want to be done with my little tantrum, but it was clear it wasn't getting me anywhere with this man.

"Can we please we go inside? I don't know about you, but I'm freezing," he said, his tone back to one of concern.

I didn't want to go back in there, but I couldn't ignore the fact that my toes and fingers were growing numb. I headed toward the door, leaving Detective Butler to trail after me.

Inside was a flurry of activity as officers gathered evidence. Where Justin's body once lay, a brown stain marred the unfinished concrete. Yellow police tape stretched from the scaffolding to a bench a few feet away before cutting back across the space to form a triangle of protection around the area where Justin had lost his life. I flicked my gaze away and headed in the opposite direction. The sooner we got this over with, the sooner I could get out of here.

I crossed to a card table, pulled out a chair that would keep my back to the room, and dropped into it, waiting silently as Detective Butler set a small tape recorder next to a yellow legal pad on the table. "Do I have your permission to record this conversation?" he asked.

"Yeah, fine, whatever," I said as I pulled the purple stocking cap off my head and ran my fingers through my hair, feeling the tangles I hadn't taken the time to brush out before rushing over here. I shifted and caught a glimpse of myself in the window behind Detective Butler. My hair frizzed out on one side like I'd stuck my finger in a light socket. The other side? Plastered down flat. No fixing it now. I shoved the hat back on my head.

"Now, Ms. Stevens, is it?" Detective Butler asked.

"Gwen Stevens," I said.

He made a note on the legal pad. "That's your full, legal name?"

I gritted my teeth. If Detective Butler stayed in Star Junction long enough, he'd learn my full name. "Gwen is short for Guinevere," I answered reluctantly. I spelled it out for him. Most people got it wrong. I'd been the last kindergartener to be able to spell my own full name. It was one of many reasons I stuck with Gwen.

Detective Butler wrote something else down before saying, "Please tell me how you ended up here this morning."

I took a steadying breath. "I got a text from my friend Chris. He owns this place. He told me there was an emergency and asked me to come," I said.

"And when was that?" he asked.

"Two this morning," I answered.

"You came immediately?" he asked as he jotted something down on the legal pad.

"Yes. Well, no. I was going to come, but then I got back into bed. I tried to go back to sleep, but I couldn't stop worrying about what the big emergency was, so I got back out of bed, and then I came here," I explained.

Detective Butler looked up from his notes, clearly confused by my choppy timeline. "You got back into bed?" he asked.

I sighed and said, "I had dinner with my friend Penny last night, and she was saying—" I cut myself off. I didn't know this man. I studied him from across the table. He sat ramrod straight, dressed more for a boardroom than a small-town crime scene.

He tapped his pen against his notepad, waiting for me to continue. Babbling anxiously was not going to help my credibility. He didn't need to know about my efforts to end my hopeless crush on Chris. "It doesn't matter what Penny said," I finally continued. "Basically, I decided I didn't need to run out at two in the morning, but then I thought what if something was really wrong? I'd never forgive myself."

He made another note and said, "We'll need your phone to get the meta-data about Mr. Crawford's communication with you. We'll get it back to you within a few days."

I clutched at the pocket of my sweater where my phone was safely in my possession. "I need my phone. The ordering software for the store is on there. Phone calls from customers get routed to my number when my parents are out of town. My whole life is on this phone," I argued.

"It wasn't a request," he said firmly. "I'll get the phone back to you as soon as possible."

I put on my best *don't mess with me* face, trying to channel Penny's teacher-energy. "That's not acceptable." I tightened my grip on my phone. All those late nights watching *Law & Order* reruns was about to come in handy. "Unless you have a warrant, I'm keeping my phone," I said resolutely.

Detective Butler's chest heaved with a frustrated sigh, but instead of arguing with me, he said, "Tell me more about why you need this phone."

"My family owns the flower shop on Main Street. Camelot Flowers. As I mentioned, we run much of the store from software on my phone," I said. We also had an iPad in the store, but I wasn't about to volunteer that information. I wanted to keep my phone.

Detective Butler was jotting a note on his legal pad when he froze. It was happening. He was putting it together. "The flower shop is called Camelot Flowers?"

"Yep," I said simply. I wasn't about to fill in the blanks for him.

"And your name is Guinevere?" he asked slowly.

"Also correct," I said.

He held my gaze for a beat before returning to his notes.

While I hadn't wanted to make the connection for him, I felt the need to explain now that he'd made it. "My dad's really into LARPing, renaissance fairs, really anything connected to King Arthur and the Knights of the Round Table."

"LARPing?" he asked, looking up from his notes, clearly confused.

"Live action role playing," I explained, my tone somehow strained and patient at the same time. It wasn't that I was embarrassed by my dad's hobby, although hobby might be too polite of a word. More like obsession. What I didn't love was the need my dad had felt to name his only child Guinevere. I had no doubt that if I'd been born a boy, Detective Butler would be talking to Lancelot right now.

The door banged open, and I yelped, clutching my chest. Hundreds of years ago, I'd have been clutching my pearls or complaining of having the vapors. What was it with people barging into this building and scaring me half to death?

"Sorry about that." An officer with a beer belly hanging over his utility belt carrying a large box kicked the door closed behind him as he apologized.

I willed my heart to slow down, but it wasn't working. Maybe I needed to work out more.

"You okay?" Detective Butler asked. He was back to concerned. I'd take that over annoyed any day. And he hadn't made fun of my name. He'd earned a check in the nice column.

"Just a little jumpy," I explained.

"That's understandable. You've been through a lot this morning," he said, his tone kind.

More niceness.

"A phone number where I can reach you if more questions arise?" He wrote something else down while he waited for me to answer.

I rattled off my phone number as I leaned forward, attempting to see what he was writing, but he angled the pad away from me. Annoying. I tugged the edges of my bulky sweater together over my chest, once again keenly aware of how ridiculous I looked. I should've stopped to put the jeans on. Or brushed my hair.

He stretched out his hand and said, "Your phone?"

How did he expect to use that phone number to reach me if I didn't have a phone? If mentioning his need for a warrant, which I wasn't even sure was true, hadn't stopped him from asking for my phone, nothing was going to. I reached into the pocket of my sweater, grumbling about police brutality. He didn't look amused. "Don't lose it. Or break it," I said firmly.

He looked down at the phone, the shattered screen protector still in place. "How would I know if it was broken?" he asked, his tone teasing.

I just barely restrained myself from sticking my tongue out at the man. Instead I said, "I dropped it when I found Justin's body. Forgive me for having a human reaction to murder."

I didn't know if his change of heart was because of the reminder of the ordeal I'd been through or not, but he said, "If you'll unlock the phone for me, I'll verify the time the text came in. Then you can have it back. If we need it again, I can let you know."

I perked up at that. "That's the first good news I've heard all night," I exclaimed as I unlocked the phone. Detective Butler spent a minute finding what he needed, took some photos with a small camera, and returned it to me.

I shoved it back into the pocket of my sweater as Tommy jogged over. He leaned down and whispered something to Detective Butler, who leaned back in his chair and studied the ceiling. I quirked an eyebrow at Tommy, who simply shrugged. Detective Butler sat back up and said, "Leave someone there in case he returns."

"Sure thing, boss," Tommy said before jogging toward the door, clearly eager to please.

"You're his boss?" I asked.

The only boss I knew of at the police station was Stan MacNamara, or Uncle Stan as I called him. Not my real uncle, but he was my godfather, my dad's best friend, and an uncle in every important sense of the word.

Detective Butler shrugged. "I report to the police chief. The officers report to me."

"The police chief is good friends with my dad," I said lightly. I wasn't above using a little nepotism if it was going to help me get more information from him about the investigation.

"Of course he is," Detective Butler grumbled under his breath.

"What's that supposed to mean?" I said suspiciously.

Detective Butler scribbled something in his notes and answered without looking up. "It means I've only been in town a week, and I've already learned everyone is either related to or best friends with everyone else."

I batted my eyelashes and said, "It's one of Star Junction's many charms."

"It's something," he muttered. "Let's get back to the case."

"You know my full, legal name. How about you, Detective Butler?"

"How about me, what?" he asked. His question sounded genuine, but there was no way he didn't know what I meant.

"What's your full, legal name?"

"I don't see how that's relevant," he said dismissively.

"It's relevant because it's only fair," I challenged.

He looked at me appraisingly, as if deciding whether or not to answer my question. He twirled the pen in his hand, his gaze never leaving mine. He finally answered, "It's Finn. Finn Butler."

I had a strong feeling he was holding something back. "If I saw your driver's license, would it say Finn Butler?"

I was very familiar with nicknames. Guinevere provided a few options. While almost everyone called me Gwen now, I'd been Gwennie for years as a child. Then there was an embarrassing two months in seventh grade when I insisted everyone call me Gwenna. It had seemed cool at the time. Boy, was I glad that hadn't stuck.

Detective Butler's gaze shifted behind me at the officers still moving around the scene before returning to meet mine. "What Finn is short for is irrelevant to this conversation," he said.

My smile widened. "A challenge. I like a challenge. I'll figure it out," I promised.

He folded his hands on the table. "Knock yourself out, Gwen." A flash of amusement sparked in his eyes.

"Give me time, *Finn*," I shot back.

Our gazes held before Finn, breaking the fragile moment, crossed his arms and looked down to study his notes. Back to business.

Back to business and back to reality. "I'm worried about Chris," I said. "He's not here, but he clearly asked me to meet him here."

"I've got officers looking for him," Finn said casually. "He'll be very safe down at the station."

"Down at the station?" I yelled. The few people left in the room stopped what they were doing and stared. "You're arresting him?"

Detective Butler appeared unfazed by my outburst. "I'm bringing him in for questioning," he said.

"But, but…" I sputtered.

"Gwen." He sighed. Again. He seemed to sigh a lot in my presence. "I'm just doing my job." He ticked off the points on his fingers. "Mr. Crawford's text puts him at the scene of the crime. You show up to find a dead body." He looked me up and down. "Unless I'm mistaken, you don't have the physical strength to shove a screwdriver up to the hilt into the victim's chest."

I flinched at his callused description of what had happened to someone I'd known my whole life.

He continued, "Reports are Mr. Hunt ran into a local restaurant last night looking for Mr. Crawford, and he was quite angry."

"How do you already know that?" I waved my hands through the air. "You just got here."

"One of the officers told me. I was on the scene for thirty minutes before waking you," he explained.

My cheeks flooded with heat. How many officers had walked past the car while I slept? Had I snored? Drooled? I'd just pretend I'd looked like Sleeping Beauty. I had to. The delusion was the only way I'd survive the embarrassment.

Finn raised his eyebrows and said, "I also heard you were at the restaurant when the victim showed up, and he seemed to think you might know where he could find Chris."

Shoot. It wasn't like I was trying to hide the fact, but maybe I hadn't been about to volunteer the information, but Justin demanding I tell him where to find Chris pretty much ensured everyone at Bucky's had noticed I was there.

"I was having dinner with a friend," I offered as a way of explanation.

The severity of the situation hit me all at once. I knew Chris better than I knew anyone. There was no way he would murder someone, but it wasn't looking good. I shoved my hands into the pockets of my sweater. "I'm tired. Can I go?" I asked.

Finn looked over his notes before meeting my gaze and saying, "I have a few more questions. Can you do five more minutes?"

"What else do you need to know?" I said wearily.

True to his word, we spent five minutes walking through exactly what I'd done, what I'd seen, and what I'd touched since entering the building. Once we finished, I trudged to my car, started the engine, and pulled out of the parking lot.

How had this happened? Justin was dead. The police were looking for Chris. Chris had texted me to meet him at the center, but he'd never responded to my text about Justin showing up at Bucky's. What was going on with him?

At least I could tell Penny I'd met the new police detective. Not exactly what she had in mind when she'd suggested he might be cute enough to date. I wouldn't deny he was classically handsome. Strong jaw, wide shoulders. He was like Superman. The Clark Kent version, minus the glasses, plus a beard. Kind and caring one minute, impatient and frustrated the next. I was too exhausted to figure him out.

I pulled into my driveway and stared at my small white house with navy blue shutters. Snow lay in fluffy piles around the bushes lining the bottom of the large picture window. The lamp I always left on in the living room glowed through the curtains. The house looked all tucked in for winter. That's what I needed. Sleep first, and then I was going to figure out who killed Justin, because I knew one thing for certain—it wasn't Chris.

CHAPTER FOUR

———

Sunday. A day of rest. At least, that's what it was supposed to be. I'd woken up at noon, after a morning of fitful sleep plagued by nightmares, to four missed calls and twenty text messages. My parents, Penny, the girls from my book club, even Finn, who requested I come in Monday for a follow-up interview. The one person I hadn't heard from was Chris.

The little I'd been able to overhear between Finn and the other officers the night of Justin's murder indicated that Finn was also interested in finding Chris. Finn would likely have an officer watching Chris's house, but I had to see for myself.

By five, I couldn't handle it anymore and chased the setting sun across town to where Chris had a house near the high school. I parked in the driveway, which was empty, and picked my way over the icy sidewalk to the front door.

No police cruiser sat across the street. Maybe Finn had already interviewed Chris and determined he wasn't a suspect. Maybe Chris was busy helping Finn find who did it.

An Amazon package leaned against the storm door. I picked it up and knocked. No answer. Stamping my feet against the cold, I walked carefully back to the garage and jumped, trying to see in through the windows that ran across the top of the door. The garage was empty.

Standing in the driveway, I was at a loss as to what to do. I pulled my phone from my coat pocket and called Chris again. I'd listened to his voicemail message so many times, I practically had the thing memorized.

At the beep I said, "Chris, this is getting ridiculous. I'm at your house and your car is gone. Please let me know you're okay. I don't know what happened with Justin, but we can work it out. Call me." I almost ended the call but added, "And there was a package on your porch. I'm taking it home with me so no one steals it. Call me,"

I added one more time.

By that night, I'd worked myself into a frenzy about Chris's disappearance. I stared at the ceiling most of the night, praying my phone would ring and it would be Chris. It hadn't, and I'd started Monday morning exhausted and wrung out.

After two cups of coffee and a stale protein bar I'd found in the back of my nearly empty pantry, I walked through the front door of Camelot Flowers, my home away from home.

I'd grown up sitting on a tall stool behind the counter, coloring pictures of My Little Ponies. I'd spent my teen years helping my mom make bouquets. I'd majored in business in college so I could come back and take on more of the workload from my parents as my dad's health got worse.

Turning on the lights, I went through my opening routine. Thirty minutes later, soft music played over the store speakers, the live plants had been watered, the orders checked for the day, and the shelves of cute knick-knacks dusted.

I flipped the sign to open. Before I made it back behind the counter, the bell jingled cheerfully from above the door. Donna Mayor walked in wearing purple from head to toe. Even her cane had a purple bow on it. Everything Donna wore was always coordinated, whether it was all red, all yellow, or all green. Today, she looked like a plump eggplant.

Although she'd been my fourth-grade teacher, now that she was retired, she insisted I call her Donna. "Good morning, Donna," I said cheerfully. "What brings you in so early?"

"Good morning, Gwen. You look lovely this morning," Donna said as she made her way to the counter.

My smile grew wider. "Thank you," I said. I'd channeled my nervous energy about not hearing from Chris into curling my light-brown hair this morning, although the maroon sweatshirt with the words *Camelot Flowers* written in curling white script was nothing special, I'd also taken extra time with my makeup, something I didn't do on a daily basis.

Donna reached out and patted my hand where it rested on the counter. "I'm here because I heard about Justin. Don't you worry yourself, honey. No one really thinks that nice, young Chris hurt anyone," she said kindly.

Her words soothed the ache in my chest. "Thank you," I said gratefully.

"You know, I've been thinking about Justin," she said as she leaned over and sniffed a small bouquet of marigolds I'd put on the counter to cheer the space up. Not that there was any absence of cheer in the sunny space filled with flowers and other plants. If you ignored the snow piled on the edges of the sidewalk outside, you could pretend it was spring in the warmth of the store.

"I'm sure the whole town's been thinking about him," I said quietly.

"Now I'm not one to gossip…" Donna paused, waiting for my customary response.

I tried to shake away my sadness and focus. Donna hadn't just stopped by to check on me. Not if she had gossip to share. Maybe I'd learn something important. "No, of course not," I said, reassuring the good Lutheran woman that she was absolved of any wrongdoing in sharing whatever she'd learned with me.

She leaned in, her watery blue eyes sparking with excitement. "I heard Justin and Samantha Weston broke up Friday," she said in an excited whisper.

First, I hadn't known the new detective had started. Now I didn't know about the breakup? I needed to get back in the loop and fast. Especially with Justin dead and Chris missing. "Why didn't I know that?" I asked in bewilderment.

Donna shook her head as if saying she had no idea why I was so out of the loop but continued, "I heard it was a pretty bad breakup. Margie told me Samantha's just a mess about it."

I picked up the pen next to the order pad and tapped it against my chin as I said, "Why would they break up again? I heard things were going well this time."

Donna leaned in even closer. If the woman leaned in any farther, she'd end up in my lap. "Well, you didn't hear this from me…" she said before trailing off once more.

"No, of course not," I answered more quickly this time, fully engaged in Donna's little game.

Donna glanced around the room, despite the fact that we were clearly alone in the small store, before saying, "I heard he cheated on her."

"What?" I shrieked.

Donna shrugged casually, but her eyes gleamed with excitement. "That's what I heard," she said simply.

In a small town, it was hard knowing what rumors had a thread of truth, which ones were completely true, and which ones were flat-out lies. I would need to ask around. Cheating could be a motive for murder.

Samantha was a few years younger than me, but her sister had been in my graduating class. Samantha was sweet. Too sweet for Justin. I had a hard time imagining her killing anyone. But if I'd learned anything from all the true-crime podcasts I'd been listening to, you could never really know what someone was capable of.

"You're sure about this?" I asked Donna.

Donna shifted her weight, leaning on her cane. "I'm sure that they broke up. I can't say I'm sure about the cheating," she replied.

"Who else might know?" I asked absently, more to myself than Donna.

"You could ask his friends," Donna suggested.

I mentally scanned through Justin's friends. Chris wasn't an option until he got back to me. If Penny's husband, Jack, didn't know about the reason for the fight between Justin and Chris, he wasn't going to know anything about Justin's love life. There was one person…

The coffee turned in my stomach at the thought of talking to Derek Thompson on purpose.

"What's that look for, dear?" Donna asked, clearly concerned.

I pushed forward a smile. "It's nothing. I just realized I could ask Derek Thompson about Justin and Samantha."

"Ah, Derek," Donna said, smiling fondly. "He always did have trouble spelling the word *canoe*."

I shot her a confused look. What an odd thing to remember about somebody. It made me wonder what she associated with me from the fourth grade. "I'll find him later today and see if he knows anything. Thanks for the tip," I said.

I'd have to wait for Hailey, the teenager who helped out in the store after school, before I could hunt down Derek. We didn't have many custom orders today, and as a senior in high school, Hailey had been working at Camelot Flowers for three years. She could handle the store alone for a couple hours while I talked to Derek, and I knew just where I'd find him.

Derek loved two things—himself and working on his body. If I waited until Hailey arrived, I'd find Derek at Titan Fitness just down the street. I'd pop in, get my answers, and start a list of who could have murdered Justin.

"Interested in any flowers today?" I asked Donna.

She smiled sweetly. "Not today, but I will take one of these." She plucked a handmade caramel from a baby blue dish in front of the cash register. Not handmade by me, but Josie at Fairytale Sweets across the street kept us well stocked.

"One caramel," I said. "That will be fifty cents."

Donna leaned her cane against the counter and dug an embroidered coin purse from her quilted purse. She counted out one quarter, two dimes, and five pennies before handing them to me. "Now, Gwen, you keep me posted on anything you find out," Donna said, pocketing the caramel in her purple pants. "We all want to know who really killed Justin."

"I will," I promised.

While keeping Donna posted wasn't high on my list of priorities, I had no doubt she'd keep herself in the know. I foresaw more trips to Camelot Flowers in her future. At least until Justin's murder was solved.

Donna left, and I straightened the already straight order pad on the counter. I sent Chris another text. *Call me.* I'd already threatened bodily harm if he didn't get back to me on text number ten. Better to keep it simple now.

I pulled my hair over my shoulder and started braiding it. Penny called it my nervous tic. I called it keeping my hands busy while my brain worked overtime. I needed to get the bouquets made for the orders that had come in over the weekend, but I also needed to get back to Margie at the police station and schedule my next interrogation with Finn. Who cared if Finn called it an interview? He'd had the gall to imply Chris had something to do with Justin's death, so interrogation it was.

Finn might exude safety and strength with his broad shoulders and warm smile, but his stuffy suits and, as far as I was concerned, stuffy attitude made it impossible to enjoy. It didn't help that the warm smile seemed to turn icy every time I opened my mouth.

I dialed the non-emergency number for the police station before I could put it off any longer. Margie, the receptionist who took her job as the gatekeeper to the precinct very seriously, answered the phone. Margie had been my Sunday School teacher twenty-five years ago, was my mother's friend, and represented one of the many people in town who still doted on me, despite the fact that I was only months away from the end of my twenties.

As expected, Margie was delighted to hear from me. "Gwen, dear, I'm so glad you called. How is it, running things at the shop with your parents out of town? I know your mom was worried about leaving you to do all of it alone," she said with concern.

"It's going great, Margie. You can tell my mom to stop worrying and enjoy Florida. Maybe she'll actually do it if she hears it from you," I said with a laugh.

Margie chuckled warmly before changing the subject as only Margie could do. "And when are you going to find a nice young man to settle down with? You know, I was just telling your mother about this app I heard about on a podcast. It's a dating app called Bumble. I guess they're hoping you'll bumble your way into a relationship." She laughed heartily at her own joke.

Part of me wanted to stab myself with the pen I was holding, while part of me couldn't help but smile at Margie. She loved me like a mother, so I could forgive her meddling. "I'll let you know if I decide to download Bumble. You know," I said slyly, "maybe we should join together."

It took a lot to stun Margie into silence. I held back my own chuckle.

"I don't think Bumble is for old ladies like me," she finally said, sounding equal parts scandalized and amused by my suggestion.

"Sixty is the new thirty," I teased.

"Coming from someone who's almost thirty herself, that's saying something," Margie teased right back.

"Anyway…" I said. Margie wasn't the only one who could change the subject. "I got a message from Finn Butler asking me to come in for another interview today."

Margie's voice lowered, and I could tell she was cupping her hand around the receiver. "It's just awful what happened to Justin. He had such a good heart, even if he found himself in trouble sometimes. I always said that young man could go far if he'd just—"

"Margie," I said, cutting her off. When Margie really got going, there was no end in sight. "It's awful what happened." I swallowed past the lump in my throat. Dang it. The unpredictable tears were a new thing and something I was working hard to control. I wasn't being very successful. "Finn said I could come in any time after one. I have to wait for Hailey to get here at two thirty, and then I have to run one more errand. Does four work?"

"Oh, for sure, honey. I'll put you on his schedule." Then Margie switched gears again and said, "That Finn Butler sure is a handsome young man. Your mom and I were just discussing the possibility of—"

"Margie," I interrupted again, the warning clear in my tone. I had no doubt what Margie and my mother had been discussing.

Margie chuckled and said, "Okay, honey. I'll put you on his schedule at four. But you keep an open mind. He's a very handsome fellow. And no wedding ring. Maybe wear something nice. Maybe low cut, even. It couldn't hurt."

I grinned at Margie's good-hearted meddling. "I was thinking of going for a good long run first. You know, really get the sweat flowing," I teased.

Margie chuckled but didn't let me off the hook. "I'm sure it would give you a lovely glow," she said.

We said our goodbyes, and I slid my phone into the front pocket of my sweatshirt. I should count my blessings my dad hadn't insisted on full renaissance garb for Camelot Flower employees. Not that he hadn't tried. My mom had been the only thing that saved me from having to look like my namesake, Queen Guinevere, every day.

By the time I sat down for lunch with the tuna sandwich I'd been able to cobble together from my nearly empty shelves, my anxiety over Chris's silence had robbed me of my appetite.

I spent the rest of my lunch break ignoring my sandwich as I mindlessly scrolled on Facebook. If I didn't hear back from Chris by the time I was done at the police station, I was going to call Uncle Stan and officially report him missing. What good was having the police chief as an unofficial uncle if I couldn't call in a few favors?

I checked the time and was about to get back to work when a Facebook status update near the bottom of the phone screen stopped me. It read, *Sad to hear about Justin, but it seemed like it was a long time coming. That guy was always in some sort of trouble or another.* It was the last sentence that made my blood run cold. *Looks like Chris Crawford did the whole town a favor.*

It couldn't possibly be true. My gaze flicked off the accusing sentence to see the name of the person who'd posted it—Tony Reagan. Tony? I flashed back on his weird behavior at Bucky's Saturday night after Justin had shown up. While not seething with anger like Justin had been, Tony's words toward Justin had carried their own bite. If the police were talking to people in town, someone was going to see Tony's accusation of Chris and tell them about it. I made a mental note to ask Penny what she thought of Tony's words.

Hailey walked through the door right at two thirty. Her bright blonde hair was up in a high ponytail, and she blew a bubble with pink bubble gum as she set her backpack behind the counter.

"Hey, Gwen," she said, shrugging out of her blue and white Star Junction High School letter jacket. She'd lettered in swimming, band, and the debate team. The fact that she had any hours in her week to devote to Camelot Flowers still astounded me. "Busy today?" she asked.

"A few custom orders," I answered. I pulled a clipboard from beneath the counter. "I made a list of things to get done if it's slow this afternoon. I have to run out for a bit. Think you can handle things on your own?"

"For sure," she said, nodding enthusiastically. "I can handle it. Totally."

I smiled at her. I had no doubt she'd do great. "I'll be back around six to help you close up," I said.

Hailey perched on the stool behind the counter. "I heard you were the one to find Justin's body," she said bluntly.

The reminder of Justin's murder socked me in the gut, and I sucked in a steadying breath. The rest of my afternoon was going to be about Justin. Especially if I could catch Derek at the gym. I needed to get used to talking about it. "I did," I said to Hailey.

"Was it awful?" She sounded more intrigued than horrified. "We were talking about it at school today and decided finding a dead body must have been so weird. A lot of kids know I work here at Camelot Flowers, so everyone was asking me about it today."

It made sense that the teens in town were just as interested in Justin's death as the senior citizens, but I was keenly aware that several blocks off Main Street, Justin's parents were grieving the loss of their son. I made a mental note to send them flowers. It's what my mom would've done if she were here.

"Listen, Justin's death isn't something cool or funny," I said to Hailey, keeping my tone light but hoping the message sank in. "Just be careful that someone who might be sad he's dead doesn't overhear you guys speculating about it."

Hailey nodded gravely. She was a sweet kid, and I could see she was taking my words to heart. "We won't, Gwen," she said. "I promise. I'll tell everyone to chill out."

"Thanks, Hailey." I gave her a wide smile to make sure she

knew I wasn't upset with her. "Any questions before I go?" I asked.

"Nope," she said brightly. Her ponytail swung back and forth as she shook her head. "I've got this."

I pulled my coat on and grabbed my purse from the back room before heading for Titan Fitness. I had just enough time to find Derek and get the truth about Justin and Samantha before I needed to be at the police station.

While I hadn't heard from Chris, I knew he was Finn's number-one suspect. Maybe I'd learn something from Derek to take the heat off Chris. If not, I was going to have to keep searching.

CHAPTER FIVE

———

I walked into Titan Fitness a few minutes later, my nose and fingers freezing after the short walk, even though it was only a block away from Camelot Flowers. Scanning the room, I looked for Derek's tanned skin and blond buzz cut. Three women were on treadmills side by side all chatting with one another. Another woman and a man were busy near the free weights, but there was no sign of Derek.

"Hey, Gwen. Looking good today," Derek's smarmy voice came from behind me.

I closed my eyes and prayed for patience. I'd come looking for him but somehow regretted finding him. This conversation wasn't going to be easy. Not with Derek Won't-Take-No-For-An-Answer Thompson. I just needed to keep the conversation focused on Justin.

I turned to see Derek in his gym "uniform" of tight muscle shirt over baggy shorts. He smiled at—no, scratch that, he leered at me. Derek asked me out incessantly. I said no just as incessantly. He crossed his arms over his chest, clearly pushing his biceps into view. "Too bad about Chris," he said, although he didn't sound the least bit upset.

Guess I wasn't going to have to find a subtle way to bring up the Justin situation after all. "It's awful," I said, agreeing with Derek for once in my life. "Just when he was getting the building ready to open, he had to lose a friend there."

Derek put his hand on my shoulder, giving it a little squeeze as he said, "I was talking about how he got arrested yesterday."

I took a step back, forcing his hand to drop from my shoulder. "Chris wasn't arrested," I said incredulously. "The police just wanted to ask him some questions. Besides, no one's even heard from him."

"That's not what I heard," Derek said. He kicked his right foot up behind him, caught it in his hand, and pulled on it to stretch his leg. "I heard the police have got motive and proof. Everyone knows what Chris did to Justin."

Derek thought the only reason I wouldn't say yes to a date with him was because I had a thing for Chris, which was another painful reminder that I wasn't that great at hiding my crush from the rest of the town. Because of that, he'd say anything to stick it to Chris.

I swallowed back the sick feeling gathering in the pit of my stomach and pushed on with why I'd come to find him. Derek had information I needed. Maybe he even had information about the fight between Chris and Justin.

"What do you know about what Chris did to Justin?" I asked suspiciously.

Derek switched legs in his stretch. "I know it had something to do with money. Don't know the details," he said.

I threw my hands up. "That doesn't help me at all," I said.

"Why don't you ask Chris?" Derek said. It was impossible to miss the bitterness in his tone when he said Chris's name.

I decided to ignore his taunt. Getting into an argument with him about Chris wasn't going to get me anywhere. "What about Justin and Samantha? Did Justin cheat on her?"

Derek's eyes were such a pale-blue color, they were almost silver. Right now they looked anything but friendly. "That's my friend you're talking about," he said, the message to tread carefully obvious in his tone. "My friend who was just murdered. Show him some respect."

"You're saying he didn't cheat on Samantha?" I pressed. I couldn't let this go. I wouldn't. Not when Chris was a suspect.

"I'm not saying nothing," Derek said as he crossed his arms over his chest.

I took a step toward him, closing the distance between us. While Finn's cologne had smelled expensive and made me inexplicably want to wrap my arms around him, Derek's cologne tickled my nose and made me want to sneeze. "Tell me what you know about Justin cheating on Samantha," I challenged.

"No," Derek said emphatically.

There was a small part of me that was tempted to flirt with him to get the information, but I had a feeling that wouldn't work, not in this case. Plus, the thought of flirting with Derek Thompson, even to get information out of him, threatened to give me a case of those old-fashioned vapors once again.

"I'll find out one way or another," I said.

Derek sneered. "Good luck with that. I've got to get back to my workout."

He walked away without another word while I resisted the urge to scream in frustration. So much for learning something useful by talking to Derek. I'd learned Chris had been arrested, which couldn't possibly be true, the fight between Chris and Justin was about money, which told me practically nothing, and Derek knew something about Justin and Samantha but wouldn't rat on his friend.

It could only mean one thing. Justin had cheated. Otherwise, Derek would've denied it. I pulled out my phone and opened the Notes app. *Talk to Samantha* went on the top of the list. Right underneath it I wrote, *Send flowers to Justin's parents* and *Ask Penny about Tony's Facebook post.* Then in all caps, I added, *FIND OUT WHERE CHRIS IS.*

I hurried back to Camelot Flowers to get my car. Talking to Derek hadn't taken as long as I thought. Showing up early to the police station wasn't going to do me any good. I picked at the bottom of my sweatshirt. Maybe I would run home and change. First impressions were everything, my dad always said.

The first impression I'd given Finn had been something between homeless woman and crazy cat lady. There was nothing wrong with my current sweatshirt and jeans. They were certainly an upgrade from the pajama pants, oversized sweater, winter boots, and bed head I'd been rocking the first time we met, but I had extra time, and having Finn's second impression of me be a good one couldn't hurt.

I walked into the station thirty minutes later and was greeted with a warm hug by Margie. "Gwen, honey, I'm so glad whoever murdered poor Justin didn't get you too. Just think, you could've stumbled in at the wrong time, and *bam*!" Margie clapped her hands in my face with her final word.

I flinched back. "Uh, thanks?" I said hesitantly.

Margie held me at arm's length and looked me up and down. I'd changed into dark skinny jeans, a black V-neck sweater, and black suede high-heeled booties. The sweater wasn't exactly low cut as Margie had suggested, but it definitely showed more skin than my Camelot Flowers sweatshirt. I'd touched up the waves in my long hair with the curling iron and added a swipe of berry-colored lip gloss along with an extra coat of mascara.

A wide grin deepened the smile lines on Margie's plump cheeks. "You certainly didn't come right from work looking like this. Maybe you care a little bit what Finn Butler thinks of you?" she said suggestively.

"What are you talking about, Margie? I got dressed up for you," I said enthusiastically.

Margie threw her head back and laughed. "I love you, Gwen," she said affectionately.

"You too, Margie," I said.

Not having extended family in the area and being an only child, I'd taken for granted how many adults acted as surrogate aunts and uncles for me growing up, but it was something I appreciated more than ever as an adult.

"I'll let Finn know you're here," Margie said, heading back to her desk.

This was my chance to solve one mystery. Margie knew everything about everyone. "Do you know what Finn is short for?" I asked.

Margie's smile grew impish as she said, "I do, but if he hasn't told you, I'm not going to either. Life's more fun with a little mystery, isn't it?"

I folded my arms across my chest. "*This* is where you draw the line at gossip? Telling me what his full name is?" I said in disbelief.

Margie chuckled as she headed back to her desk and said, "The line has to be drawn somewhere."

"Fine," I said, maybe pouting just a little bit.

"What's fine?" Finn asked as he appeared at the end of the hall wearing another dark suit fitted perfectly to his muscular frame. My stomach gave a little flip, which only served to darken my mood.

I shot a look at Margie that said *keep your mouth shut* and turned to Finn with a sly smile. "Nothing," I said in a sing-song voice.

He pinched his lips into a tight line as if holding back whatever retort was running through his mind. "Thanks for coming in today," he said stiffly.

"Did I have a choice?" I challenged.

"Why can't you just say you're welcome?" he asked, annoyed.

I shuffled my feet and adjusted my purse. Margie was

watching us, the delight evident on her face. "Sorry," I said reluctantly. "You're welcome. How can I help?"

"Let's head back to my office," he said as he turned and extended his arm, inviting me to take the lead.

I gave Margie a little wave.

"Behave yourself," Margie crooned as we headed down the hall.

Which one of us she was talking to, I couldn't be sure.

I walked into Finn's office and sat in the chair opposite his desk. Behind the desk, a bulletin board displayed papers advertising everything from upcoming community events to the standard OSHA compliance sign.

Finn closed the door and settled behind the desk. He'd paired a golden tie with his blue suit, which made his golden-brown eyes glow. His beard looked slightly longer, as if he hadn't had time to trim it since Justin's murder.

Finn clicked a button on his laptop and said, "I want to go over the timeline one more time to make sure I didn't miss anything."

"Sounds like a plan," I said.

See. I could be polite, although I had a feeling pointing out how polite I was being would ruin the goodwill I was attempting to build. I'd been treating Finn like the enemy, when I really needed to be treating him like a source. And as the saying goes, you can catch more flies with honey than with vinegar.

Finn opened a document on his computer and started with, "You had dinner with your friend, Penny, at Bucky's Saturday night."

"Yes," I answered, determined to be helpful. If I helped Finn, maybe he'd tell me something about the murder investigation I could use to prove Chris didn't do it.

"At six thirty, Justin came in looking for Chris," Finn said.

"I guess. I'm not really sure what time it was." I leaned forward, curious how he knew what time Justin had shown up at Bucky's. "Actually, I don't remember mentioning what time Justin came into Bucky's."

Finn kept his gaze on his notes as he said, "You're not the only person I've been talking to. Others said it was six thirty."

He was talking to other people. I was dying to ask him what else he'd learned but knew even from our short interaction in the early morning hours of Sunday that it wouldn't go over well. "That makes sense," I finally said after concluding my internal debate about whether or not to risk annoying him with my questions. "I got there around six."

"Justin left five minutes later after Mitch Alcomb calmed him down and said Chris wasn't there," Finn added. He fixed me with a pointed look. I imagined it was a very effective tool in an interrogation room.

"Correct," I said. Feeling uncomfortable under the weight of his stare, I crossed my legs and shifted in the hard, wooden chair. Why did he need me to answer the same questions again? Did he think I was lying?

"Did you see Chris later that night?" Finn asked.

I tugged on a loose string hanging from the sleeve of my sweater. It came off in my hand, and I proceeded to twirl it around my finger. "No. I told you I didn't see Chris after I left the center. After dinner, I was tired and went home. Why would I have seen Chris?" I asked.

"People say you two are close," Finn said casually. Almost too casually.

My cheeks grew warm as the meaning of his words sank in. Like at dinner with Penny, I found myself defending my unrequited relationship with Chris. "I mean, we're close, but we're just friends." How to explain this clearly? "I'd have no…reason…to see him late on a Saturday night," I finally managed to say.

Finn held my gaze for a moment then exhaled lightly before turning his attention back to the computer. "So, no one saw him that night," he said quietly, as if talking to himself. "You got a text from him at two in the morning asking you to come to his building," he continued through the timeline.

"Yes, he said it was an emergency," I said as I shifted again, but this time it wasn't due to physical discomfort. I didn't like how specific Detective Butler was getting with his questions about Chris. My stomach squirmed, and I clutched my hands together in my lap. "I haven't been able to get ahold of Chris. Is he okay?" I asked.

"You arrived at the building at what time?" Finn asked, ignoring my question.

I looked up at the ceiling, scanning through my memory of that morning. "I believe it was about two thirty," I said.

Detective Butler looked up from his computer. "And Mr. Crawford wasn't there when you arrived?" he asked.

"No, it looked like the building was empty," I said. "It was dark. There were no cars in the parking lot."

"But you went in anyway." It could've been a question, but Finn's tone held a sting of reproach.

Being like honey instead of vinegar was proving more and more difficult. "Of course I went in. What if Chris had hurt himself? What if he needed help?" I said.

Finn must have noted the change in my tone, because he looked up, his eyes softening slightly as he said, "Gwen, I'm just making sure I have everything clear so the right person pays for Justin's murder."

I loosened my death grip on the arms of the chair and tried to see things from his perspective. He had a job to do. Ensuring he had the details straight was part of that job.

Finn walked me through the events of the rest of the night, and I tried my best to be cooperative. As he finished typing something into his computer, he looked up and smiled for the first time since I'd arrived. "That was helpful, Gwen. Can you think of anything else I should know?" he asked.

I scanned through my memory like a movie on fast forward, landing on Tony's behavior at Bucky's. Finn had been interviewing other witnesses, it seemed, but he hadn't mentioned Tony. "There was this one thing," I said slowly as I thought through Tony's seeming dislike of Justin.

Finn had been checking something on his computer. He looked up in surprise, clearly not expecting me to have something else to add, even though he'd asked the question. "Yes?" he asked expectantly.

"There was this guy at Bucky's Saturday night. Tony. He graduated high school with us but moved to Chicago after college. He was in town visiting his parents this past weekend and ended up at the bar with Mitch and some of the other guys who played football together. Anyway, he seemed upset with Justin," I explained.

"Upset how?" Finn asked.

"Justin came in yelling about looking for Chris, as you know," I said. "But Tony was making all these snarky comments about Justin, and then he said if Justin was staying, he was leaving." I shook my head. "It was weird. They used to be friends."

I left out the part about Tony's Facebook post practically accusing Chris of murdering Justin. I couldn't risk Finn adding another check in the guilty column for Chris.

"Thanks for sharing that," Finn said as he made another note on his computer. "No one else mentioned it."

I shrugged and said, "Justin was kind of the star of the show. I'm sure everyone was focused on him. Even Andy, the owner of Bucky's, was worried Justin was going to start some kind of fight."

Finn didn't ask more about Andy. He must have already talked to him. Funny that Andy hadn't mentioned Tony, since it seemed that Tony's slightly drunk statements had been a possible ignition point for the fight between Justin and Tony that Andy had successfully prevented.

Finn stood and said, "Thank you, Gwen. That was helpful. I'll walk you out."

Finn followed me into the hall, where a booming voice called out, "Guinevere?" The police chief walked toward us, his arms outstretched, a smile under his bushy mustache. He was wearing the dark-blue police uniform. Despite being in his early sixties, he'd avoided the spreading girth of a lot of men his age. His hair, what was left of it, was snowy-white despite his sandy-brown mustache. Margie's husband had passed away ten years ago from cancer. I'd always thought she and Uncle Stan would be a good match, but they'd resisted my efforts over the past year to push them together.

"Uncle Stan!" I said as I greeted him with a hug.

Finn looked back and forth between us. "*Uncle* Stan?"

"Oh, I'm not her real uncle, but I've been best friends with her dad since before she was born," Stan said as he looked at me with what could only be described as fatherly pride. "I held her in the hospital. I've gone to every school function she's ever had. Never had a family of my own. Gwen is like a daughter to me."

To say Finn's smile was strained would've been an understatement. "That's great," he said, sounding like he thought it was anything but great.

I turned my attention back to Stan. "I haven't been able to get ahold of Chris. I'm worried about him. I can't imagine what losing Justin has done to him," I said.

Stan looked to Detective Butler. "No one told her?" he asked.

"I didn't think it was prudent," Finn said tightly.

"Told me what?" I asked, fear gathering in my gut.

"Chris is here," Stan said softly.

"Chris is—? What?" The meaning behind Stan's words clicked into place, and my eyes narrowed to slits. I pivoted to Finn. "*You* arrested him?" I spit the words, my voice like ice. So much for honey. We were full-on vinegar now.

Uncle Stan took a step back and said, "The only time I've seen her like this was in fifth grade when she found out little Billy Masters was picking on Tammy Goldberg. She got calm like this right before she punched Billy in the face." Finn snorted out a laugh, but Uncle Stan said, "I'm not kidding."

The smirk slid off Finn's face, and his eyes widened in disbelief. "You think she's going to punch me?"

"Probably not," Stan said. "She's matured since fifth grade. Right, Guinevere?"

"I'm not going to punch anyone," I said through gritted teeth. It didn't mean I wasn't picturing it.

Uncle Stan continued, "Guinevere gets feisty when faced with injustice, especially if someone she cares about is involved."

"Injustice?" Finn objected.

"Gwen is also standing right here," I said, referring to myself in the third person. I shot Finn one more icy glare before turning back to Stan. "I want to see Chris."

"What? No way!" Finn's attempt to control his temper in front of his new boss was admirable, but his flexing jaw and bulging eyes gave away his disbelief we were even having this conversation.

Stan rested his hands on his utility belt. "Sweetie, I wish I could," he said.

"But you can!" I leaned forward and whispered loudly enough for Finn to overhear, "You're the boss. You don't have to listen to him."

Stan smiled sadly, placing a hand on my shoulder and giving it a squeeze. "I know I am, and that's why I can't do it. This is serious. I don't know how Chris got himself messed up in murder, but until we can clear some things up, I can't let you see him. I'll tell him you stopped by," he said.

Uncle Stan's attempts to soothe my temper were lost on me. I turned on Finn. "This is your fault," I snapped before spinning on my heels and marching back toward the front of the station.

Finn sputtered something about following procedure, but I didn't care. Procedure shouldn't matter more than people, and Chris was my people. I turned before rounding the corner and pointed a finger at Finn. "This isn't over."

Finn's eyes widened in shock, and he shook his head. "Unbelievable," he muttered as he headed back to his office. "Move to a small town, they said. It'll be less stressful, they said." His office door slammed shut.

I stomped into the foyer to see Margie typing away on her computer. "Unbelievable," I said, echoing Finn's words but for a very different reason.

Margie eyed me over her reading glasses before sliding them off her face. "What's the matter, dear? That sounded like quite the commotion."

I stopped my pacing and leaned on Margie's desk, trying to calm my racing heart. "Why didn't you tell me Chris is here?" I asked.

"You didn't know?" she asked, clearly shocked.

"No." I shot my best look of death down the hall toward Finn's office. "Uncle Stan won't let me see him because stupid Finn won't shut up about procedure."

"I don't think we should blame Finn—" Margie started.

I cut her off with a bitter laugh and resumed my pacing. "Margie, I need to see he's okay. He can't go through this without me. What am I going to do? What if I never see him again? What if he goes to prison for the rest of his life for a crime he didn't commit? It'll be all Finn's fault. That man—" I was just getting started, but Margie cut me off.

"Now, Guinevere." Her voice held a hint of reproach. Having a group of second mothers was wonderful. Until it wasn't. "Calm down. Everything will work out the way it's supposed to."

I planted my hands on my hips and stared out the front window at the watery blue sky. I sucked in a sharp breath and held it for a moment before letting it out, releasing some of my anger with it. My chest tightened, and my eyes filled with tears. Without the anger, the fear was too real.

Margie's gentle voice broke through my thoughts, "I *said*, everything will work out the way it's supposed to."

I turned to see an impish smile on Margie's face and a set of keys jingling in her hand.

"Are those…?" I asked, too afraid to hope.

"Yep." Margie's smile grew wider.

The desire to see Chris warred with my need to protect Margie. "I can't let you do that. You'll get in trouble," I said.

Please don't listen to me. Please don't listen to me.

"Pshaw, I've been here since Stan was just an officer writing speeding tickets, and I'll be here long after he finally decides to retire. You let me worry about me. Now, do you want to see Chris or not?" she said with a wide grin.

CHAPTER SIX

I couldn't believe Margie was going to sneak me in to see Chris. "Really?" I asked.

"Really. Now let's get going. I happen to know Stan stepped out to meet a friend for lunch and Finn is on some kind of conference call. Now's our chance." Margie jumped up from her desk and practically danced toward the hall that led to the holding cell. "Oh, this is so fun. It's like one of those *Mission Impossible* movies." She crouched and peeked around the corner like we were infiltrating an enemy base.

I should have known better than to worry about Margie. Margie lived for this sort of thing. If push came to shove, she'd be able to take care of herself.

I couldn't contain the sly grin that twitched the corners of my lips as I followed Margie to the back of the police station, where a single holding cell ran along the back wall. My heart pumped with excitement. I wanted to see Chris, but I took pleasure in defying Finn with his formal procedures and uptight attitude.

Any lingering worries I had over Margie getting into trouble for helping me died at the sight of Chris sitting on the bed in the corner of the holding cell. He stared at the floor, his arms on his knees, his head bent low.

"Chris?" I said hesitantly, not wanting to startle him.

His head snapped up. He stared at me like he was seeing a mirage. "Gwen?"

I rushed over, wrapping my hands around the thick bars. "Oh, my word! I've been so worried about you." I looked over at Margie. "How much time do I have?"

Margie looked through the window in the door to the hallway. "Maybe ten minutes. I'll keep my eye on Finn and detain him if necessary." She searched through the big ring of keys and unlocked the door to Chris's cell.

"Detain him?" I asked suspiciously. She seemed really into this *Mission Impossible* fantasy. How far was she going to go to keep Finn away?

"You know, make small talk," Margie said. "I don't think I've told him about my trip to the Hosta convention in Springfield last summer."

I turned my head to hide my smile. I'd heard the story. Maybe *detain* was the right word after all.

Margie turned to Chris and said, "I'm sorry about all of this. Hopefully they'll get it cleared up real soon."

"Let's hope," Chris replied.

The resignation in Chris's normally confident voice arrowed through my heart. I slipped into the cell, and Margie shut the door behind me. "I'll be back in ten to let you out." She lifted on her tiptoes and slinked down the hall, hugging her back against the wall.

Chris watched Margie's stealthy exit. "What's that about?" he asked.

"That's Margie living her dream of being an international spy." The smile at Margie's antics slipped off my face as silence descended between Chris and me. Shifting my weight from one foot to another, I was unsure of what to say or where to start.

"Thanks for coming," Chris finally said.

I gave him a sad smile and said, "Of course. Anytime."

"Want to sit?" He patted the bed next to him, the only place to sit in the small room.

I sank down onto the thin mattress.

Chris resumed staring at the floor as he said, "The new detective says I have a motive for killing Justin. And then there's the text to you that makes it sound like I'd done something stupid and needed help."

I shifted to face him. "What was that about? You asked me for help, and then you weren't even there," I said.

Chris jumped up and paced the length of the cell. "That's just it." He ran his fingers through his sandy blond hair. "I accidentally left my phone at the center that night. By the time I realized it was missing, I was already home and too tired to go back and get it. I figured I'd just get it in the morning. I'm not the one who texted you." He stopped in front of me, pain etched across his face. "You have to believe me, Gwen."

"If you're not the one who texted me…" I looked up at him,

reading the concern in his blue eyes as if he already knew the answer to the question my mind was trying to ask. My hand tightened around the strap of my purse. "If you're not the one who texted me," I said again, my voice just above a whisper, "then whoever did probably killed Justin."

Chris pinched the bridge of his nose and squeezed his eyes shut as he said, "Probably."

Goosebumps raced across my skin. "They lured me there?" I asked, my voice rising in fear.

Chris dropped to his knees in front of me, running his hands up and down my arms.

"Why me?" I blinked rapidly, trying to stop the rising swell of tears in my eyes.

"Think about it," Chris said. "Who else would jump out of bed for me in the middle of the night? Everyone knows you're my best friend." He gave me a half smile, but it did little to penetrate the fog that was wrapping itself around me with a blanket of icy fear. "Everyone knows we'd do anything for each other," he added.

"Someone wanted me to find Justin?" I whispered. The tears I'd been battling since finding Justin's body broke through my defenses, streaming down my cheeks, leaving dark spots on my jeans as they fell.

Chris hung his head, dropping his hands from my arms. "I'm sorry," he said, his voice breaking. "This is all my fault."

I swiped at the tears. "What? Don't say that." I lowered my voice and glanced at the door to the rest of the precinct. "Especially don't say that in here. You didn't kill anyone." I paused, studying him. "Right?" The man I'd loved since he was a boy wasn't capable of killing anyone, but I needed to hear it from him.

Chris's gaze snapped up to meet mine, and he rocked back on his heels. "No! I would never!" he said insistently. He ran a hand across the blond stubble covering his face, evidence that he'd been locked in here while I'd been desperately trying to get ahold of him. "But everyone knew we were fighting. Justin made sure of that," he added bitterly. Pushing himself to standing, he walked over to the bars, looking out on the empty room. "I never should've gotten mixed up with him."

"Why was Justin mad at you?" I asked, not sure I was ready to hear the answer but knowing I needed to know everything if I was going to help Chris. "Maybe if I understand what's going on, I can help explain to Stan that he's got the wrong guy."

"They haven't charged me with anything," Chris said, dodging my question. "I guess they can hold me for seventy-two hours before doing that."

"That doesn't answer my question," I challenged. "I saw how mad Justin was when I was leaving the center Saturday. I was at Bucky's when he came bursting in looking for you that night."

Chris stood with his back to me, silent.

"Chris?" I asked hesitantly.

"I can't tell you," he said quietly.

His tone, filled with shame and regret, cut right through me. I shifted on the thin mattress, growing more uncomfortable both physically and emotionally the longer I spent in the cell. "You can tell me anything," I said. "We tell each other everything."

Chris turned to face me, pain etching lines across his handsome face. Walking over, he sat down, taking my hand in his. I expected my stomach to flutter at his touch, but instead it filled with dread. "You're the best person I know," he said. "I can't tell you this. You'll never look at me the same way again."

I gave his hand a squeeze. "If I don't know, I can't help you."

Chris rubbed his bloodshot eyes and studied the floor. I'd never seen him like this. Always the class clown, the life of the party, he was quick with a smile and even quicker with a hug.

He pulled his hand away, refusing to meet my gaze. The toe of his shoe traced a small crack in the cement floor. "Six months ago, I learned the building on Lincoln was going up for sale." He looked at me, and a glimmer of the charming, confident Chris flickered in his gaze. "You know I'd had my eye on it for a long time. It's the perfect location for a youth center, and I knew it would be cheap if it ever went up for sale because of the condition it was in."

I nodded, remembering how excited he'd been. He'd rushed over without calling, catching me in the middle of trying to hang new curtains in my living room. He'd burst through the door, which I had a bad habit of leaving unlocked, and scooped me up in a hug before I'd even registered he was in the room.

"I planned to start fundraising, but my real estate agent called the next day. Another buyer wanted to level it and put in a parking lot," Chris said in disgust. "We don't need a parking lot downtown. We need a place where teens can hang out after school when their parents are still at work. I couldn't let the other buyer get it, which meant I needed the down payment as soon as possible.

Justin and I were out fishing that weekend, and he told me he could loan me the money. In cash." He looked up at me, waiting for the response he had to know was coming.

"Oh, Chris," I said, not bothering to hide the disappointment in my tone.

Chris's shoulders slumped. "I know. I didn't want to see my dream disappear."

"How did Justin have that kind of cash?" I asked. My fear over the answer to the question pressed heavy against my chest.

"I didn't ask," Chris said. He sighed deeply before saying, "The truth is, I didn't want to know."

"What happened?" I asked. I couldn't help him if I didn't know everything, but part of me wanted to childishly plug my ears and sing *la-la-la* until it all went away. I wanted to hold on to the idealized Chris that lived in my fantasies.

Chris continued, "He showed up the next day with ten thousand dollars cash in an envelope, and I took it. He was demanding an exorbitant interest rate, but I figured I'd worry about that later. I closed on the building a few weeks later."

"You know the rumors about Justin," I said quietly, as if by my keeping my voice kind, I could soften the gravity of the situation.

"About drugs?" Chris said. "Yeah, I know."

"And you never stopped to think maybe you shouldn't fund your keep-kids-off-drugs youth center with possible drug money?" I asked.

"Of course I thought of that," Chris said, his voice rising.

I glanced at the door, and Chris followed my gaze, lowering his voice. The last thing either one of us needed was for me to get caught back here.

"I told you," Chris said. "I messed up."

"So, what was Justin so upset about? Did you not make a payment?" I asked. We needed to speed this up. I didn't know if I could get back in here again, and if I was going to get Chris out of this cell, I needed to know everything.

"I couldn't live with the thought that Justin's money might have come from him dealing drugs," Chris answered. He paused long enough that I began to worry about what I was going to hear next. "Last week, I called my dad." His face pinched, and he shoved his hands into his pockets, watching me closely.

"You called your dad?" I couldn't have been more shocked if Chris had told me he'd murdered Justin himself.

"I didn't know what else to do," Chris said. He stood and leaned back against the bars, folding his arms across his chest.

The Crawford family had moved to Star Junction when we were in second grade. Mr. Crawford was a lawyer, which made Chris's family one of the wealthiest families in Star Junction. Not only did Mr. Crawford hate Star Junction, but he made sure everyone knew it.

Moving here to take care of Chris's grandma was supposed to be a temporary arrangement. By the time she passed away, Chris was established in school and sports. His mom had insisted they stay.

As soon as Chris left for college, his dad took the opportunity to move the two hours back to Chicago. Chris was a disappointment to his dad, not only because of his decision to become a school guidance counselor and eventually open a youth center, but also because he'd moved back to Star Junction. For him to call his dad meant he was beyond desperate.

"What'd your dad say?" I asked tentatively.

"First he yelled," Chris said, his tone resigned. "Then he lectured. You know, the usual." We shared a brief smile. We'd spent a lot of time in high school trying to avoid his dad's lectures. Chris continued, "Then he said he'd take care of it and hung up. Two days later, there was a check in my mailbox for ten thousand dollars. I used the money to pay Justin back in full. No more payments. No more interest."

I sat back and considered the situation. "That doesn't seem so bad," I finally said. "I don't understand why Justin was so upset."

Chris started pacing again. "I don't get it either. When I gave him the check, he lost it. He started yelling about how he couldn't believe I backed out of our agreement. He said he invested the money and expected the interest he was due. I asked how much he wanted. He wanted his money doubled. Ten thousand more dollars?" Chris said incredulously. "I didn't have that kind of money. I told him a real friend wouldn't rob me blind while I was trying to do something good for the town. He said he'd get his money from me if it was the last thing he did."

"Your dad?" I asked hesitantly.

Chris shook his head. "No way was I going to ask him for more money, and I'd already invested all my own savings into buying the supplies to fix up the building."

I glanced toward the door. I had no idea how much time we

had left. I needed Chris to pick up the pace. "Justin thought you cheated him out of money. That's what he was so mad about?"

"And now this new detective is convinced I killed him," Chris said in frustration.

"It doesn't look good," I replied.

He sank down onto the bed next to me, his face buried in his hands. "I know."

A new thought occurred to me, and hope flared in my chest. "Did they find your phone? I bet whoever sent the text left fingerprints on it. They'll be able to figure out it wasn't you."

Chris shook his head and said, "Detective Butler has been stingy with information, but he's asked me repeatedly about where I hid my phone." Chris scoffed. "Like I'd get rid of the phone and not the murder weapon."

I groaned and said, "While I agree with your logic, let's not sound too much like a criminal mastermind. Especially not when you're in police custody."

I tried to see down the hall through the small window in the door that led to the rest of the precinct. From this angle, it was impossible to tell if anyone was coming.

"Let's review," I said, all business. "You have a motive for killing Justin. You have no alibi?" I figured that's what Detective Butler was getting at when he'd asked if I'd seen Chris Saturday night.

"I was home alone," Chris said.

I folded my arms across my chest. "You need a girlfriend. Then maybe you'd have an alibi and all of this would be over."

"Know anyone who's interested?" It was his usual flirty banter, but there was no heart behind it.

I ticked the points off on my fingers as I said, "No alibi. It looks bad that your phone was used to get me to the center and now it's missing. It happened in your building with your screwdriver." A new thought occurred to me. "How'd Justin get in? Did you leave the door unlocked? It was unlocked when I got there," I told him.

Chris shook his head and said, "I'd never leave it unlocked with all those tools in there. He must have broken in. But why?"

"Maybe he was going to steal the tools?" I theorized. "Get his money another way?"

"Then someone else had to have known he was going to be there," Chris said.

"The same person who texted me." My skin crawled at the

thought of someone luring me to find Justin's body. "I told you a passcode of 0000 on your phone wasn't a good idea." Maybe now wasn't the time to nitpick. There were a hundred things Chris could've done differently.

"I'm sure my fingerprints will be all over the screwdriver," Chris said, sounding dejected.

"I'll just have to figure out why Justin was at the center after you left and who knew he'd be there. Maybe I can find your phone," I said.

"You'll… What?" Chris said in horror. "No, you're not going to do anything."

"Someone has to get you out of here," I said. "I don't know if you realize this, but you're in real trouble."

"You don't think I know that?" he practically shouted. "I'm in jail."

"Which is why I need to figure out what happened to Justin," I argued.

Chris launched himself off the bed, his eyes flashing with anger. "No, I don't want you digging into this."

"Well, I'm not going to do nothing while this new detective builds a case to put you away for murder," I said, my voice rising in intensity to match Chris's.

"Gwen, I said no. It's not safe!" Chris yelled.

Margie came bursting through the door. "Everything alright in here?" she asked, sounding out of breath, as if she'd rushed down the hall.

I stared at Chris. "Yeah, it's fine," I said to Margie. "I'm ready to go."

Margie looked back and forth between us as she unlocked the cell door.

I reached for Chris's hand and said, "There's no way you'd leave me sitting in here to rot, and I'm not going to leave you in here either. I'll figure this out." I gave his hand a squeeze and walked out the door before he could object again.

I said goodbye to Margie and glanced through the window into Finn's office as I walked by. He was on the phone, but our gazes met. The smile slipped off his face. I gave him a little wave, hoping he would read the sarcasm in it.

As far as I was concerned, he was the reason Chris was in jail to begin with. Uncle Stan needed to follow procedure, but having this new guy running the investigation likely pushed Chris's detainment more quickly than if Uncle Stan had been handling it himself.

I held my head high as I walked into the cold sunshine. It was time to get to work and prove someone else killed Justin.

I dug around in my purse as I cut across the parking lot to my car. I needed to talk this over with Penny, brainstorm, make a murder board. Something. I found my phone and tapped out a quick text. *Just left police station. Chris is in jail. Need to process. Is Jack at the station tonight?*

Penny was more likely to be available on the nights her firefighter husband was working. Fingers crossed this was one of those nights.

Penny texted me back before I made it to my car. *Yes, he's working. Want to do dinner?*

I climbed into my car before responding, turning the heat up and the radio down. *I don't have any groceries.*

She texted back, *Me neither. Let's go out.*

Not local though. Too many interruptions. Too many listening ears.

We can do Rose Lake. Pick you up at six?

I sent her back a thumbs-up and headed back to Camelot Flowers to help Hailey close the store. I had a few hours before dinner, which gave me time to work on my to-do list surrounding Justin's murder. I needed to add a column for possible motives, which meant I needed to get information from people close to Justin. Derek had stone-walled me about the affair rumor, but it didn't mean he wouldn't talk to me about other things in Justin's life. I couldn't get stuck on one theory, or I might waste all my time heading down the wrong path.

CHAPTER SEVEN

———

Penny and I made it to the neighboring town of Rose Lake in record time. Saying nothing about Justin's murder, or Chris being in jail, Penny talked about the upcoming vacation she and Jack were planning for spring break. As a high school teacher, Penny liked to say spring break was the only thing that kept her alive between Christmas break and summer break.

It might have seemed bizarre in light of what was happening around us, but I was grateful for the hint of normalcy, even if it wasn't going to last forever.

Not much bigger than Star Junction, Rose Lake offered a change of scenery from the same old restaurants, not to mention the same people we ran into every day. Dos Gringos was our favorite place. Run by Jose and Maria Ramirez, a couple originally from Mexico City, it was a breath of authentic Mexican cuisine in the center of America's heartland.

The server stopped by with a large bowl of chips and two smaller bowls of salsa. She took our orders and walked back toward the kitchen.

Penny leaned across the table, her hazel eyes twinkling. "Now, I know we need to talk about Chris and the mess he's gotten himself into, but first we're going to talk about Detective Hottie and exactly what you're going to do to get a date with him."

I pulled a chip from the pile. "Detective Hottie?" I said, complete with an eyeroll.

"You don't think he's hot?" she asked in shock. She shook her head, her black hair swinging around her shoulders. Her signature hot-pink lipstick matched her equally hot-pink sweater tonight. "I saw him at the Piggly Wiggly this morning. He was in a suit. A well-fitted suit," she added, wiggling her eyebrows suggestively. "Who wears a suit in Star Junction?"

"Plenty of people. The mayor wears a suit," I said.

"Fine," Penny said as she scoffed. "Who wears a suit and is young and handsome? And what do we think about that beard?"

She had me there. I definitely had a thing for that beard.

I shifted in my chair and scanned the room, pretending to search for our server. "Excuse me," I finally said when it became obvious no well-timed interruption was coming to change the subject, "but I was too focused on answering questions about finding a dead body to pay much attention to Finn's suit or his hotness."

It was a lie. I'd definitely noticed both, but the lie worked. Sort of.

Penny looked ready to apologize before her eyes narrowed. "Did you just call him Finn?"

I was at a loss as to how this was news, but from Penny's tone, I could tell she was building up to something. "I did."

"Not Detective Butler. But *Finn*. Getting pretty familiar with the hot new detective."

It was time to redirect the conversation. Again. "If I can figure out who would want Justin dead, the police would let Chris go and focus on arresting the real killer. Once he's in the clear, we can talk all you want about my nonexistent love life."

"If *you* can figure out who killed Justin? Are you crazy? You'll get yourself killed. You'll end up on *Dateline*. Maybe even a true-crime podcast. When you turn up dead, I'll try to avoid watching the media coverage because it'll be too painful to hear all about how you got yourself killed by meddling in this investigation, but the story will be everywhere. Unavoidable. Do you really want to do that to me?" she asked, verging on hysterics.

I stared at Penny. She'd lost her mind.

The server dropped off our food, and I rearranged some things on the table to make room for a small plate where I could assemble my fajitas. I unwrapped the foil holding the tortillas, flattened one out on my plate, and dropped a generous dollop of guacamole in the center.

Penny ignored her enchilada. "Last time I checked, florists aren't also forensic experts," she said.

I took a bite and let out a contented sigh. "I'm not a forensic expert, but I am a Star Junction expert," I pointed out.

Penny cut off a bite of her enchilada. "That might be true, but where would you even start?" she asked.

I took another bite, using the time it took me to chew and

swallow to come up with an answer. I waved my hand through the air. "I'll just ask around. I already started making a list."

"You'll just ask around?" Penny said skeptically.

"I'll just talk to people who knew Justin," I said.

"So, everyone in town. You're going to talk to five thousand people?" Penny challenged.

I supported her harebrained schemes all the time. The one time I have one, and she's suddenly Miss Logical? "Just the ones who knew him well. I already heard he broke up with Samantha, when Donna came into the flower shop this morning. I followed up with Derek to see if he knew anything about it," I said.

"And…" Penny prompted.

"Hey, ladies, got out of town tonight, huh?" Mitch said as he sauntered toward our table, adjusting his beat-up Texaco baseball cap on his head.

So much for leaving town for some privacy, but this was the perfect opportunity to show Penny what I was capable of. I turned to Mitch and explained, "We needed a change of scenery from Bucky's. What are you doing in Rose Lake?"

"I have a job over here for the next several months," he said. "The guys and I stopped for dinner before heading back to town." Mitch had started a construction business a few years ago. From the looks of things, it had really taken off. He'd bought a nice house on the edge of town on Star Lake last summer.

Penny grabbed her napkin and wiped her mouth. "What are you working on? Please say building a spa," she said, her hazel eyes pleading for it to be true.

Mitch chuckled and said, "Unfortunately, no spa, although I heard Lucille's Clip and Curl back in town added some kind of acupuncture."

Penny scrunched up her nose in disgust. "I heard she took a weekend class through a brochure she found on her last cruise. No way am I letting that woman stick needles in my face," she said.

Mitch laughed and said, "I wouldn't either." He turned to me, his smile slipping. "I'm sorry about Chris. How's he holding up?"

I shot Penny a smug look. *See? I didn't even need to bring it up.* People were going to be falling all over themselves to talk to me about the murder. "I got to see him today," I said. "He's hanging in there."

Mitch leaned in a little closer and his bushy, caterpillar-inspired eyebrows pulled together. "I hope he gets a good lawyer. I had to tell that new detective about how angry Justin was when he was looking for Chris at Bucky's that night." He grimaced. "It doesn't look good."

"Chris is innocent," I snapped, feeling the betrayal of Mitch's comment deep in my gut. Chris was his friend. How dare he think Chris would murder Justin?

Mitch leaned back and folded his arms across his chest. "Then who do you think did it?" he asked.

"I don't know, but I'm going to find out," I said defiantly.

"You?" Mitch chuckled. "Good luck with that."

"Speaking of Justin's murder," I said, not willing to lose the opportunity to add to my motives list no matter how frustrated I was with Mitch, "do you have any theories?"

"Besides Justin finding Chris at the center Saturday night, their fight escalating, and Chris killing Justin in a of fit of rage?" Mitch asked.

"Yes, besides that," I gritted out through clenched teeth.

Mitch stared off into the distance, his dusty work boot tapping on the wooden floor. He lifted his cap, ran his hand through his dark hair, and resettled the faded thing back on his head. "I don't know. Justin was a likable guy."

"He was also a screw-up," Penny said emphatically.

I grimaced. It was true, but it felt wrong to speak ill of the dead. At least I hadn't been the one to say it.

"I don't know what to tell you," Mitch said. "I know you think Chris is innocent, but people do all sorts of things in the heat of the moment. If I hear anything different, I'll let you know. Have a nice dinner." He rejoined the group of guys sitting at a high top next to the bar.

Mitch's insistence that Chris was guilty grated on my nerves, but it was clear I wasn't going to convince him otherwise. I turned to Penny and said, "See? Finding out information about Justin won't be hard."

"But did you really learn anything useful?" she asked skeptically.

She had a point.

"I think you should let Detective Hottie handle it," Penny said, turning back to her enchilada.

"If I let Detective Hot—seriously, you've got to stop calling him that. If I let Finn handle it, Chris will end up in jail for the rest of his life. He's already decided he's guilty," I said glumly.

Penny took a sip of her Dr. Pepper and sighed dramatically. "Finn Butler. A name straight out of a soap opera."

"You need to focus," I said, although I couldn't help but laugh.

"I am focused. I'm focused on getting you a date." Penny stared off into space, her expression dreamy. "I bet it's Irish. You know what they say about Irish boys."

"That they're a little too attached to their mamas?" I deadpanned.

"No, that they like their women feisty." Penny narrowed her eyes at me as if eyeing a choice cut of meat. "I bet you're right up his alley."

Heat flooded my cheeks. We needed a change of subject. Now. "Let's figure out who else I can talk to about Justin so we can get Chris out of jail," I said.

"*We're* not going to get Chris out of jail." Penny gestured between the two of us. "I'm sure his parents will send him a lawyer, and *that person* will get him out of jail."

"I don't know," I said slowly. "You know what his dad is like."

Penny gave me a pained look. "Yeah, I do." She gazed down at her food for a moment before looking up and saying, "Finding out who really killed Justin can be plan B in case his parents don't send a lawyer." She pointed her fork at me. "A dangerous plan B." Her expression brightened as she said, "What about the pie social? Lots of people all in one place. I bet you could learn all sorts of things to add to whatever list you've got going."

The pie social. Without Chris there, who would serve as a buffer between me and my mother's well-meaning friends intent on setting me up with someone? "You have to agree to protect me though. I can't end up with Derek, who thinks if he asks me out one thousand times, I'll eventually say yes, winning my pie. Even when I talked to him this afternoon at the gym, he was a total creep."

"Jack will bid on it," Penny reassured me. "Believe me, he won't mind taking home two pies."

The server dropped off our check, and I scooped it up. "Ah, the pie social. Star Junction—" I started.

"Tradition," we finished together.

We dissolved into a fit of giggles. *Star Junction tradition* was code for anything you didn't want to do but you had to because the town expected it. I'd come to peace with it a long time ago, but it didn't mean I couldn't complain about it.

The month of January was the coldest, grayest, longest month of the winter. The Friends of the Library had started the pie social when Penny and I were in high school as a way to raise money for the summer reading program and provide a social remedy for the winter blues. It was actually a pretty fun night. There was always good-natured arguing during the pie auction, and the spread of food was amazing.

As I approached thirty years old, it became less fun as my mom's friends made it their mission to use the pie social to set me up with their sons, nephews, or any other man with a pulse. Every woman brought a pie to be auctioned off. Whoever won my pie would get the pleasure of sitting down and sharing a slice of it with me. It was old-fashioned, and some might even say sexist, but it was all in good fun.

Unless one of us happened to be dating someone, Chris had always bid on and won my pie. We'd sneak away and spend the rest of the night laughing about what other matchmaking was going on in the church hall. The smile slipped off my face and my heart sank at the thought of Chris not being there this year.

"Let me show you my list," I said as I dug through my purse to find my phone. I opened the note I'd started earlier that day.

Penny leaned over to see the list, shaking her head when she saw Samantha's name.

"What?" I said, maybe a little defensively.

"How're you going to talk to Samantha without making it seem like you think she killed Justin?" Penny asked.

"Who's to say she didn't?" I challenged.

Penny's hazel eyes widened, the shock clear on her face. "Listen, I'm all for helping Chris. Do I think he killed Justin? No way, but you need to be careful. You have to live with these people long after this mess with Justin is over. The fine residents of Star Junction are not known to be quick to forgive," she said.

Penny's words gave me pause. I hated to admit she was right, but I was wading into a minefield. If Chris didn't kill Justin, then someone else did. Probably someone I knew. Maybe even someone I trusted.

CHAPTER EIGHT

———

I pulled into the parking lot of the grocery store the next morning, driving cautiously. A cycle of snow—melting and freezing—had plagued Star Junction since Christmas. The city had done its best to stay on top of the ice, but some of the sidewalks and parking lots were like skating rinks.

I would've preferred to stay home, nice and cozy by the fire, before heading to Camelot Flowers to have the shop opened by ten, but I couldn't ignore the fact that the pie social was tonight, and not only did I have no pie, but I didn't even have enough food in my house to make one.

I usually rushed into the pie social with a store-bought pie, much to the chagrin of my mother, who'd never bought a pie from a store in her life. Figuring out who killed Justin was going to take some time and effort, but baking a pie from scratch? I could do that. Right?

Pinterest had been my salvation, and the list of ingredients I needed for my lemon blueberry swirl cheesecake was tucked in my purse. While not technically a pie, it looked delicious and seemed like an elevated version of the cheesecake my grandma used to make every fourth of July. I didn't think anyone would object to having a taste of summer in the middle of winter.

I grabbed my purse and shoved a wool hat on my head before ducking my chin against the icy wind and hurrying toward the entrance of the store. If it was going to warm up today like the weather app predicted, it hadn't started yet.

Choosing a cart, I headed toward the baking aisle, sending up a silent prayer I'd make it through this trip without having to recount the events of finding Justin's body. Gossip was practically an Olympic sport in Star Junction, and securing the story directly from the source was like winning a gold medal.

Passing the cereal aisle, I pulled up short at the sight of

Samantha Weston, Justin's girlfriend. Or, if the rumors were true, ex-girlfriend. She was standing in front of the Fruity Pebbles, but it was clear from the look on her face that she was mentally somewhere else.

While I was frozen with indecision, she pulled in a shaky breath and headed in the other direction. This was my chance. I pushed my cart forward. If I could "bump" into her, I'd have a chance to ask her about Justin.

She skipped the baking aisle, and so did I. When she turned down the next aisle, I mimicked her movements, until we were on a collision course. Metaphorically of course. Our carts approached each other near the canned soups, and I put on my best shocked impression when I said, "Samantha?"

She glanced in my direction blankly for a moment before recognition dawned on her face. "Hey, Gwen," she said glumly. Her bleach-blonde hair hung limp around her face like she hadn't washed it in several days. Dark circles rimmed the bottom of her blue eyes. She sniffed, wiping her button nose with the back of her hand.

"How are you doing?" I asked.

Samantha sniffed as if holding back tears and said, "It's been a rough week."

I scooted my cart over so we weren't blocking the aisle, although we were mercifully alone for the moment. "I'm sure it's been tough," I said in agreement.

This brought on a fresh wave of tears. I awkwardly patted Samantha's shoulder as she snuffled into her hands, her hair covering her face. I rooted around in my purse, came up with a napkin from the coffee shop in town, and handed it to her.

"Thanks," Samantha said as she took a shaky breath and pressed the palms of her hands over her eyes for a moment like she was plugging a leaking faucet. She gave me a wan smile. "Justin's mom called to ask some questions about a memorial service. The police still have his body." The tears started again. "But you don't need a body for a memorial service," she finally managed as she wiped her nose with the napkin.

I stood in silence, dying to ask questions that might help Chris but not wanting to be insensitive.

"I'm sorry you had to be the one to find him," Samantha said, breaking the silence. "I can't… I can't believe…" I braced myself for more tears, but Samantha took a shaky breath and continued, "I can't believe he's really dead."

"Stuff like this doesn't happen in Star Junction," I said. "At least not to people we know." It was time to take a risk and ask her some questions. Better than having to track her down later. "I'm trying to help Chris," I started. "The police have pretty much decided he's guilty, but I can't believe he did it. Plus, he says he's innocent." I looked down at my hands. "How many murders can the police here have investigated? I'm worried they'll get it wrong."

Samantha reached out and squeezed my hand. "I can't believe Chris would do anything to hurt Justin. Or anyone," she added.

You should be the one comforting her, blared through my mind like a siren. For all my bluster at dinner the night before, I was flying blind in this investigation. Navigating the line between helping Chris and not hurting people close to Justin might be harder than I thought.

"But that new detective is from Chicago," Samantha continued. "I'm sure he's investigated murders before. The police will figure this out."

I met Samantha's gaze, her eyes red and puffy from crying. "He's from Chicago?" I asked.

Samantha shrugged and said, "That's what I heard. Hey, I better get going. I told Justin's mom I'd drop off some pictures she could use for the service. That's why I was here. I was getting them printed. Who prints pictures anymore?" She let out a shaky laugh. "I don't even know how I ended up by the soup."

"Grief is a funny thing," I said. After my dad's heart attack five years ago, I'd wandered all sorts of places, my brain turning off as if trying to escape the worry and sadness. "I just wanted to make sure you were okay."

"Thanks," she said sweetly.

I pushed my cart forward to give Samantha room to leave but paused and said, "Can I ask you one more question? It's kind of personal."

Samantha's eyes widened slightly, as if taken aback by my request. "Uh, okay."

I rushed on before I could lose my nerve. "It's just that I heard you and Justin broke up last week, and I was wondering if it was true." I held my breath. Was I being a jerk?

Samantha stared across the aisle at the shelf of pasta sauce. A single tear snaked down her cheek. "It's true," she finally said, her voice not much more than a whisper. "I loved him. Very much. But I found out last week he was cheating on me with some girl from Rose Lake." She hung her head and picked at the edge of her fingernail. Her next statement was so soft I almost missed it. "The same person who told me about the cheating told me the other girl might be pregnant."

"The same person? Like a friend of yours?" I asked, itching to add another source to my list.

Samantha shook her head and said, "Someone random contacted me on Instagram. The account is clearly fake, because there are no pictures on it, but they knew enough about Justin for me to believe them."

Samantha picked up a can of chicken noodle soup and added it to her cart without even looking at it before adding, "When I asked Justin about it, he didn't deny it, but he didn't say it was true either. That was the last straw. I broke up with him Tuesday." Her gaze grew distant. "I didn't talk to him again. The last thing I said to him was that he was an awful human being." Her eyes flooded with tears again.

My mind was going a million miles a minute trying to figure out how to find out who told Samantha about the affair, but I couldn't ignore her suffering. I pulled her into a hug, patting her on the back as she sniffled away.

My mom once told me that when someone is suffering, you let them end the hug, so I held on to Samantha for what felt like forever as she cried. Finally, she pulled away and asked, "I shouldn't have said Justin was an awful human being. Am I a bad person?"

"No way," I said, adamantly. "You couldn't have known Justin would end up murdered just days later, and if he really cheated, then he did do an awful thing." I made a mental note to tell Finn about what Samantha shared if I ended up running into a dead end trying to find out who sent the message on Instagram. The police might have better luck than I would. It didn't mean I wouldn't try. "Do the police know this?" I asked Samantha.

"I assume they do," she said. "Seems the whole town knows we broke up."

"Not about you guys breaking up," I clarified. "I mean, did you tell the police about the affair? The possible pregnancy?"

Samantha reared back as if I'd struck her and said, "No. Why would I do that? It's embarrassing."

"But it could be another motive for murder," I said.

"Are you saying I have a motive to murder Justin?" she practically shouted.

"No, that's not what I'm saying at all." I reached out a hand reassuringly, but Samantha flinched out of reach. "But maybe the other girl had a boyfriend who got jealous," I added.

"Why are you being so mean to me?" Samantha said right before she burst into tears again.

My gaze darted to the ends of the aisle. This was turning into a scene, which is the last thing I wanted. "I'm sorry. I'm sure it's nothing." I reached over and gave Samantha one more pat on the back before she stomped toward the front of the store.

I hurried through the store to find the rest of the items on my list, pondering Samantha's words. Pulling out my phone, I added, *Baby?* to the line about Justin cheating. Being cheated on could lead to all sorts of feelings, including the desire to murder the no-good boyfriend, but finding out there was a baby? That had to cut even deeper.

Finn was convinced a woman couldn't have committed the crime, but accounts of moms lifting cars off their trapped kids argued differently. Adrenaline could make people strong enough to do all sorts of things, even commit murder.

An hour later, I dropped my bags on the kitchen counter. Before I could make it out of the store, I'd been stopped four times by people who wanted to express their concern about how I'd been the one to find "poor Justin" and twice more by people who had their own theories about who had murdered him.

The theories were wild, including a gang from Chicago driving the two hours from the city to murder Justin. When I'd asked why some random gang would do that, the person had just shrugged and said, "That's what I heard," before walking off.

Even if I wanted to stop investigating, it wouldn't stop people from talking to me about what had happened. I couldn't help it if people shared things with me. I tucked that little argument away in case Finn found out I was investigating. I had a feeling he'd want me as far away from this investigation as possible.

I got the groceries put away and set out to make the cheesecake, thinking about the timeline of my day. I had to open the shop at ten, but it was only eight. The recipe indicated I could get the pie done within an hour. I looked over the list of things to follow up on about the investigation. *Bring Mrs. Hunt flowers* caught my eye.

If I hurried, I'd have time to swing by the shop, grab a bouquet, and pay Mrs. Hunt a visit before I had to open. Besides feeling like the right thing to do, she might know something about Justin's life that I didn't.

I sent a quick text to my mom saying, *How's the weather in Florida? We're looking at another hard freeze tonight. You picked a good time to head south. Can I get Mrs. Hunt's phone number? I want to take her flowers.*

When I didn't see the little bubbles indicating my mom was writing back right away, I turned on some music and lined up the ingredients on the counter. I was halfway through belting the lyrics of "Jailhouse Rock," an ironic song to come through my streaming service considering the mess with Chris, when the music stopped, interrupted by a text alert.

I wiped my dirty hands on a dish towel before unlocking the phone to read the text. My mom had written back, *That's a lovely idea, Gwen. So thoughtful. I've attached her contact info. Your dad says hi. We're heading to ride bikes on the beach path. Let me know how it goes with Justin's mom. I can't stop thinking about that poor boy.*

Thanks, Mom, I wrote back. *I'm jealous of your bike ride by the beach. Send us some sunshine. Love you.*

A text saying she loved me too and sunshine was on the way came through as I dialed Mrs. Hunt's number.

The call connected, and a woman said, "Hello?" Her voice sounded hollow and weak.

"Mrs. Hunt? This is Gwen Stevens," I said. "I wanted to say how sorry I am about Justin and see if I could drop off some flowers later this morning. Maybe around nine thirty?"

I heard quiet crying on the other end of the phone.

My heart broke for her. "I'm so sorry about Justin," I said again.

"Thank you," she said, her voice teary. "Nine thirty would be perfect. I'll look forward to it."

I ran my finger along the edge of a stain on my old kitchen table as we said our goodbyes. I scanned the mess on my kitchen counter and turned on a podcast, not in the mood to listen to music after hearing the grief in Mrs. Hunt's voice. Maybe my visit would give Mrs. Hunt some peace. Who knew? Maybe it could give me some answers too.

* * *

Precisely at nine thirty, I parked in front of the two-story brick colonial where Justin had grown up. A dried-out Christmas wreath still hung on the door. Although Justin and I hadn't been particularly close, I'd spent most of my teen years across the street at Chris's house. Chris and Justin's friendship had started the day Chris's family moved in.

The memory of simpler times tightened my throat with unshed tears. I checked my reflection in the mirror on the visor. "You can do this," I said to my reflection.

Hopefully I was right. I'd put together a bouquet with flowers in shades of purples, hoping they'd feel cheery in light of her tragic loss. I rang the doorbell, the dulcet tones barely audible through the bright-red door. I glanced over my shoulder as I waited for someone to answer. New owners had repainted the house Chris grew up in a deep navy blue, but they'd left the porch and front steps a brilliant white.

I flashed back to summer nights sitting on those front steps, talking, laughing, looking for shooting stars. Chris's arm would brush against mine as he pointed out the different constellations. Things had been easier back then.

My wistful thoughts were interrupted by the click of a deadbolt. Mrs. Hunt answered the door, dressed in jeans and a thick red sweater decorated with Scandinavian designs stitched in white. She smiled, but her bloodshot eyes and blotchy skin told of recent tears. She gripped a crumpled tissue in her hand. "Thank you so much for coming. Come on in. It's cold today," she said.

She backed up, and I stepped into the large foyer. A formal living room sat in darkness to my right. I wiped my feet on the mat, and we stood staring at each other for a moment.

"I thought we'd chat in the kitchen. It's cozy with the fireplace this time of year," said Mrs. Hunt, ever the hostess, even under these circumstances.

I extended the bouquet. "I know this does nothing to replace what you've lost, but I wanted to create something special for you," I said as I handed her the flowers.

She took them, bringing them to her nose. A ghost of a smile graced her lips. "They're just beautiful," she said, her voice thick with emotion. "Purple is my favorite color."

I'd had no idea, but my mom always said I had a knack for knowing what kind of flowers or plants a person needed. She called it magic. I called it coincidence, but I was happy the magic had surfaced this time.

Mrs. Hunt turned, and I followed her down the hall toward the back of the house. Pictures of Justin covered the wall of the short hallway. Justin as a baby, Justin without his two front teeth, Justin with his older sister, and Justin standing in a graduation cap and gown with his parents as they beamed at the camera. It was a potent reminder of why I was here.

The hallway opened into a large sunny kitchen, a fireplace in the corner warming the room. Mrs. Hunt pulled out a barstool that had been tucked under the island. "Have a seat. I have both coffee and tea. What would you like?" she asked.

I settled into the chair and removed my coat, draping it over the back. "I couldn't put you to any trouble," I said.

"Nonsense," she said firmly. "Let me do this small thing for you."

"In that case, I would love some tea," I replied.

"Coming right up." Mrs. Hunt bustled around to the other side of the island and lit the gas burner under a bright-yellow tea kettle. She pulled two cherry red mugs out of the cabinet to the right and set them down in front of me. She added a small woven basket that held a variety of tea bags and sweeteners.

"Thank you again for the flowers," she said. The kettle whistled, and she poured the hot water into the two mugs before coming around to sit on the stool next to me. "I've been so lonely rattling around the house during the day. It's nice to have some company."

I looked through the tea bags and chose a vanilla spice black tea. I ripped open the foil packet and dropped the tea bag into the steaming water. "Where's Mr. Hunt?" I asked.

"Oh, he's been busy at work this week," she said. "You know men. They hide in their work when life gets stressful."

My dad wasn't like that, but I wasn't about to contradict Mrs. Hunt.

She fiddled with her mug, turning the handle side to side. "I know you were the one…" she started.

She trailed off, but there was no doubt to what she was referring. I was the one who'd found her son dead. I dunked my tea bag up and down, watching the brown tea swirl into the hot water. "I'm so sorry." It was all I could think to say.

Mrs. Hunt blinked, and a tear escaped the corner of her eye. "I'm sorry," she said, wiping at her cheek as more tears fell. "I promised myself I wasn't going to do this. My emotions have been all over the place."

I wrapped my hands around the mug, allowing the warmth to anchor me. "Please don't apologize. I can't imagine what you're going through right now," I said compassionately.

Tears continued to slip silently down Mrs. Hunt's cheeks. "It doesn't even seem real most of the time. Justin had his issues…" She leaned forward with a small smile on her sad face. "Don't get me wrong, Justin was a great son. He was so helpful around the house. He was handsome and charming. Everyone loved him. I don't understand how this happened." The tears fell faster as she took a shaky sip of her tea.

"I can't believe this happened either. I can't believe it happened to Justin. I can't believe it happened in Star Junction," I said.

Mrs. Hunt looked down at her tea and shook her head. "What is this world coming to?" she asked quietly.

There was no good answer to that question.

Mrs. Hunt slowly lifted her head and met my gaze. "Who could've done this? Who would've wanted to hurt my Justin?" she asked.

I wished for a magic wand. I wished I could go back to Saturday when Mrs. Hunt was a happy mother and the biggest thing I had to worry about was when I was going to find time to go grocery shopping.

But I didn't have a magic wand. All I had was the opportunity to find some answers for Mrs. Hunt, and to do that, I was going to have to ask some uncomfortable questions. "I'm sure you heard about Chris," I started cautiously. After the interaction with Samantha this morning, I was going to tread carefully when it came to people who loved Justin.

"Chris is like a brother to Justin," Mrs. Hunt said firmly. "There's no way he had anything to do with this."

A weight lifted off my chest. It would have broken my heart to think Mrs. Hunt suspected Chris. "You mentioned Justin was helpful around the house. Did he live here? I thought he rented a house over on Beeker," I said.

Mrs. Hunt swiveled her chair to face me and crossed one leg over the other. Despite my fears I would make Mrs. Hunt upset with my questions, she seemed eager to talk about Justin. "He moved back in about a month ago," she said. "The owners of the house he rents were doing renovations. Justin told them he'd move out for a couple months to make it easier. I loved having him here."

"What did you think when he didn't come home Saturday night?" I asked.

"Well, it wasn't that unusual." She swiped at her nose with a napkin and balled it up in her fist. "He's a grown man. He has some friends in Rose Lake he'd stay with sometimes," she said.

Could one of these "friends" be the mystery woman he was having an affair with? "Do you know those friends?" I asked. "Maybe they'd know something that could help the police."

Mrs. Hunt shook her head. "He'd say he was staying late in Rose Lake or heading over there to meet friends. I didn't ask a lot of questions. He doesn't like that." She caught herself, her eyes welling with tears again. "*Didn't* like that," she said, changing to the past tense.

I fiddled with my cup, not knowing what to say.

"Anyway," Mrs. Hunt continued after taking a shaky breath. "Whitney is flying in next week before the memorial service. It'll be a comfort to have her here."

Justin's older sister had gone to Harvard and stayed in Boston after graduation. She worked at some kind of biotech firm. To say the two siblings were different was the understatement of the century.

"I'm so glad she'll be here," I said.

Mrs. Hunt nodded and took another sip of her tea.

Maybe Mrs. Hunt knew something that would help the police without even knowing she knew it. "Did Justin seem worried about anything lately?" I asked.

Mrs. Hunt seemed to consider my question. "Nothing I knew about." She tapped her finger against her lower lip. "I keep thinking maybe it was a case of him being in the wrong place at the wrong time. I'll never believe Chris would hurt Justin, but he was killed in Chris's building. Maybe someone wanted to hurt Chris and got Justin by mistake," she theorized.

The thought twisted my gut. I hadn't considered Chris could've been the real target. That would change everything. The murderer would realize they got the wrong person. Chris wouldn't be safe.

But Chris and Justin looked nothing alike. With his blond hair, vivid blue eyes, and chiseled jaw line, Chris looked like a surfer from California, despite his Midwestern roots. Justin, on the other hand, was half Italian, and it showed. Dark hair that curled at the nape of his neck, olive-toned skin, dark eyes. How did I know he was Italian? Because of our family tree project in high school when Justin wouldn't shut up about going to Italy someday and meeting a hot Italian babe.

Mrs. Hunt interrupted my thoughts by saying, "I'm sure that new police detective will figure out who hurt Justin."

"Have you spoken to the new detective?" I asked. Maybe she'd learned something about Finn's investigation that would help me with my own.

"Oh yes, he was so kind. He came over yesterday and went through Justin's room," she said.

Maybe Justin's room could give me some kind of clue as to what he'd gotten himself caught up in that could've led to his death. Although if Finn had already been in there, the chances I'd find anything he hadn't already were slim. Still, it was a lead, and I couldn't pass up the opportunity.

Asking to see Justin's room felt awkward, but I decided to just go with the truth. "It feels like the new detective is set on Chris being guilty. Any chance I could look over Justin's room? Maybe I could find something the detective missed. He's not from Star Junction. He might not even know what's important," I said.

I was prepared for Mrs. Hunt to say no, but she immediately agreed. "That's a great idea. Chris's mom called me yesterday to say how sorry she is about Justin. I already lost my baby. I can't stand the thought that her son might be blamed for something he didn't do," she said.

It was one thing to ask people I knew questions about Justin's death. It felt like a whole other level to conduct a search of Justin's room. Did I need to wear gloves? My pink wool mittens wouldn't give me much dexterity. Plus, according to Mrs. Hunt, Finn had already been through the room. I couldn't mess up an investigation that had already been conducted, could I? I had no idea what I was doing, but hopefully if there was something worth finding in Justin's room, I'd know it when I saw it.

CHAPTER NINE

———

Mrs. Hunt led me toward the front of the house and up the stairs. She opened the second door on the right. The phone rang downstairs. From the sound of it, it was a landline. "Excuse me," Mrs. Hunt said. "I'll be right back. Go ahead and look around." Her smile grew nostalgic. "Not much has changed since he was a teenager."

As she left me alone, I stood in the doorway for a moment. The room didn't show signs of a police search. At least not like what I'd seen on TV. The bed was slightly rumpled but still covered with a dark blue and green plaid comforter. I had a hard time picturing Justin's tall body being comfortable in the twin size bed.

I scanned the room, noting the desk, a dresser, and a closet. Where to start?

I moved to the desk first and pulled open the middle drawer. A few pens rolled around, but besides that it was empty. I checked the other drawers, but they were much the same. I found an old notebook labeled *Math*. It was empty of notes, which tracked with what I knew of Justin in high school.

The sound of Mrs. Hunt chatting with someone on the phone floated up from downstairs. I went to the dresser next. The clothes were unfolded as if someone had rooted around in the drawers. I checked anyway, running my hands under the clothes. What was I even searching for? A note detailing how Justin feared for his life and if I was reading this, it meant he was already dead? I huffed out a frustrated sigh. This wasn't some *Lifetime* movie.

The closet looked how you'd expect a closet to look— hanging clothes, shoes on the floor. I moved the clothes aside, patting the pockets as I went. Something crinkled in the pocket of a flannel shirt.

Bingo! Evidence. I pulled out a receipt to a gas station in Rose Lake and pursed my lips in frustration. I already knew Justin went to Rose Lake all the time.

I continued my search, more out of an obligation to the opportunity than out of any real hope I'd find anything. I dropped to my knees and riffled through his shoes. Nothing. I rocked back on my heels and scanned the room one more time. If there'd been any clues in Justin's room, Finn must have found them.

From the sounds of it, Mrs. Hunt was wrapping up her phone call. Justin's bed caught my eye. The navy-blue dust ruffle was tucked up on one end, as if it had gotten caught in the mattress. It wasn't going to be pretty, but I knew what I had to do.

Before I could change my mind, I crawled to the bed, dropped to my belly, turned my phone flashlight on, and scooted under Justin's bed. People stored things under their beds all the time, and Finn definitely wouldn't have fit in the narrow space.

I sneezed as the flashlight panned past dust bunnies and random candy wrappers. I pointed the light toward the back corner and hit pay dirt. A shoebox was shoved all the way into the corner. It could've been nothing. It could've been there for years. I scooted closer and sucked in a breath of surprise, promptly coughing past all the dust I'd just inhaled. *Real nice, Gwen.*

The shoebox was suspiciously free of dust. If this was some kind of evidence, I didn't want to move it and ruin chain of custody, or some other police lingo. I flipped the lid off and looked inside. Now we were getting somewhere. A thick roll of money lay next to several baggies of white powder.

The doorbell rang. I could hear Mrs. Hunt saying goodbye to whoever was on the phone. A moment later, she answered the door and said, "Detective Butler, I didn't expect to see you today. What can I help you with? Did you find who killed my Justin?"

Finn was here? My heart stopped. Sweat seemed to pour from everywhere on my body all at once, and those dreaded old-fashioned vapors threatened to overwhelm me. I couldn't get caught snooping in Justin's room. Finn would have a fit.

"I had a few more questions I was hoping we could go over?" Finn's deep voice rumbled from downstairs.

With panic pumping through my body, I snapped a picture of the contents of the box and replaced the lid. Shoving my way backward, I bit back a yelp as my elbow banged into the underside of the bed.

"Of course, come on in," Mrs. Hunt replied. "A friend of

Justin's stopped by to bring me flowers. Gwen Stevens. She's just upstairs. Let me see if she needs anything."

"Gwen Stevens is here?" Finn asked, sounding suspicious.

"Oh that's right. You probably met her during the investigation," Mrs. Hunt said. "She's the sweetest. I'll be right back."

"I'll come with you," Finn said. The sounds of their footsteps coming up the stairs was unmistakable.

The vapors were back. I sucked in another sharp breath and inhaled more dust as I scooted the rest of the way out from under the bed, banging my head for good measure. I bit back a yelp of pain, jumped to my feet, and caught my reflection in a mirror hanging on the wall near the door to Justin's room. My shirt was covered with dust, and my hair was a mess.

I frantically brushed the dust off my shirt and yanked my hands through my hair. I jumped into the hallway and examined a series of family photos as if my life depended on it as Mrs. Hunt and Finn reached the top of the stairs and rounded the corner.

"Look who's here," Mrs. Hunt said. "Find anything helpful?"

"Find anything helpful?" Finn echoed, eyeing me suspiciously.

There was no way I was telling her I'd found drugs and cash hidden under her precious son's bed. And I definitely wasn't going to bring it up with Finn here. The last thing I needed was a lecture in front of Mrs. Hunt. "Nope, nothing in these pictures was helpful," I said, grasping for some kind of explanation for her question that would make sense to Finn.

Both Finn and Mrs. Hunt gave me weird looks, which was fair. I could no longer see my reflection, but I was guessing I looked a little deranged, if how I was feeling was any indication. "I better get to work," I said. I gave Mrs. Hunt a quick hug. "Let me know if you need anything."

She returned my hug and said, "Thank you, dear."

I followed Mrs. Hunt and Finn downstairs where she'd hung my coat on the coat rack by the door. She asked about my parents as we walked to the door and said our goodbyes.

"I'll follow Gwen out to make sure she gets to her car okay," Finn said.

So much for my clean getaway. "That's not necessary," I said with a saccharine smile. "It's perfectly safe."

Finn's grin matched mine in level of insincerity, but

thankfully Mrs. Hunt didn't seem to notice. "Can't be too careful, Guinevere."

It took every ounce of self-control I had to not stick my tongue out at the man who was clearly goading me. It was clear he wasn't going to take no for an answer. I said one more goodbye to Mrs. Hunt and headed outside with Finn on my heels.

He closed the door, and I turned to face him, giving him that overly cheerful smile again. "What can I do for you, Detective Butler?"

"What were you really doing upstairs?" he asked pointedly.

I kept the smile on my face, but my stomach flipped as if I'd be caught doing something I shouldn't have been doing. But I hadn't been caught, and there was nothing wrong with looking around Justin's room with Mrs. Hunt's permission. "Mrs. Hunt was telling me about Justin," I said. Not a lie. "And she mentioned some pictures she wanted me to see upstairs. She couldn't remember how old we were when we went to the field trip to Shedd Aquarium. She had a picture and wanted to show it to me." Definitely a lie.

Finn stared at me a moment longer as if he could read the truth of my statements through sheer force of will, and then his eyes, the color of warm whiskey, softened. "It was really nice of you to bring Mrs. Hunt flowers. I wanted to see how you're holding up. Finding a dead body can be traumatic."

My face warmed, despite the frosty wind blowing across the yard. I'd come outside ready to defend my presence, and all he'd wanted to do was be nice. "It was nothing. Besides," I added, completely taken off guard by his change of attitude, "I wondered if maybe Mrs. Hunt knew of someone who might want to hurt Justin."

Finn's expression darkened, the warmth draining from his gaze. "You asked her about the case?" he asked.

I rubbed my hands together against the cold creeping through my winter layers. "There's hardly any other topic of conversation to be had around here. I just asked her—" I started.

"You shouldn't be asking her anything," he snapped. "This is a job for the police."

I folded my arms across my chest, my chin jutting into the air with defiance. "Whether you like it or not, I'm involved in this," I argued. "I found his body."

"You're involved as a witness. Not an investigator," he countered.

"Maybe I wouldn't have to be asking questions if you were focused on finding the real killer and not on trying to find evidence to pin this on Chris."

Finn's cheeks reddened, and his brown eyes flashed. "I don't need to *try* to find evidence that points to Chris," he said. "It's everywhere."

"Exactly," I said, pointing my finger at him. "Don't you find that suspicious?"

He huffed out a breath and rested his gloved hand on the gun at his side. "I find it—" He stopped and looked to the sky as if praying for patience. "Let me do my job. If your boyfriend's innocent, the facts of the case will bear that out." He opened the door and moved to walk inside.

"He's not my boyfriend," I called after him.

He threw a dismissive wave over his head before disappearing into the house.

I stomped back to my car. Any inclination I had to show Finn the photo of what I'd found evaporated in the face of his accusations. He was upset I'd asked Mrs. Hunt about Justin. What would he do if he found out I'd searched Justin's room?

I drove to Camelot Flowers, guilt mixing with the indignation I was feeling. I needed to tell Finn about the box. No matter how frustrated I was, I couldn't withhold possible evidence. Even if it wasn't related to Justin's murder, it was evidence of a crime.

But I didn't have to tell Finn about the box before I figured out more about what it meant. Had the drugs been for personal use? Was Justin selling drugs like the rumors indicated? How did someone even get drugs to sell? My innocence around this sort of thing was going to be a major roadblock in this investigation. I was going to need help, someone with some dirt on their hands. Too bad I didn't know who that might be.

* * *

I arrived at the church hall at five thirty, exactly an hour and a half early as requested by Margie, who'd texted me to say they needed some young blood to help with setup for the pie social. I'd do anything for Margie, especially after she'd broken the rules to let me see Chris.

I clutched the cheesecake in my hands as I picked my way

across the icy parking lot. The weather had warmed up as promised but dropped to below freezing as soon as the sun set. I'd need to make sure Margie got someone out here to put salt down on the sidewalks. We didn't want anyone slipping and hurting themselves.

I walked through the side door into the bright, warm multipurpose room of the church. Ladies rushed around setting up tables and hanging decorations. Penny's mom stood holding the bottom of a ladder as Penny's dad strung twinkle lights around the edges of the black curtains on the stage.

I scanned the room for the pie table, but movement off to my right caught my attention. A crisp, white tablecloth billowed in the air. As it floated onto the rectangular table below, it revealed Finn.

A dark-gray Henley stretched across his wide chest. Biceps flexed as his wrists flicked the tablecloth again, releasing a crease that had settled into the middle. His well-fitted suits, all buttoned up and stiff, had been replaced by faded jeans that moved with his body as he ran his hands over the top of the table.

I'd never considered myself attracted to men with facial hair, but Finn's short, dark beard was doing it for me. In his suits, he looked like he'd stepped off a cover of *GQ* magazine, but dressed casually, I imagined him using those muscles to chop wood, and a butterfly took up a dance in my stomach.

Mrs. Johnson walked over to Finn, her reading glasses bouncing against her ample bosom from the silver chain around her neck. In her seventies, she seemed in no rush to retire from her position of head librarian at the Star Junction Public Library. With the proceeds of the pie social going to support the library's summer reading program, tonight was a big night for her. Mrs. Johnson said something to Finn that prompted a wide, genuine smile.

He patted her on the shoulder and replied to whatever she'd said. Mrs. Johnson laughed and said something again, this time nodding her head in my direction. Finn turned, and his gaze locked with mine like two puzzle pieces fitting together. I blinked, my body rooted in place. He ran a hand through his perfectly gelled dark hair and ducked his head.

Mrs. Johnson called out to me, and the spell was broken. I tried unsuccessfully to slow my racing heart before ungluing my feet from the floor. Setting the cheesecake on the table closest to me, I shrugged out of my navy-blue dress coat and draped it over the back of a chair.

I'd paired black jeans with an emerald green blouse with sheer long sleeves that gathered at my wrists. The front was lower cut than the sweater I'd worn to the station the day before. Margie, who wanted me to "show off all my assets," would be proud.

I'd freshened the waves I'd put in my hair the day before, even taking the time to stop in at Lucille's Clip and Curl to have my long curtain bangs trimmed. She'd offered to throw in some acupuncture for free, but I'd declined as sweetly as possible. Penny had been right. The thought of Lucille getting anywhere near with me with needles threatened to give me those dreaded vapors again. As I made my way across the room to them, my gaze flicked to Finn in time to catch him watching me approach.

"Guinevere, it's just so awful that you had to stumble onto"—Mrs. Johnson grimaced and waved her hand through the air—"you know, Justin like that. How are you holding up?"

"I'm okay, Mrs. Johnson. Thanks for asking," I replied, giving her a soft smile. Whether or not I was truly okay seemed to change from moment to moment, but no need to worry Mrs. Johnson.

Mrs. Johnson turned to Finn and asked, "Any progress in finding the killer?"

Finn smiled, but it looked strained, a little too polite, a little too forced. "It's still early," he said. "We're working on it though."

I wanted to argue that he seemed to be making plenty of progress, if locking Chris in a holding cell counted as progress, but I didn't want to get into that argument in front of Mrs. Johnson.

"Anyhoo," Mrs. Johnson said, already moving on. "Thank you for coming early, Guinevere." She waved her hand around the room, where volunteers bustled about getting things set up. "We can use all the help we can get."

"Of course," I said. "What can I do to help?"

Mrs. Johnson held up a finger as if asking me to wait. "One moment," she said before turning to Finn. "The situation in the parking lot is dire. I don't know if you noticed, but it's an icy mess and, and the church is out of salt. Would you be a dear and run to the store? The Friends of the Library will reimburse you for the cost."

"I did notice," Finn said. "I'm happy to help."

Mrs. Johnson reached up and patted his cheek like he was the grandson she'd always wanted. Never mind the fact that she not only had seven grandchildren, but her first great-grandchild was due in a month. "Thank you, dear," she said to him.

This could be an opportunity to pump Detective Butler for information. A little alone time with the man was just what I needed. Plus, I still felt guilty about not sharing the photo of the box from under Justin's bed.

There was no way I was going to share that anywhere public. All it would take was one person overhearing us or getting a glimpse of the picture for the whole town to be buzzing about where all that money came from and what that white powder could be.

"There's ice on the roads," I said to Mrs. Johnson, making sure I sounded very concerned. "Why don't I go with Detective Butler. I can show him where to go and make sure we get back safely."

Finn's eyes narrowed slightly as if he could read my intentions. "I don't think that's necessary," he said. His voice was friendly, but his smile looked strained.

"No, no," Mrs. Johnson said. "That's a great idea, Guinevere. Hurry back." She bustled away. We'd been dismissed.

Finn turned to me, the full charm he'd used on Mrs. Johnson long gone, replaced with suspicion. "We're going together? Is that really necessary?"

"You heard Mrs. Johnson. She thinks it a great idea," I said sweetly, although I sensed the smile on my face bordered more on triumphant than sweet.

Detective Butler sighed heavily before saying, "Okay, let's go, Guinevere."

I gritted my teeth at Finn's use of my full name. "Right behind you, Phineas," I shot back.

I grabbed my coat, spun on my heels, and marched out the door. My suede ankle boots clicked on the icy sidewalk as I headed toward my car. Detective Butler's footsteps sounded behind me, but I didn't stop to wait.

"Phineas, huh?" he said into the silence.

I stopped and turned, expecting to see anger in his eyes, but instead they glimmered with amusement. I shifted my coat in my arms. I should've put it on, but the irritation coursing through my veins was keeping me plenty warm. "As I've mentioned before, I have two goals—get Chris out of *your* jail and figure out what Finn stands for."

I headed in the direction of my Jetta without waiting for a response. My mind shot back to our encounter at Mrs. Hunt's house earlier. I spun on my heels, ready to explain, once again, that Chris was not my boyfriend, but Finn had narrowed the distance between us, and I slammed into his solid chest.

My shoe caught on the edge of the icy sidewalk as I bounced off him. My feet slid out from under me as my body tilted backward. Finn's hands shot out and wrapped around my arms, keeping me on my feet.

For a moment we stood frozen, the warmth of his hands radiating through the thin sleeves of my blouse. His gaze flicked to my lips ever so briefly. The butterfly in my stomach woke up and started fluttering around again. I took a step back, breaking the contact that had me feeling so confused.

"You must be cold," Finn said as he took my coat from my arms and held it open for me.

I didn't want his help, but saying no seemed petty, even for me. I turned and slipped my arms into the sleeves. "Thank you," I mumbled.

"No problem," he said. He scanned me as if checking for injuries, despite the fact that he'd prevented me from actually falling. "Are you okay?"

"Good thing we're getting salt," I joked. I attempted a chuckle, but it sounded thin. Anger was the solution. I didn't have any problem focusing on the murder investigation when I was infuriated with Finn and his stupid rules and procedures. I pictured him adjusting the tie of his overpriced suit. "And another thing, don't call me Guinevere. Only my parents call me that," I added.

A grin played at the corner of his lips. "And Mrs. Johnson," he teased.

I huffed in frustration. "Okay, anyone over the age of fifty can call me that."

There was that look of amusement again. "Aye-aye, captain," he said as he leaned closer, the clouds from our breath swirling together in the space between us. A car pulled into the parking lot, its headlights washing over us. I squeezed my eyes shut against the offending light then eased them open as the car turned the corner.

He gave me a nod as if we'd struck some kind of détente and headed off down the first row of the parking lot.

"Where are you going? My car's right here," I said, gesturing toward my green Jetta.

Finn eyed it briefly. "If the roads are icy, we need a car with four-wheel drive. We'll take my truck," he said.

"Excuse me," I said indignantly. "I don't even know you. I don't get into cars with men I don't know unless I'm driving. And you're new to town. You don't know where you're going. We're taking my car."

Finn looked up at the stars as if praying for patience as he had earlier that day at Mrs. Hunt's house. "I'm a police detective. Not a serial killer. Why does everything have to be an argument with you?"

I folded my arms across my chest and said, "Everything's not an argument with me."

"I rest my case," he said resolutely. "Come on, it's freezing out here. Please get into the truck, and let's get this done so we're back in time to finish helping."

As much as I hated to admit it, Finn was right. It was freezing out here, and it was clear he wasn't going to budge. "Fine," I said pertly. I followed him to a black pickup truck parked at the end of the lot. Whatever cease-fire we'd reached when he'd been gazing into my eyes and that beard had been close enough to touch seemed to have vanished.

Finn's truck was immaculately clean. The smell of leather mixed with brief notes of something both spicy and sweet tickled my nose. The truck started with a low growl. "Where to?" he asked as he backed up.

"Let's try Henry's Hardware downtown," I replied. "Turn right on Elm, and you'll see it up ahead."

Finn nodded his understanding. I watched him out of the corner of my eye. His left hand casually gripped the top of the steering wheel while his right hand tapped out a beat on his knee.

What was happening with the case? Had he found more evidence? Did it point back to Chris? If only Chris had an alibi. If only he hadn't left his phone at the center. If only Justin hadn't been killed in the first place.

CHAPTER TEN

―――

We pulled up to Henry's Hardware, and I jumped out of the truck before Finn could offer to help. An inviting light, promising warmth, spilled from the large windows lining the front of the old hardware store. I pushed the door open, Finn close on my heels.

Aisles of everything you would imagine a hardware store carrying, plus things you'd never expect, were crammed into the small store. I looked to my left where bags of rock salt usually sat. The space was empty, stray pellets of salt the only indication of what had been there before.

Finn ran his hand across the back of his neck, eyeing the dusting of crushed salt on the hardwood floor. "You'd think they'd have stocked up on salt." He glanced around. "And you'd think someone would be around to help."

Finn was right about one thing. Not having salt was an anomaly. "Henry?" I called out.

"Is that little Guinevere I hear?" A bald head with a small fringe of white hair ringing the edges peeked out from aisle ten.

Finn's grin let me know the endearment "little Guinevere" hadn't escaped his notice.

"It's me," I answered.

Henry adjusted his wire-rim glasses and headed in our direction.

"And who's this tall young man with you?" Henry asked, clearly excited at the sight of Finn. "A new boyfriend? Your mother was in here right before they left town last week. I can't believe she didn't mention anything." I tried to jump in and stop him, but Henry was on a roll. "You two make such a handsome couple. I'm so glad you found our little Guinevere. She's a special one." Henry's face beamed at the two of us.

I said a prayer that the floor would swallow me up and save me from this humiliation. Unfortunately, God didn't seem interested in defying the laws of matter to help me today. Instead, Finn's eyes danced with laughter. He threw his arm around me and said, "Guinevere sure is something special. I can't put my finger on it, but when she's around, the day is never boring."

I attempted to slide away, but Finn tightened his grip. I looked up at him and widened my eyes, trying to communicate the severity of the situation. This was how rumors started in Star Junction. I didn't need any flying around about this new detective and me.

My bugging eyes didn't work. Finn was taking entirely too much pleasure in this. Time to take matters into my own hands. I jabbed him in the ribs with my elbow, coughing into my arm to cover the movement.

Finn doubled over, and I maneuvered out of his grip. I beamed at Henry while Finn rubbed his side. I risked a look at Finn to see how angry he was with my elbow attack. Instead of anger clouding his features, his whiskey-brown eyes sparkled with delight. He thought this was funny.

"This isn't my boyfriend," I explained to Henry. "This is Finn Butler, the new detective Stan hired."

Henry's pale blue eyes lit up with interest. "The new detective." He reached out and shook Finn's hand. "Welcome to Star Junction, young man," he said.

Finn accepted Henry's handshake. "Thank you very much," Finn said sincerely.

Henry rubbed his hands together before saying, "What can I do for you two?"

Finn replied, "We're on the hunt for salt for the church parking lot. The pie social is tonight, and it's getting slippery out there."

Henry pulled off his glasses and cleaned them with the edge of his flannel shirt. "Here's the thing. I'm plum out. Everyone's out. People have been coming in all weekend buying up my supply because of the forecast with the warming and then the freezing. My next shipment won't come in until tomorrow," he said regretfully.

"What do you mean everyone's out?" I asked.

"Just what I said," Henry replied with a shrug. He settled his glasses back on his hook nose. "I made some calls this afternoon to see where I could direct people when they came in looking, and everyone's out—the grocery store, the gas station. Everyone."

This was not good. "What are we supposed to do?" I asked, feeling desperate. "The social starts at seven. It's not safe in the church parking lot right now. I don't want someone slipping and breaking something."

"I'd head to Rose Lake," Henry replied. "You can be there and back in forty minutes. Plenty of time. I talked to Jim at the Mobile station, and he says they got a new shipment this morning."

I looked over at Finn, who shrugged.

"Okay, thanks, Henry," I said. "Say hi to Rita for me."

"Will do, darling," he said to me with a grandfatherly smile. "Good luck with the salt." He moved to walk away but stopped. "One more thing," he said to Finn. "My Rita is plumb scared over the thought of a murderer in Star Junction. Any good news I can pass along?"

Finn ran his hand over his beard and gave Henry the same line he'd given Mrs. Johnson. "It's still early. We're working on it though."

"I understand," Henry said with a sigh. "Rome wasn't built in a day and all that." Henry turned and walked away, whistling a tune as he adjusted a barrel filled with yardsticks before disappearing down aisle ten again.

We walked back to Finn's truck. "Is that the official line?" I asked as Finn opened the car door for me. "You're working on it?"

"It is now." His tone held some bite, as if he was offended by all the questions.

"People are going to ask, you know," I said. "It's a small town. They're worried."

Finn huffed out a breath, his expression softening. "I know. Should we drive to Rose Lake?" he asked.

"I hate driving there if the roads are getting slippery, but we need salt," I said. "I don't want to waste time driving around town asking people to use some of theirs if we're going to end up empty-handed."

Finn pulled onto the street and turned toward the highway to Rose Lake. "We'll be fine. I have the four-wheel drive on."

Finn turned on the radio, songs of attraction and love filling the car. I hummed along as we cruised down the dark highway toward Rose Lake. I'd driven this stretch of highway more times than I could count. Finn pressed down on the accelerator, taking us up to sixty-five.

"Don't get going too fast," I said as I eyed the speedometer.

"There are some turns up ahead that get icy."

"I'm fine," Finn said casually. "I've been driving in snow and ice all my life. I don't want to be late getting back."

"Okay, but black ice can develop—" I started.

The truck slid to the side. I gripped the handle on the door. Finn's jaw flexed in concentration as he worked to steer us out of the skid. My heart slammed against the walls of my chest as I braced myself against the dashboard.

The truck straightened for a moment but caught another patch of ice. We careened across the road and down a steep embankment, plowing through several inches of snow. The front bumper skidded to a stop inches from a thick pine tree.

The sound of our frantic breathing filled the truck. I loosened my grip on the door handle and straightened in my seat. The headlights played off the sides of the embankment. There was no way we were going to drive out of this mess. Not without some help.

"Are you okay?" Finn asked as he pushed himself back from the steering wheel and surveyed me from head to toe.

"I-I'm okay," I stuttered out. "I think." I moved my head from side to side and groaned. "I'll be stiff tomorrow." As the initial fear faded, frustration burned in my chest. A simple task, go get salt for the parking lot, had us stranded. Finn's jaw flexed as he took in my accusatory glare.

"I can't believe you got us into this!" I yelled at the exact moment Finn shouted, "Don't even start with me!"

We glared at each other, Finn on the defensive, and me on the attack.

Frustration pulsing through my veins, I collapsed back into my seat. "Maybe next time you'll listen," I muttered.

He leaned forward and scowled. "What makes you think there'll be a next time?"

I turned to make a face at him, but a drop of fresh blood on his shirt caught my attention. "You're hurt," I exclaimed, my tone softening as my concern eclipsed my frustration. I put my hand on his shoulder, searching for the source of the blood. Above his eye, a cut intersected his eyebrow. "That looks deep."

Finn reached up and fingered the cut, his fingers coming away red. "I hit my head on the driver's-side window when we slid off the road," he explained. "It'll be okay. There's a first aid kit in the glove box."

Flashes of Justin's chest, smeared the same color as the blood on Finn's face, slammed into me. My eyes swam with tears as I reached for the handle of the glove box. *Not now. Don't do this now.* I pushed the memories of Justin from my mind. I couldn't do anything to help Justin, but I could help Finn. "It's locked," I said, my voice shaky.

"Sorry," Finn said as he pulled the keys from the ignition, plunging us into darkness. He leaned across the seat, his shoulder brushing against my arm. He used a small key on his keychain to open the glove box and leaned back, starting the truck again.

I opened the glove box to see a red bag with a white cross on the front. Right next to it—a handgun. No wonder it had been locked. Pulling a large, square gauze from the zippered pocket of the first aid kit, I scooted closer and held it to his forehead. He winced as I touched the laceration, gripping my arm.

Silence descended between us as I tended to his wound. It didn't escape my notice that this was the second time I'd played nurse this week. First Chris. Now Finn. I leaned closer as I dabbed the cut.

Finn caught my gaze. "Thank you," he said softly. The look of genuine gratitude in his gaze disarmed me.

If I were being honest with myself, his prior defensiveness wasn't unwarranted. I'd done nothing but criticize him since we met. "Sorry for yelling," I said quietly. "This could've happened to anyone. At least we're okay."

He may have been more surprised by my apology than the fact that we'd slid off the road. He rubbed his hand across his bearded chin. "I'm sorry too," he said. "I should've listened and slowed down."

"Black ice is invisible," I said, making an excuse for him. "You were just trying to get us back to the church on time."

I pulled the gauze away from his forehead. The bleeding had stopped, and the cut didn't look as deep as I'd initially thought. "I think a couple of Band-Aids, and you'll be good to go."

I rummaged through the well-stocked first aid kit. "Or we could go for the full-on head wound look," I teased as I pulled out a roll of white bandages. The incredulous look on his face made me laugh. "No, seriously, I think it could be a good look on you," I continued to tease.

"I think no," Finn said with a grin on his face. He reached over me, pulling butterfly bandages from the first aid kit. "These will be sufficient."

"If you insist," I said lightly, shooting him a grin. "I've been going to renaissance fairs and Live Action Role Playing events with my dad since before I could walk. At some point around middle school, I got roped into applying bandages to the faux-wounded. If you want to look like a knight who took a blow to the head, I'm your gal."

"I'll keep that in mind, but let's go for the modern look this time around," he said.

How quickly we'd gone from *who says there's going to be a next time* to *next time around.*

I pulled the butterfly bandages from their wrappers and carefully applied them to Finn's wound. He winced but stayed silent as I tugged the strips tight, pulling the ends of the cut together. "Sorry." I pulled the second one taut and pressed it to his skin.

He gave me a pained smile. "I'll live. Let me call someone from the precinct to get us out," he said.

I eyed the steep embankment. "No offense to anyone on the fine Star Junction police force, but I think we need more than a pickup truck with a tow cable. I'll call a professional. I've got the full roadside assistance package courtesy of my overprotective dad," I explained.

"Remind me to thank your overprotective dad," Finn said as he turned up the heat and settled back in his seat.

I waited for the call to connect, reflecting on the truce that once again seemed to have formed between us. Would this one last?

The call connected, and I answered the operator's questions, giving her our location and assuring her we were safe. The tow truck would be there within the hour. I called Margie to explain what had happened. After reassuring her about a thousand times that we were fine, I was finally able to end the call.

Finn looked over the dashboard. "At least we have enough gas to keep the heat going," he said.

This was it. I had a captive audience. Unless Finn wanted to wait out in the cold, he couldn't walk away from my questions. Or my suggestions. I recommitted to my original plan of using honey instead of vinegar to get Finn on my side. "How did things go with Mrs. Hunt today?" I asked, making sure my tone was friendly and approachable.

"You know I can't talk about that," he said, sounding resigned but not offended.

This wasn't going to be easy. "Come on, Finnegan! I'm trying to help you," I said.

Finn barked out a laugh. "Finnegan?" he asked incredulously.

"Finn could be short for Finnegan," I said flirtatiously. I couldn't help it. Bantering with Finn was as exciting as arguing with him.

"Strike two," he said. "No to Phineas, and no to Finnegan. You're getting colder."

I rubbed my hands together with glee. "A clue. I'll have to put some thought into what would make me hotter."

Finn's gaze heated at my innocent comment that ended up sounding not-so-innocent, but instead of coming back with a flirty retort, his eyes tightened and he said, "You're not helping me with this case. And I can't give you an update on Chris."

"Who asked for an update on Chris?" I said indignantly.

"It was coming," he said.

Well, shoot. He wasn't wrong. "I think you're making a mistake," I said.

Finn folded his arms across his chest. "What kind of mistake is that?" he asked.

"The mistake of forgoing my expertise," I said.

"You're an expert on murder?" His tone left no doubt as to what he thought of my assertion.

I was tempted to argue that I listened to more true-crime podcasts than anyone I knew, but I suspected he wouldn't count that as real experience. "My expertise on Star Junction," I explained.

Finn paused as if considering my argument before saying, "Tell me more about what you mean by that."

I was so shocked by his genuine interest that it took me a moment to answer. "Cops have informants, right? People who hear things on the street they're not privy to because people don't always want to talk to the police. That can be me. I know everyone in town. People underestimate me all the time. People might tell me things they wouldn't tell you."

"People underestimate you?" he said incredulously. "I find that hard to believe."

Was that a compliment? I was too afraid to ask just in case it wasn't. "Using my connections makes sense. Even you have to admit that," I said.

"I can't give you details of the case," he said earnestly. "I also can't let you put yourself in danger. Let me handle this. Believe it or not, this isn't my first rodeo."

"I won't be in danger," I argued. "I'm going to talk to people I already know. I graduated with Justin. We know all the same people, and they'll trust me."

"One of those people might have killed Justin," Finn explained. "What happens if you're poking around and you get too close?"

His argument mirrored Penny's, but I was undeterred. "Let's have a job interview. I'll tell you what I know, and you decide whether or not I could be helpful," I said.

"Let me ask you a question first," he said, clearly hedging. "Would you be this invested in finding Justin's murderer if Chris Crawford wasn't my prime suspect?"

The question stung in more ways than one. I wanted to say yes, to say I'd want justice for Justin no matter what. But was that the truth? The other thing I needed to consider was whether or not this was the right time to show him the picture of the box beneath Justin's bed.

Finn was going to be mad when he saw it. I was getting somewhere with him. I could feel it. I didn't want to jeopardize it by tipping my hand too soon. Waiting too long wouldn't be good either.

"Your silence tells me a lot," he finally said.

My embarrassment at the implication of his statement flared into irritation. "My silence says I'm trying to give a thoughtful answer," I snapped. I paused again, just long enough to shoot him a dirty look. "I'd like to think I'd want to find Justin's killer either way." There. That was pretty honest.

"Fair enough," Finn said. "Tell me what you know."

"There's a rumor about Justin being mixed up with drugs," I said. "Drug dealers kill each other all the time. That's a motive that has nothing to do with Chris."

"I've heard that rumor and am following up on it," Finn said simply.

"Did you know he cheated on his girlfriend Samantha, and the other woman is pregnant?" I countered.

"Yes, and allegedly pregnant," he pointed out. "I have an officer looking into it."

If I couldn't give him something new, he was never going to let me help. "It's possible the other woman has a boyfriend who's not very happy with Justin. Or there's Samantha. You said it would take a lot of force to drive that screwdriver into his chest, but adrenaline can enable people to do crazy things. Maybe Samantha did it. Or the girl he got pregnant. Maybe he's not supportive, and she's mad."

"That's a theory," he said blandly.

"You don't seem impressed." As far as job interviews went, I was failing miserably.

"So far, you've only told me things I already know," he explained.

I got my phone from my coat pocket. Like it or not, it was time to pull out the big guns. I opened my photo app and showed him the picture. "I found this under Justin's bed today. It was shoved way back in the corner against the wall. I didn't move it or touch it besides taking the lid off," I said.

Finn's jaw worked as he studied the picture. "So you weren't just upstairs looking at old family photos," he finally said, his tone tense.

I grimaced. "No," I admitted. "I was never going to keep this from you, but I didn't want to say anything in front of Mrs. Hunt. She worshipped the ground Justin walked on. I didn't want her to hear about anything related to drugs."

"Can you send this to me?" he asked as he handed back my phone.

"Sure," I said, sounding hopeful. Maybe he really was trying to solve this case the right way. "What's your number?"

Finn rattled off his phone number, and I texted him the photo. I saved the number. Who knew when having direct access to Finn might come in handy?

I tucked my leg onto the seat and shifted so I could face him. "Did I pass the test?" I asked.

Finn rubbed his hands across his eyes, suddenly looking weary. "There wasn't any test," he said.

"I mean, if I learn something helpful, do you want me to tell you?" I clarified.

"I want you to stay out of this, but if you happen to learn something helpful, I'd like to be informed," he said, sounding resigned.

I'd gotten my way. Sort of. Even so, somehow the victory felt hollow. We had at least thirty minutes before the tow truck would arrive. Time to wade into safer topics. "So, why Star Junction?" I asked.

"Why Star Junction?" he repeated.

"Yeah, you used to be a cop in Chicago," I said. "At least that's the rumor. So, why Star Junction?"

I wasn't sure he was going to answer. Even I had to admit it wasn't the smoothest segue, but if I was going to help him solve this murder, I wanted to get to know the guy.

To my surprise, he answered with more detail than I'd been expecting. "I've lived in the Chicago area all my life. All I ever wanted to do was become a cop. I got my wish, but it wasn't exactly what I'd thought it would be.

"I worked rough neighborhoods as a new patrol officer. I thought the job might get easier once I made detective, but it was almost worse. We weren't helping people. We were just cleaning up messes. We were chasing a serial killer last year. It was a gruesome case. The one witness almost died before we caught the guy. It made me rethink my life priorities. When a relationship I was in ended around the same time, I decided I wanted a fresh start."

A relationship? How long had it been since it ended? How long had they dated? What did she look like? Were they still in touch? Maybe they weren't the most relevant questions, but I couldn't stop them from running through my mind.

Finn continued, "I didn't expect to be investigating a murder my first week on the job. Especially not after the description of the town Stan gave me during the interview process."

"Thanks for sharing all that," I said, in awe of how forthcoming he'd been.

Finn shrugged like it was no big deal.

Still no tow truck. I'd disarmed him with a personal question, but I needed more information if I was going to help Chris get out of jail. "I have another question," I said.

"Shoot," he said encouragingly.

I rattled off a series of questions, "Did you find any evidence at the crime scene that pointed to someone besides Chris? Fingerprints. Threatening messages on Justin's phone. A doorbell camera somewhere in the neighborhood that showed someone else coming and going. Or a doorbell camera showing Chris went home and didn't leave again the night of the murder?"

Finn's lips pressed into a thin line. "We're not talking about this," he said sternly. "If you want to feed me information, that's one thing. I can't share confidential parts of the investigation with you."

We descended into silence. I wasn't surprised he wasn't willing to share information, but the arrangement didn't strike me as fair.

He must have sensed my displeasure, because he said, "It's not personal. I can't share details with anyone." His tone begged me to understand.

I did understand. It didn't mean I liked it. "Okay, I have another question."

Finn looked hesitant but said, "Go ahead."

"Football or soccer?" I asked.

It was a softball question, not to mix up sports metaphors, but I was tired of pushing. Thoughts of Justin's murder dominated my days, and nightmares plagued my nights. While it felt wrong to think of mundane things with Chris sitting in jail, I needed a break, and I sensed Finn did as well.

"Football or soccer?" he repeated, clearly confused by the abrupt subject change.

"Yeah, which do you like better?" I explained.

"Football, for sure," Finn answered.

"Favorite team?" I asked.

He eyed me askance and said, "The Bears. Obviously."

I grimaced.

"What's that look for?" he asked.

I pointed to myself. "Packers fan."

He couldn't have looked more horrified than if I'd confessed to Justin's murder right then and there. Then his lips twitched as if he were struggling not to laugh. "Get out," he said.

"What?" I exclaimed.

"I can't have a Packers' fan in my truck, not when we're facing them in the playoffs," he said.

I chuckled and pretended I was going to touch him. "What? You think I'll give you Packer-cooties?"

Finn leaned away from me. "That's exactly what I think," he teased. "How did this happen anyway? How do you grow up in Bears' country and become a Packers fan?"

"My dad grew up in Green Bay," I said in way of explanation.

Finn assessed my statement before responding, "You get a pass for that."

I laughed, smacking my hand against his chest. "That's very generous of you."

"Family trumps everything," Finn said.

"Even football?" I asked playfully.

"Even football," he agreed.

"That's a relief. Making me walk back to Star Junction was not going to bode well for your reputation in town. I'm well loved by the people," I said.

A laugh burst from Finn's lips, and he flinched, reaching for the wound on his head.

"Are you okay?" I leaned over in the dim overhead light and examined my doctoring skills. The bandages seemed to be holding.

"It's fine," he said. "Just a little sore."

"Maybe when we get back to town you should go home and rest. You could just drop me off at the church," I said with concern.

"And miss my very first pie social? Not a chance. Besides," he added, "I already have my eye on one of the pies."

"We left before most of the pies even got there," I said, confused.

Finn opened his mouth to respond as headlights washed over us. A tow truck pulled over to the side of the road. I turned back to Finn, but he was already easing his door open. What was he about to say? And how worried did I need to be about the cut on his forehead? No time for answers now. Help was here, and we had a pie social to get back to.

CHAPTER ELEVEN

———

We were on the road back to Star Junction twenty minutes later. The tow truck driver had efficiently pulled Finn's truck out of the ditch, and I'd signed the papers while stamping my feet against the cold wind rushing across the barren farmland.

The front bumper of Finn's truck was dented, but it was drivable, for which I was grateful. The thought of being squished between the driver and Finn in the small cab of the tow truck had been less than appealing.

"Now I'm the one who has a question," Finn said as the headlights washed over a stand of trees between farm fields.

I was expecting something about the murder investigation, so I was surprised when he said, "What should I expect tonight? You may find this hard to believe, but I've never been to a pie social before."

I wasn't surprised, but I couldn't pass up the opportunity to give him a hard time. "What? The police detective from the big city has never been to a good, old-fashioned pie social?" I teased.

His eyes crinkled at the corners as he grinned. "I'm afraid not."

"It's pretty simple," I said. "The ladies bring in pies, and the guys bid on them. You spend the rest of the evening sharing a piece of the pie you won with the person who made it."

Finn took the last turn into town. "So, it's like a dating service," he said.

"Don't let Mrs. Johnson hear you call it that," I said, laughing. "She'll deny it, but you're not far off. I usually end up eating a slice of pie with someone like Uncle Stan. You know, someone who's known me all my life. Or Chris." My mind, now tied to the cell holding Chris, reminded me of all the reasons I had to be upset with Finn. If I didn't think about Chris, who would?

Words to pick a fight with Finn formed sentences in my

mind, but somehow I couldn't force the hurtful phrases out. A mutual silence filled the space, but instead of stewing over the way Finn was handling the investigation, I found myself regretting bringing Chris up in the first place.

The church parking lot was now full. Light poured onto the snow from the windows of the fellowship hall. Finn parked and cut the engine. "Any advice for a first timer?" he asked.

I opened the car door, a gust of wind cutting through my coat. "You don't have to bid on a pie. No one has any expectations," I reassured him.

Finn hopped out of the truck, and I met him around the front of the vehicle. We picked our way across the parking lot. Salt lay scattered across the ruts of now melting ice. Seriously? We went to all this trouble to get salt, and someone else just showed up with it?

"I came to Star Junction to build a life. I want to participate in all of it," Finn said. His interest in the town and our traditions, even the outdated ones, was sweet.

"Stick with me," I said. "I'll coach you through it."

We made it to the sidewalk and started toward the door together.

Finn paused, and I stopped, looking back at him. He took a step toward me, closing the distance between us. "Would it be okay if—" he started.

"There you both are," Margie exclaimed. She bustled toward us, her breath puffing out as tiny clouds in the cold, night air. "I was getting worried you'd miss it. I'm so glad you're both okay." She linked arms with us, putting herself in the middle, and started toward the door.

Laughter and music called us to join the party inside. Margie chattered on about how they'd called everyone in town, trying to find salt for the parking lot. I looked over Margie's head to see Finn smiling down at me, but his gaze was wistful. I tried to reassure him with my own smile. What had he been about to ask me?

Before I could wonder any longer, Margie rushed us into the bright lights and steamy warmth of a very full fellowship hall. I took in the crowd of people milling about, laughing, plates of food balanced in their hands. "It's packed," I said.

Margie beamed at the crowded room. "Biggest group we've ever had. We're going to raise so much money for the library. Don't you worry, honey. I got your pie where it was supposed to be," she said.

I patted Margie's hand, still tucked around my arm, and said, "Thanks, Margie."

"Anytime, darling. Now I better go make sure they got the microphone working. You know Donna and technology," Margie said as she rolled her eyes good-naturedly and rushed off toward the front of the room.

I turned to Finn to comment on Margie's never-ending enthusiasm and energy, but he was a few feet away, talking to Mrs. Horne, the school nurse from when I was in elementary school. She wore one of her hand-embroidered cardigans, this sporting a brown squirrel on each square pocket. Her snowy white hair was perfectly styled in curls that I knew she had reset once a week by Lucille at the Clip and Curl.

Mrs. Horne looked up at Finn admiringly, clutching his arm as she prattled on about something. Finn caught me watching him and shot me a grin before turning his attention back to Mrs. Horne.

My stomach flipped at his smile and then growled with hunger. At least it had its priorities straight. I tried to spot the food table past the crowds of people standing around chatting. There was no telling how long Finn would be sidelined by Mrs. Horne, and I needed food now. I located the buffet table set against the far wall. I'd find Finn later.

I grabbed a paper plate and piled on pasta salad, a ham sandwich, and fruit salad, forgoing the Jell-O "salad" containing a mix of fruit and vegetables in a lime green gelatin. I was as Midwest as the next girl, but I couldn't get behind "salads" inside Jell-O.

I found a smaller table a few yards away covered with standard potluck drinks—lemonade, coffee, iced tea, and water. I filled a cup with water and scanned the room for somewhere to sit.

"Gwen," Penny said as she waved and rushed toward me, pulling her husband, Jack, behind her. "You made it. I heard about the accident. Are you okay?" Penny asked as she scanned my body much like Finn had right after the accident.

"I'm fine," I said. "Nothing food won't help. I can't believe how crowded it is." I turned to Penny's husband. "Hey, Jack, how's it going?"

Jack was as warm and cozy as Penny was sleek and stylish. He matched Penny in height but was wide with muscles useful in fighting fires. Instead of looking intimidating, he looked like a giant teddy bear with his tawny brown hair and bushy beard to match.

On the surface, they seemed like a strange match, but Jack was good for Penny, grounding her, while Penny added the excitement his life needed outside of the fire station.

"Hey, Gwen," Jack said as he frowned. "Sorry about having to find Justin like that. And Chris getting arrested."

My heart sank once again and I sighed. "Thanks. It's been a rough week," I said.

Penny glanced around furtively, leaned in, and said, "I've been asking around, and I think I have some information that might be helpful. I found out—"

"No way," I interrupted her. "You should not be asking around about Justin. It's not safe."

Penny folded her arms across her chest and knitted her eyebrows together. "Why do you get to go around asking questions, and I can't?" she asked pointedly.

"It's not the same," I argued.

"How?" Penny challenged.

Oh boy. I didn't want to get into another fight about why I shouldn't be getting involved in this investigation. "Can we find somewhere to sit?" I asked, changing the subject. "I'm starving, and this plate is getting heavy."

Penny huffed out a sigh. "Fine, but then I'm telling you what I found out. I already know the information, so it's not going to hurt anyone for me to share it with you," she said.

I relented. "Deal. Do you see any open seats?" I asked.

The three of us scanned the edges of the room for an open table. Jack spotted one near the restrooms, and we weaved our way through the crowd, stopping to say hi to what felt like a million people on the way. By the time we sat down, I couldn't stand the hunger pangs any longer. I picked up the ham sandwich and took a bite, a slice of ham sliding out of the bun and slapping against my chin.

"Is this seat taken?" Finn asked, startling me, as I hadn't seen him walk up behind me. His gaze snagged on the ham falling out of my mouth and danced with amusement.

Heat flared across my cheeks, spreading to my chest as I shoved the stray piece of ham into my mouth, shaking my head like an idiot in answer to his question. He sat down and turned his attention to Penny and Jack. He stretched out his hand toward Jack and said, "I don't think we've met. I'm Finn Butler."

Jack shook his hand. "Jack Taylor. Nice to meet you. This is my wife, Penny."

Penny reached out her hand but wiggled her eyebrows at me. I shot her a desperate look that said *please, not tonight*. In a rare act of restraint, Penny rearranged her face into a sweet smile and said, "It's very nice to meet you, Detective Butler. Welcome to Star Junction."

At least she hadn't called him Detective Hottie.

"Please, call me Finn," he replied.

The sound system let out a shriek followed by Donna, who was wearing all green tonight, from the headband holding her salt and pepper hair out of her face to her green orthopedic shoes and everything in between, shouting, "Is this thing on?"

A chorus of "yeah, it's on" rang out around the room. Donna welcomed everyone to the fifteenth annual pie social and explained the rules.

Finn leaned over and whispered in my ear, his breath tickling my neck. "What's a typical starting bid?" he asked.

I turned, finding myself inches from his face. A butterfly danced through my stomach as my gaze met his. "Usually five dollars," I said, suddenly feeling breathless.

"Thanks," he said as he leaned back in his seat. He left his hand resting on the back of my chair. It wasn't around my shoulder, and it wasn't exactly touching me, but I could feel the tip of his thumb resting gently against the thin fabric of my blouse.

I kept my gaze focused on Donna, who was giving instructions for the auction, but my attention was fixed on the weight of Finn's touch. I was tempted to look around and see if the gossip machine had taken notice of Finn's hand placement, but I was nervous that moving would send a signal that I didn't want his hand there. I remained still, pretending as if my whole body wasn't centered on this simple, innocent touch.

The first pie up for bid belonged to Penny, and she jumped up and headed to the front of the room. She picked up her strawberry rhubarb pie and shook her finger at the room as she said, "I'm expecting to eat a slice of this delicious pie with my husband tonight, so let's raise some money for the library, but let's not get carried away."

The crowd laughed, and someone shouted, "But I want to eat pie with you, Mrs. Taylor."

Penny's bubbling laugh floated through the room. "It won't

help your grade in Advanced Literature, Robbie."

I'd complained to Penny about having to come tonight, but the truth was, I loved the feeling of community at events like the pie social. The bidding got hot and heavy, but it was all in good fun. A few minutes later, Jack had secured the winning bid for his wife's pie at twenty dollars, and she skipped back to the table, planting a kiss on his lips before sitting down.

Donna looked over her clipboard and called out, "The next pie was made by Guinevere Stevens."

Finn and I looked at one another. I wiggled my eyebrows playfully, which prompted a chuckle from Finn.

"Go get 'em, Tiger," he said, patting me on the back.

I could feel the goofy grin on my face as I made my way to the front of the room.

Donna continued, "Gwen has brought a Lemon Blueberry Swirl Cheesecake." She looked at me in surprise. "How delightful, dear. Did you make this yourself?" Everyone in Star Junction over the age of sixty called me dear, honey, or sweetie. Donna was no exception. She frowned. "Although not technically a pie." Donna was nothing if not a stickler for the rules.

I smiled as I leaned into the microphone. "This delicious *cheesecake*," I said, emphasizing the offending word, "is completely homemade." I held up a finger as I made my next point. "Although not technically a pie, I did make it in a pie pan, and it has all the hallmarks of a great pie—a buttery crust, a delectable filling, and lots of sugar."

"That's what I'm talking about," someone yelled from the back, prompting a smattering of chuckles around the room.

"There's that debate team experience shining through," Mr. Locke said from one of the tables near the front. As the coach of the debate team both currently and when I was in high school, Mr. Locke considered himself something of a Robin William's type character from *Dead Poet's Society*, even down to the tweed blazer with suede elbow patches.

I gave Mr. Locke a quick smile before returning my attention to Donna. Was she going to let my cheesecake slide?

Donna seemed to consider my words before looking over the crowd and saying, "Who'll start the bidding to get this delicious cheesecake and some nice company from our very own Guinevere?"

I'd won my argument.

Finn's strong voice from the back shouted, "Ten dollars!"

"Oh! What an opening bid!" Donna exclaimed, clearly delighted and no longer worried whether or not my non-pie had broken the pie social in some way.

Finn grinned confidently. My cheeks grew warm, and I ducked my head, trying to hide whatever emotions were flashing across my face. I was increasingly confused by my ever-changing feelings around him.

"Twelve!" another voice called out from the other side of the room.

I turned toward the voice to see Mitch standing with his hand raised. He'd traded his normal uniform of faded wranglers for a darker, cleaner-looking pair of jeans, but still sported the beat-up Texaco baseball cap. Mitch, Justin, Chris—we all grew up together, but Mitch and I were never particularly close. I gave him a small smile despite my confusion. Maybe he really liked cheesecake.

"Fifteen!" Finn leaned forward in his chair, looking expectantly at Donna.

"Sixteen," came another shout from the back.

I turned to see Derek watching me eagerly, his arms crossed over his chest, putting his biceps on full display once again. Oh no! That was not happening. Derek wouldn't care that I'd turned down his offer of a date at the gym yesterday. He was evidence number one of why my crush on Chris felt safer than dating in Star Junction.

I was starting to seriously rethink the appropriateness of the pie social. It was all in good fun until Derek Thompson with his smarmy smile bid on your pie and you were faced with the possibility of having to be trapped in a pseudo-date with him.

Finn knew nothing about my ongoing issues with Derek. Neither did Mitch. I turned to Finn anyway, my look pleading.

Finn sat up a little straighter and called out, "Seventeen!"

"Twenty!" Derek shouted.

"Fifty dollars!" a voice called out from near the doors to the parking lot.

I sucked in a sharp breath.

I knew that voice.

I turned to the back of the room along with everyone else.

There, in the doorway of the fellowship hall, stood Chris Crawford.

CHAPTER TWELVE

———

Chris grinned, his hands in the pockets of his jeans, his blue sweater intensifying the cornflower blue of his eyes. His blond hair lay damp on his forehead.

I squealed and closed the distance between us, throwing myself into his arms. The sound of his deep laugh wrapped itself around me as he lifted me off the ground. The clean smell of fresh soap mixing with the fresh hope that Chris was actually here made my heart feel as if it would burst.

Chris set me down. "Bet you weren't expecting to see me tonight. Are all the good pies gone?" he said loudly enough for everyone to hear.

"You're bidding on the best one," I teased as he surveyed the room, nodding and waving at friends. The hubbub Chris's sudden appearance caused reached my ears, but I was too focused on his crooked smile and sparkling eyes to pay any attention to it. I reached out and gripped his arms. "How are you here?" I asked.

"How about I win this pie, and we can sit and talk all about it," he replied with a charming grin.

"Technically it's not a pie," Donna corrected from the microphone.

It felt like I was eleven years old again and we'd been found huddled in the woods. Relief, joy, and disbelief flooded my body, making me not care that Donna was still stuck on that. "Sounds like perfection," I said to Chris.

A low murmur hummed through the room as people expressed their shock at Chris's sudden appearance and probably their theories about whether or not he had killed Justin.

Donna tapped on the microphone to get everyone's attention, which resulted in another squeal from the sound system. I winced but then laughed, my relief at seeing Chris out of jail making me giddy.

"I say we call this cheesecake sold. What do you all think?"

Donna said to the crowd.

Applause filled the air.

Chris walked up to Donna and planted a kiss on her lined cheek. "I'll take that," he said confidently. He lifted the cheesecake off the table, grabbed two forks, and walked back to me with a patented Chris Crawford smirk on his lips. "I've been in jail for two days," he said loudly enough for the room to hear. "I think people will understand if we dig into this pie before the rest of the auction is over."

This prompted a wide variety of responses from the crowd—catcalls mixed with light applause joined by a few "you got that right's" let me know that most of the crowd was just as thrilled Chris was out of jail as I was.

"I think you're probably right," I said, laughing.

I followed Chris as he sauntered to the back corner of the large room and ducked into an alcove used to store tables and chairs. It was almost empty, most of the chairs having been moved into the main room for the night. Chris settled onto the floor in the back corner, and I dropped down next to him. Chris dug his fork into the edge of the cheesecake, pulling out a huge bite.

"Someone's not wasting any time," I teased as he shoved the bite into his mouth.

He swallowed quickly and took another bite. "Listen," he said around a mouthful of pie, "I've been eating whatever takeout Stan brings me for the last two days. I'm hungry, and this pie looks amazing."

"You're always hungry," I said happily. I tucked my arm under his and rested my head on his shoulder. "I was so worried about you."

Chris patted my knee with his free hand while continuing to shovel bites of pie into his mouth with the other. "I know. Me too," he said.

I sat up and faced him. "How are you even here?" I asked.

Chris leaned his head back against the wall and looked up at the ceiling. He blew out a measured breath. "My dad sent a lawyer," he said.

"Oh," I said, my voice hushed with the thought of what Chris's father might expect in exchange for his help.

"Yeah," he replied, his tone flat.

We sat in silence, the cheesecake momentarily forgotten.

"I'm glad you're here," I finally said into the silence, trying to sound cheerful, "no matter how it happened."

Chris sighed and looked down at the cheesecake again, a quarter of it already gone. "The truth is, I am too. I'll figure things out with my dad," he said. "The lawyer arrived this evening, and after meeting with Stan for thirty minutes, Stan said I was free to go. I'm not allowed to leave town, but where would I even go?"

"Mexico?" I asked. I was joking. Sort of.

"Very funny," Chris said dryly. "I trust Stan to figure this out, and he says the new detective is good. I guess we'll see. Have you met him?" He started in on the pie again.

"We've met," I answered. "He interviewed me after I found Justin's body." I didn't tell Chris about the accident today. I also didn't tell him about how warm Finn's hand had felt against mine as we stumbled and laughed our way up the embankment earlier.

"What do you think about the guy?" he asked, still focused on demolishing the cheesecake.

What did I think about Finn? That was a loaded question. "He seems to know what he's doing," I answered diplomatically. I took the other fork from Chris, who'd managed to hang on to both of them despite his work on inhaling the cheesecake I'd spent all morning making.

I took a bite. The freshness of the blueberries and lemon mixed with the tanginess of the cream cheese exploded like a cool spring morning on my tongue. "This is amazing," I said in awe. "I need to bake more often."

Chris blocked my fork with his like it was a sword and we were knights battling. It wasn't going to work. He'd had plenty of the pie. I shoved his arm out of the way, laughing.

"I paid for this pie," he objected, trying to block my access again.

"Too bad, Crawford. I made it." I snatched the fork from his hand. "It's time to focus," I said, pulling his attention away from the cheesecake to more important matters at hand. "I've got some things to fill you in on about the investigation."

"I told you to leave it alone," he warned.

"Good thing I stopped listening to you a long time ago," I teased, hoping he'd be too charmed to continue to object.

It worked. Chris shot me a crooked grin. "Fine. What'd you figure out, Nancy Drew?"

I poked my head around the corner to make sure no one was

lingering, trying to listen in on our conversation. The room had settled into a low roar of conversation. The auction must be over. Finn sat at the table chatting with Penny and Jack. Maybe Penny would manage to learn something from him I hadn't.

When I was satisfied no one was listening, I broke off another small piece of the cheesecake and said, "It all started with Donna coming into Camelot Flowers Monday morning. We got to talking about Justin's murder, and she mentioned Justin and Samantha broke up last week."

Chris rubbed the back of his neck before saying, "I hadn't heard that."

In my excitement about not being the only one out of the loop, I smacked Chris's chest with the back of my hand. "Exactly!" I exclaimed. "Me neither. Anyway, Donna also said Justin might have cheated on Samantha, so it was over for good."

Chris shook his head as if trying to make sense of Justin's behavior. "So, what? You think Samantha killed him for cheating on her?" he asked.

"I don't know about that," I said. "I ran into Samantha at the grocery store and talked to her. She seemed pretty broken up about Justin's death."

"Maybe she's all broken up," he said, using my own words, "because she feels guilty for killing him."

I shook my head in doubt but said, "Maybe. Finn seems to think whoever killed Justin was really strong. Samantha is a beanpole. I'm not sure she could have done it." The more I thought about it, the less I liked my own theory that adrenaline could have enabled Samantha to shove that screwdriver into Justin's chest.

"Finn?" Chris asked, clearly confused.

I looked at him for a moment, trying to understand his one-word question, before it dawned on me that he might not have ever heard Finn's first name. I doubted Finn had been very buddy-buddy with Chris while he was questioning and detaining him.

"Detective Butler," I explained. "His first name is Finn."

Chris paused, another bite of cheesecake hovering in the air between the pan and his mouth. "First-name basis with the new detective?" he asked.

I scoffed as I turned my attention to getting another bite of cheesecake before Chris managed to eat it all. "Back to the case," I said, hoping the heat I felt flooding my cheeks wasn't obvious to

Chris. "Samantha confirmed the cheating rumors but doesn't know who he cheated with. I thought maybe that person killed Justin or that person's jealous boyfriend."

"And?" Chris asked.

"I went to talk to Derek to see if he'd know anything, but he blew me off," I said.

"Makes sense," Chris said. "Even if Derek knew what Justin was up to, he's not going to rat him out."

"It's not like I'm the police," I argued. "Why hide anything from me?"

"You're not the police, but those good old boys stick together," Chris explained.

"Maybe he'd talk to you?" I suggested. "As one of the good old boys?"

Chris hedged, "I'm not sure I count as one of the good old boys. Not that I'm complaining. There's being buddies with those guys, and then there's being truly *in* with them."

I took a deep breath before launching into the biggest piece of news. "Speaking of being in with whatever they've got going on, I went and saw Mrs. Hunt this morning." I gave Chris a brief smile. "She believes you're innocent, by the way," I added.

The relief on Chris's face beamed through the stress of the last few days. Hopefully what I was about to share with him wouldn't wipe that away.

"She let me look around his room," I explained. "I found a stash of cash and drugs under Justin's bed." I showed Chris the picture.

Chris let out a low whistle. "The rumors were right," he said.

"It has to be connected to his death, right?" I said, hopeful that this would prove to be the solution to Chris's problem.

Chris set the cheesecake aside like he'd lost his appetite. "I don't know," he said slowly. His gaze grew distant. "My lawyer said I need to stay home as much as possible, keep a low profile."

"Do whatever the lawyer says," I replied. "I'll keep you posted on what I find out."

"I still don't like this," he said. He put his arm around my shoulder and tucked me against his side. Moves like this were familiar between us but not helpful in my quest to get over him. "I worry about you," he continued. "Whoever killed Justin went to great effort to set me up, including pulling you into it."

"Whoever killed Justin is going to want to keep as low of a

profile as your lawyer is asking you to keep," I argued. "They're not going to go on a killing spree."

Chris pressed a quick kiss into my hair. I steeled my body, willing it to remain neutral, but butterflies danced in my stomach. In all the years we'd been best friends, we'd never kissed. Not on the lips at least. Not even when we went to prom together.

There had been moments, late at night on his front porch—the night we graduated, the day before we'd both left for college—moments when I'd thought he was going to kiss me. I'd never read the moment right.

"There you are," Penny said as she appeared in the doorway, giving me a meaningful look at how close Chris and I were sitting. Thankfully she didn't say anything about it. "People are starting to head out." She turned to Chris. "Mr. Jacobson is looking for you."

Chris ran his hand through his hair. "This can't be good," he said, his voice tight with worry.

As the principal of the high school, Mr. Jacobson was Chris's boss. Being a guidance counselor was the perfect job for Chris and something he planned to keep doing while he was getting the youth center up and running. He was still cool enough for the kids to listen to, and he cared enough to be dedicated to his job.

"Maybe he just wants to tell you he's glad you're out," I said.

"I guess there's only one way to find out," Chris said as he stood, brushing dust off his jeans. "Thanks, Penny." He turned to me. "I'll call you later."

I stood too. "I'm so glad you're out of jail. Now we just need to keep you out for good," I said, determined to make it happen.

Chris nodded his agreement before heading off to find Mr. Jacobson. Penny took his place, picking up the pie, which had the semblance of one crooked piece left. She held out her hand and wiggled her fingers, her meaning clear. I handed her my fork. She took a bite. "Oh my gosh, Gwen. This is actually good," she said in awe.

I laughed. "Don't sound so surprised," I said, faking offense.

Penny took another bite before saying, "I need to tell you what I learned about Justin."

It still seemed like a bad idea for Penny to get involved, but like she'd said, she already knew the information. It would be almost criminal for her not to share it with me. "Okay…" I said.

"Lena heard from Jackie who heard from Matt that Justin

was fired from Palmer's Gravel and Rock," Penny said with gusto.

"Fired?" I replied. "That doesn't seem like Tom. He's always giving people second chances." Tom was father to Tommy Jr., the police officer first on the scene the night of Justin's murder. Most of us dropped the *Junior* part of his name, opting to simply call him Tommy, although his dad still called him Junior.

Penny nodded knowingly and said, "That's what I thought. Maybe Justin used up too many second chances."

Information that started with the words *I heard* should never be trusted blindly. I pulled out my phone and added *Talk to Tom* to my growing list. "That's helpful," I grudgingly admitted.

"I knew it would be," Penny said triumphantly. "And I'm finishing the rest of this pie."

It was almost gone anyway.

I followed Penny into the main room as she scooped the last of the pie from the disposable tin and tossed the tin into the garbage can by the door. "Staying to help clean up?" she asked.

"I should," I said hesitantly. I stifled a yawn. I'd been going to bed at a reasonable hour but waking up in the middle of the night, heart pounding, covers tangled around my legs. Justin's vacant eyes haunted my dreams, leaving me too wound up to fall back asleep.

I glanced around at the groups of people breaking down tables and stacking chairs. "Have you seen Finn anywhere?" I asked Penny.

While Chris showing up had been a dream come true, I was disappointed at the lost opportunity to spend more time with Finn. We'd reached some sort of fragile peace while trapped in the ditch together, and I was curious what talking to him about something other than murder might be like.

"He took off shortly after the auction," Penny answered with a shrug. "Something about crime never sleeping."

"He didn't bid on any other pies?" I asked, keeping my tone casual.

My attempt at an innocent question failed as Penny gave me a meaningful look and said, "Just yours."

"Okay, okay," I said, brushing off her insinuation. "Let's get this place cleaned up." I'd help clean up the fellowship hall then get to cleaning up the mess of Justin's murder.

CHAPTER THIRTEEN

———

My car tires crunched over the gravel parking lot of Palmer's Gravel and Rock. I'd spent another sleepless night staring at the ceiling, images of the people I'd known my entire life lined up behind one-way glass like some sort of police line-up. Someone had killed Justin. Probably even someone I knew.

I'd finally surrendered and gotten out of bed an hour before the sun was up. I'd nearly gone crazy puttering around my house. The moment the rock yard had opened at six, I'd been in my car heading to the outskirts of town to talk to Tom Palmer.

I parked next to a small building tucked between piles of rock of every size and color imaginable. A large sign reading *Palmer's Gravel and Rock* hung above the gray metal door.

I'd spent many an afternoon as a child riding with my dad out to the rock yard to drop off Kiwanis business, which usually resulted in cups of coffee and long chats about sports, hunting, or their next poker game. I opened my car door to be greeted by a large black dog barking and sniffing around my legs.

"Hi, Gus," I said as I scratched his furry neck.

"Well, Guinevere Stevens, as I live and breathe. What are you doing out here without your dad?" Tom Palmer asked. He stood in the doorway to the office building, his hands on his hips and a smile on his round face.

"Still using Gus as a living doorbell, I see," I said, laughing as Gus licked my hand.

Tom laughed too, and his large belly shook under his faded flannel shirt. "Keeps me aware of who's coming and going. I don't need someone shoveling off a pile of rock without my knowing."

I locked the car and started toward him, Gus dancing around my feet. "You know, there are these things called security cameras," I teased. "You hang 'em up, and they tell you exactly who's coming and going."

"That's true," Tom said, running his hand over his short, gray beard. "But Gus is more fun to pet."

I reached down and ruffled Gus's silky-smooth coat. "You've got me there," I agreed.

"Come on in," Tom said. "To what do I owe the pleasure?" He took a step back, leaving room for me to walk into the office.

The small space hadn't been remodeled since the Carter administration. I walked across the green shag carpet that had seen better days and settled on a floral sofa under a large window that looked out onto a pile of river rock. "I wanted to talk about Justin Hunt," I answered.

Tom let the door close behind him and blew out a breath. "It's a darn shame what happened to that boy." He walked over to an ancient coffeemaker and poured himself a cup. "Do you want some?" he asked.

"No thanks," I said, waving away the offer. "I heard a rumor you fired him last week."

Tom perched on the edge of his desk, which groaned under his weight, and took a sip of the coffee, eyeing me over the top of his mug. "You heard a rumor, huh? Why do you care?" he asked, his gaze shrewd.

I shifted in my seat and set my purse on the Formica coffee table. "I'm sure you heard I'm the one who found Justin's body," I started.

Tom nodded and said, "Junior mentioned he was first on the scene." Tom shook his head. "It really shook him up seeing a friend like that."

"I don't blame him," I said. "I will say it was nice to see a friendly face in that moment, although I'm sorry Tommy had to see it at all."

"It's part of the job," Tom said, referring to Tommy Junior's role on the police force. "What does any of this have to do with me?" he asked.

"Well, the police think Chris did it," I explained. "You know Chris. He'd never murder anyone."

Tom set the mug down and folded his arms across his thick chest. "I know that when pushed, people are capable of most anything," he said.

I hadn't expected that response from Tom, who was always good-natured and friendly. He knew Chris's character as well as anyone. "I know Chris didn't do it. I think someone's setting him up, and I'm going to figure out who that is," I blurted out.

Tom's eyes narrowed. "Your dad know you're poking around in this?" he asked, the warning in his tone clear.

I gulped but held his gaze while saying, "No, and I don't think there's any reason he needs to be told."

We stared each other down before Tom barked out a laugh, slapping his knee for good measure. "Still as strong willed as ever," he said. "I'll make you a deal. You be smart about this, and I won't tell your dad."

I beamed up at him. "Deal. Now will you tell me what happened with Justin?" I asked again.

He walked around and sat at his desk, shuffling through a few papers. "I got a load getting ready to go out in a few minutes. There's not much to tell, but I'll tell you what I know," he said.

He leaned back in his chair and continued, "Justin came to work for me six months ago. You know Justin, charming as all get-out but always seems to find himself on the wrong side of situations. He needed a job, and so I gave him a chance. Two months ago, I started to notice I was filling up the trucks with diesel more than usual, even though we weren't delivering more orders."

"That's weird," I said.

"That's what I thought," Tom agreed. "I started checking the mileage on the trucks before I left for the day and then again in the morning. One of the trucks was going out some nights." Tom leaned toward the window and pointed to a green dump truck parked a few spaces away from my car. "That one right there. Someone was putting between twenty and eighty miles on it, depending on the week."

"Someone was joyriding in one of your trucks?" I said in disbelief.

"I didn't know what to think," Tom answered. He looked down at his watch and pulled himself out of his chair. "I've gotta go check this shipment before it leaves. This is an important client, and I can't risk the boys loading the wrong rock. I'll walk you out."

I stood and grabbed my purse. Gus was waiting for us at the door and continued his bids for attention. I absently patted his head.

"Justin was my only driver at the time," Tom said. "Jed was out recovering from knee surgery. When I asked Justin about the discrepancies, he denied knowing anything about it, but I had enough other offenses that I could fire him without needing proof he was taking the trucks out."

"Other offenses?" I asked, itching to take my phone out but suspecting Tom wouldn't take kindly to seeing my list of suspects. He'd agreed not to rat me out to my dad, but if he knew how many people I was talking to, he might change his mind.

"Nothing big," Tom explained. "Being late, taking longer breaks than allowed. But he'd done it enough, and I'd talked to him enough, that it was a convenient excuse."

We reached my car, and I opened the door, leaning against it. "What do you think he was doing with the truck?" I asked.

Tom reached down and scratched Gus behind the ears. "Beats me, but he was real angry when I fired him." Tom stared into the distance as if he were seeing it all over again. "He had this wild look in his eyes. He begged me to give him another chance. He told me I didn't understand, that he really needed the job."

"You think he was stealing rock?" I asked, trying to make sense of what I was hearing.

"It's not that I can count every rock on the yard, but I'd notice if a whole dump truck load was missing. He was using the truck for something, but it wasn't to steal my rock," Tom said.

"Tom!" a man shouted from across the parking lot where he stood by a loaded truck.

"I gotta go, hon," Tom said briskly. "Stay safe."

"I will," I agreed. "Thanks for the info. And for not calling my dad."

The man who'd called Tom over caught my gaze, giving me a nasty look. While I knew a lot of people in Star Junction, I didn't know everyone. What was this guy's problem? I'd delayed Tom, what? One minute? I resisted the urge to give the look right back to him.

Tom walked around the corner with the other man, leaving me with Gus standing in the cold. I tapped my finger against my lips as I considered my options. The dump truck Tom had pointed out as the one Justin was driving after hours was just across the lot. I looked around. Tom was out of sight. Maybe I'd take a little look around while I was here. As far as I knew, Finn hadn't been out here investigating Justin's work as a possible connection to his murder.

I couldn't think of a connection to Justin winding up dead in Chris's youth center, other than Tom getting angry enough at Justin for using a dump truck without permission and hunting him down to murder in cold blood.

I shook my head as I made my way across the parking lot. I just couldn't believe it was true. Tom was a gentle giant. There were a million things he might do to Justin before murder would even make the list.

Halfway to the truck, I was still undetected. A thrill moved through my body. Is this what Margie had felt as she snuck me into Chris's holding cell? Like a superhero on a mission? Mild-mannered florist by day, crime fighting detective by night. I didn't hate the thought.

I made it to the dump truck, moving to the side opposite the parking lot and office portable. Standing with my hands on my hips, I considered my next move. What was I even looking for? I ducked down and looked under the truck, but it just looked like a normal truck to me.

I huffed out a sigh. This was ridiculous. Unless the truck came with a flashing sign that said *I'm the reason Justin got murdered*, I had no idea what I was looking for. The sound of two people talking, their voices growing louder as they got closer, froze me in position. Two men were talking. I plastered myself against the side of the truck, praying the mud was frozen enough to stay on the truck and not get on the back of my coat.

"What'd that lady want?" one voice sneered, as if my very presence had offended him.

"Gwen is the daughter of an old friend of mine. She was out here asking about Justin Hunt," Tom Palmer answered, his voice friendly.

"What's her deal with Justin?" the other man asked harshly. I was convinced it was the man who'd shot me a dirty look. I hadn't seen anyone else around, and his voice matched the undeserved hatred I'd seen in his beady little eyes.

"They went to high school together," Tom answered. "The load looks good. Let's use this truck to haul it. The other has been having some transmission issues."

"Good riddance to Justin Hunt. He did nothing but make my job harder," the man said.

Made his job harder? Was this another motive for murder?

"We don't have to worry about Justin anymore. Let's get this load out so we can start working on the Hansen job," Tom replied.

His words had been casual, almost distracted, as if he were checking an order while talking to the other man, but the substance of his words bothered me. *We don't have to worry about Justin anymore?* Sure sounded like something a murderer would say.

"Why's her car still here?" the man asked.

I held my breath as my heart hammered in my chest. That was a very good question.

"Probably using the bathroom or something," Tom said. "She's been out here countless times with her dad. She knows where it is."

I nodded enthusiastically, despite having no audience. That was a good excuse. If I managed to get out of here without someone finding me hiding, I was going to use that one.

The dump truck belched to life, and I bit back a yelp of surprise. The truck vibrated against my back. They were going to move the truck, and I'd be discovered. What excuse would I use then? I couldn't find the bathroom? That wouldn't fly.

I had a vision of myself gripping the pipes on the underside of the truck and riding out of here undetected like some kind of superspy. Yeah, right. I'd probably get myself run over.

The truck turned slowly, and I inched along with it until I was on the side facing away from the office and my car. A pile of reddish-brown gravel sat a few feet away. It was taller than I was. Before I could overthink my next move, I sprinted for the pile and practically dove behind it.

For minutes, I crouched close to the ground, my breath coming in frantic puffs, fogging into the icy air. I imagined it made me look like a dragon guarding its loot. *A dragon.* My dad would like that reference. Guinevere and the dragon.

No one yelled. No one came running over. Despite the odds, I'd escaped detection. I peeked around the side of the pile. The truck was on the other side of the office. No one was around. This was my chance.

I walked briskly to my car. Sprinting would have looked suspicious. Better to get caught and make up a lie than get caught looking guilty. I slid into my car, started the engine, and drove down the road until it curved, leaving me out of sight of the rock yard.

Heart still pounding, I opened the list on my phone and added the information I'd learned from Tom, including a note to brainstorm what Justin could have been doing with that truck in the middle of the night. Delivering drugs somewhere? But why one of Tom's trucks? There had to be more low-key ways of transporting illegal substances than a giant dump truck.

I put away my phone and headed to open Camelot Flowers, my mind working overtime. Justin bounced from job to job. He was enthusiastic but unreliable. Why had losing this job been such a big deal? How did this new piece of information fit into the puzzle I was attempting to construct around Justin's murder? If I were being honest with myself, the puzzle had more holes than it had pieces right now.

I slowed as I reached the city limits. Getting pulled over wouldn't help my mission to make it to work on time. Minutes later, I parked on the street a few doors down from Camelot Flowers.

Climbing from my car, I headed toward the door, but movement across the street caught my eye, and I turned to see Tommy, the officer who'd been first on the scene to Justin's murder and Tom Palmer's son, walking toward the coffee shop at the corner.

He was in full uniform, so he must be on duty. I glanced between Camelot Flowers and Tommy. I had a few minutes and didn't know when I might get an opportunity like this again.

"Tommy, wait up," I called out as I jogged across the street.

"Hey, what's up?" he said once I reached him.

"Got a minute?" I asked with a wide smile. I didn't have the same problems with Tommy as I had with Finn initially, but I'd also never asked Tommy for inside information on a police investigation before now. No harm in getting off to a friendly start.

Tommy shrugged. "Sure. I was going to grab some caffeine. We've been working overtime trying to figure out what happened to Justin, and I'm exhausted. I've got some time unless a call comes through on the radio," he said.

Just what I wanted to hear. "By the way, I just saw your dad," I said.

Tommy tilted his head to the side. "You went out to the yard? Why?" he asked.

"I heard Justin got fired. I was hoping your dad might know something that could point to another suspect in Justin's murder. Besides Chris," I added.

Tommy opened his mouth to respond, but I held my hand up to stop him and said, "And before you tell me this is police business and I should let you guys do your jobs, I've heard it all before from Detective Butler." While he'd insisted I call him Finn, it didn't feel right to call him that in front of one of his officers.

Tommy laughed and said, "I was going to say no such thing.

Truth is, we could use any insight the public has about this case. It's turning out to be more complicated than the interpersonal politics of the pie social."

"In what way?" I asked, curiosity blooming in my chest like a spring tulip.

"We're tracking down every lead we come across, but the location of the murder, the murder weapon, the fight between Justin and Chris, it's not looking good for Crawford," Tommy explained in a matter-of-fact tone.

Finn wouldn't give me any details, but Tommy was a small-town cop and a friend from high school. Maybe he'd be more open to sharing. "What about forensic evidence?" I asked.

Tommy shook his head. "That stuff takes forever to come back, especially since we don't have our own crime lab here. We send it over to the county labs, but we're in line behind everything that came in before us," he said.

"Surely murder trumps any of the nonviolent crimes," I argued.

"It does, but Justin's isn't the only murder in the county. It'll be a few weeks," Tommy said, his frustration with the sluggishness of the system obvious in his tone.

"A few weeks!" I exclaimed. "Chris doesn't have a few weeks."

"Crawford will be fine. He just needs to keep his head down and stay out of trouble," Tommy replied.

I glanced at my watch. The store was supposed to open two minutes ago. I needed to get going. "Thanks, Tommy," I said, truly feeling grateful that he'd been willing to talk to me. "If you think of anything that could help me, can you let me know?"

"Isn't that supposed to be my line?" he teased.

I shot him a grin and turned to head across the street.

"Oh, hey," Tommy called after me.

I stopped and turned back toward him.

"There is one thing." Tommy looked around as if to make sure we weren't overheard. "Detective Butler found nasty messages on Justin's phone between him and Tony Reagan. Remember him?" Tommy asked.

Remember him? I'd seen him at Bucky's the night Justin was murdered. "Nasty how?" I asked.

"Angry," Tommy explained. "Tony blaming Justin for

ruining his future."

"Ruining his future? Tony has an amazing job, lives in Chicago. What could Justin have ruined?" I said, thinking back to Tony's rude behavior toward Justin at Bucky's Saturday night. The same night he was murdered.

Tommy shrugged. "We're checking it out. We're also looking for a woman he was dating in Rose Lake."

"What about Samantha?" I asked.

"Detective Butler talked to her," Tommy said. "I don't know the details of their interview."

It wasn't much, but it was more than I knew before. "Thanks, Tommy," I said before hurrying across the street.

The police were checking it out, but I would too. The nasty text messages shed some light on what I'd seen at Bucky's, but I had no idea how Justin could've ruined anything for Tony. I didn't know the details, but there were plenty of people in town who might know exactly what happened.

* * *

Hours later, I hadn't had a moment to think about Justin, Tony, Tom, or anything else related to the case. Customers had kept me occupied until the store closed and my friends showed up to the store for my favorite part of the month—book club.

"Why do we always choose these depressing books?" Emma complained as she plucked another cookie from the floral plate on the table covered with a rose-patterned tablecloth.

My mom went all out when designing what she called "The Family Room" at Camelot Flowers. Not a break room, which she envisioned as boring and drab, but a comfortable room that would make spending long hours at the store feel more like home. My only complaint as I'd gotten older was that she'd painfully stuck to the flower theme in the décor. It was cheery. It was also a little sickening.

I'd been hosting the monthly book club for a year at Camelot Flowers. There were seven of us total, but with busy schedules we were never all there. Take Penny for instance, who had an event at school tonight.

We used "The Family Room" to meet so no one had to worry about cleaning their houses to host. Easy-peasy was our motto. Except when it came to literature, apparently.

"Don't blame me about the book choice," I said, joining Emma in having another cookie. They were homemade snickerdoodles courtesy of Kristi, the only one of us who consistently showed up with baked goods not from a store.

We all turned to look at Kristi, who'd chosen this month's book.

"What?" Kristi said defensively. "It was on the *New York Time's* Best Seller List for weeks."

"I bet there are some steamy romance novels on that list too," I countered.

"Or a mystery," Amy said with glee. "I love a good who-done-it." She glanced down at her watch. "Ugh, I've got to run. It's bedtime for the kids, and I promised I'd be home in time to tuck them in."

"Yeah, I need to get going too. Early morning tomorrow," Emma said. "Do you want us to wait while you lock up?"

I stood and gathered everyone's empty cups. "You guys go ahead. I've got to clean up and finish some paperwork from earlier today. I'll be fine," I said.

The group stood to help clear the table, but Amy said, "Are you sure? I've been jumpy since Justin got murdered. I used to feel like Star Junction was the safest place in the world. Now I'm not so sure." She tossed used napkins in the trash by the small kitchenette. "You're the one who found him," she said to me. "Aren't you scared?"

I packed up the rest of Kristi's cookies and handed them to her. "No," I said. "I mean, I haven't really been thinking it could be dangerous for anyone else. I figured it was personal. I don't think there's a serial killer lurking around town or anything."

Kristi shivered and said, "Don't even say that. I've been freaking out. I ask Matt at least twelve times a night if the doors are locked. He's getting pretty annoyed."

I rinsed off the one real utensil we'd used, a large spoon to dish out the pumpkin mousse Emma had brought. "I'd be annoyed too," I said to Kristi as I chuckled. I turned from the sink to see the group standing in a line watching me. "You guys, I'll be fine," I reassured them. "I lock up here all the time. This week's no different."

"If you say so," Amy said hesitantly. She clearly thought I was being foolish.

"I'll lock the door after you leave, and I'll text you when I get home. Deal?" I said to Amy.

"You'll text all of us," Emma said, pointing a finger at me.

"Yes, ma'am," I agreed, giving her a little salute.

I followed them to the front door and locked myself in. I watched through the glass door until they made it safely to their cars before heading to the back room. They were being paranoid, but it was nice they cared.

I brushed crumbs from the table before surveying the room to make sure we'd cleaned everything up. I scooped my copy of this month's book off the couch, where I'd tossed it halfway through our meeting. Emma was right. It really had been depressing. I had a feeling my copy was going straight to the library to be donated.

I straightened one of the throw pillows on the couch, both in floral prints. The room was clean, but I was exhausted. Forget the paperwork. I'd come in early tomorrow to finish it.

Riffling through my purse, I searched for my keys. Before I could find them, the room plunged into darkness. With no windows in the room, not even the glow of the moon could light my way.

My hands hovered over the bag in the dark. A blizzard could knock out the power, but the weather was clear. Maybe we'd tripped a circuit breaker. If so, there would still be power to the front of the store.

I straightened and started feeling my way toward the door to check the rest of the building. My knee slammed into something, and I yelped. I reached down. I'd run into a chair, which meant I was heading too much to the left. I shifted my position and reached out in front of me, moving one step at a time until I felt the smooth wood of the door. I pushed lightly, opening it a crack.

This wasn't a tripped circuit breaker. The entire building was dark.

I took a step back, letting the door swing closed. I didn't know what could cause a blackout in the whole building, but I wasn't afraid of the dark. I'd find my phone in my bag and call Penny. Her husband, Jack, was great at fixing things. I'd need to make sure the power was on before we opened tomorrow. He'd know what to do. As I turned back toward my locker, the unmistakable sound of breaking glass shattered the silence.

CHAPTER FOURTEEN

―――――

I threw my hand over my mouth, muffling the shriek that escaped from my constricting lungs. Heart hammering, I raced back in the direction of my purse, running into the table and another chair before finally reaching it.

A second crash shattered the silence.

And then another.

Tears coursed down my cheeks. I riffled through my bag, searching desperately for my phone. Where was it?

I whimpered. Was someone in here with me? Silently walking toward me? A strangled cry escaped my throat as I thrust my hand deeper into my purse.

My fingers closed around my phone. I whipped it out, thrusting the light from the screen between me and the door. I half expected to see someone standing there ready to strike, but the light panned across the table and the chair I'd knocked over.

I sagged onto the couch, my hands shaking as I unlocked the phone. I had a new text from Chris. *Police released the building. Just wanted to let you know. I can get back in there tomorrow.* I dismissed the message with a swipe of my finger, barely registering what it said.

I called 9-1-1 and waited for the operator to connect. "9-1-1, what's your—"

"I'm at work," I whispered. "At Camelot Flowers in downtown Star Junction. All the lights went off, and then I heard breaking glass."

"Are you alone, ma'am?" the operator asked calmly.

"Yes," I whispered as I kept my gaze focused on the faint outline of the door across the room. "I'm in the back room."

"Stay where you are. I'm sending a unit to you. What's your name?"

"Okay. Um, my name? It's Gwen. Guinevere Stevens."

"Okay, Guinevere. Help is on the way."

I pressed my back into the couch, wishing I could melt into it and disappear. I didn't hear anything coming from the front of the store, but if I couldn't hear them coming, how could I keep myself safe?

I counted my breaths. One hundred breaths. Still nothing. I flinched. Had the door moved? Was it a shadow?

Then I heard it—feet crunching on broken glass. The phone fell from my hands. I fumbled for it, but the darkness swallowed it. I jumped to my feet, my body torn between running or fighting. Where would I run to? I was trapped.

"Gwen?" a deep voice called from the front of the store.

Finn? A sob escaped my throat, and I crumpled onto the couch.

"Gwen?" Finn called out again.

"I'm in here," I tried to say, but my sobs intensified, and I couldn't seem to catch my breath.

The door banged open, and Finn's large frame filled the doorway. The flashlight in his hand played light around the room until it landed on my tear-streaked face.

"Gwen!" Finn shouted as he ran to me, setting the flashlight on the bench, the light tossing shadows around the dark room. He dropped to his knees in front of me and scanned my body, his hands moving lightly along my arms. "Are you hurt? Did someone hurt you?" he asked.

I buried my face in my hands, wracking sobs overtaking my body. All the fear I'd been carrying since finding Justin poured from my body in salty tears. Every time I'd told someone I was fine had only added to the growing pit in my stomach. I'd convinced myself I could live with the pit. Justin was dead. Chris was a suspect. What did I have to complain about?

Finn eased my head up, his hand warm against my chin. "Are you hurt?" he asked again.

"No." I hiccupped and wiped my sleeve across my wet face. "I'm not hurt," I said.

The fear in Finn's eyes melted into relief. "I have officers sweeping the building and surrounding area. Whoever broke the windows is gone," he said.

I nodded my understanding, my tears slowing. The hiccups continued. I pulled in a deep breath and held it.

"You want to get up?" he asked gently. "There's more light out front shining from the street through the broken windows."

"Yeah. Okay," I murmured.

Finn let go of my shoulders and grabbed my hands. "Come on, here you go." He pulled until I was standing. We stood there, a breath apart, his hands still wrapped around mine.

"I dropped my phone," I said vacantly. It felt like I was mentally wading through quicksand.

Finn let go of my hands and said, "Oh, okay. Let's find it." He talked to me in low, soothing tones I would've normally found condescending. Right now, though, it was the only thing tethering me to the small bit of composure I had left.

He picked up the flashlight and swept the beam over the floor. My brain was moving at half speed, and my body seemed to be following suit. "How are you here?" I asked. "I called 9-1-1."

Finn picked up my phone and my purse, looping it over his shoulder. He directed me toward the door, his hand planted on the small of my back. "I was home, and I heard the call go out on the scanner. When I heard your name, I jumped into my truck and raced over here," he said.

We reached the door, and I faltered. What if Finn was wrong? What if whoever had broken in was out there waiting for me? Finn set his hands firmly on my shoulders and spoke soothingly into my ear as if reading my mind, "I promise it's safe. No one is out there."

I took a slow, shaky breath and nodded, steeling myself. Finn reached over my shoulder and pushed the door open. I turned the corner and circled the front counter. An officer stood with his back to us. The light from his flashlight played across a scattered pile of broken glass. In the center lay a large rock. He glanced over his shoulder, and I recognized the boyish face of Nick Holmen.

With Uncle Stan being the police chief, I'd spent time with all the officers and their families at summer BBQs, fall bonfires, even precinct Christmas parties.

"Hey, Nick," I said weakly.

"Gwen," he said in greeting before turning to Finn, all business. "You need to see this."

Finn gave my shoulder a squeeze of reassurance and walked over. The officer handed Finn a pair of gloves, and he snapped them on while crouching down to examine the rock.

I wandered closer as Finn flipped the rock over. It was about the size of a grapefruit but flatter. I'd seen rocks like that in large piles at Palmer's rock yard. The words *BACK OFF* were scrawled in white across the craggy surface of the rock.

My breath caught in my throat, and Finn twisted to look up at me. He grimaced and stood. "I'm taking you home," he said resolutely. He looked back at the officer. "I'll be back in twenty minutes to process the scene. Don't let anyone touch anything."

"Got it," the officer said.

Finn turned to me and asked, "Where's your car? I'll follow you home and make sure you get in okay."

"Make sure I get in okay? Why wouldn't I get in okay?" I asked in confusion.

Finn glanced at the officer and took my elbow, leading me back toward the front counter. "I think whoever killed Justin just made it very clear how they feel about you asking questions around town," he said, his tone firm but his expression worried. He ran his hand over his short, dark beard. "Am I safe to assume you've still been talking to people about this?"

I shrugged noncommittally.

Finn's lips tightened into a thin line. "That's what I thought. Let's get you home," he said.

We headed toward the shattered front door as the space flooded with light. I winced against the sudden brightness. Tommy came jogging around the corner. "The breaker box is outside," he said, holding up a large padlock. "The padlock's been cut. Whoever did this flipped the main breaker."

I shivered, both from the cold night air whistling through the broken glass and the thought of someone plotting to plunge me into darkness.

"Thanks, Tommy," Finn said. "I already told Nick, but make sure no one touches anything until I get back."

"Understood," Tommy said before stepping through the hole in the glass of the front door. Both windows on either side were also shattered.

"The flowers," I said, groaning. "They're going to die from the cold air."

Finn set his hands on his hips and surveyed the damage. "We'll board up the windows and doors before we leave tonight. We wouldn't want to leave the scene unsecured anyway," he said.

This was all too much. "You don't have to do that," I argued.

"I'm sure that's not in your job description." A new thought occurred to me, and I tunneled my hand through my hair. "I'm going to have to tell my parents. They're going to insist on coming back from their trip early."

"Let's worry about one thing at a time," Finn reassured. "Where's your car?"

"Just over there," I said, pointing down the street to where my car was parked alone this late in the evening.

I moved toward it, but Finn put his hand out and said, "Hold on."

"Finn, I just want to go home," I complained.

"Something's not right with your car," he said warily. He jogged toward the car, stopping on the passenger side and staring at the front tire with his arms crossed. "Change of plans," he said briskly as he headed back toward me. "I'm going to drive you home in my truck. It's just around the corner."

"No, I need my car. I need to run errands tomorrow, and I have to come to work. It's cold. I can't walk," I said. I was vaguely aware I sounded like something between a whiny child and a petulant teenager.

Finn stepped between me and my car and said, "Driving your own car home isn't an option. I'll get you home, and then we'll figure how to get you where you need to go tomorrow after everyone's gotten some sleep."

I pushed past him. "Why can't I drive my own…" I started, but I trailed off, staring dumbfounded at the front tire of my car. The red handle of a giant screwdriver glinted in the light of the streetlamp. Just like the one used to kill Justin.

The next ten minutes were a blur as I let Finn guide me to his truck without further complaint and leaned against the window as he drove me home, my thoughts scattered. Before I knew it, we were pulling up in front of my house.

"Stay in the truck," Finn commanded as he parked the truck by the curb. "Lock the doors. I'm going to check and make sure everything's okay with your house. I'll be right back."

Before I could respond, Finn was out of the truck and jogging toward my front door. Finn disappeared around the corner of the house. I waited for a minute, but he didn't reappear. I pulled my phone out of my pocket to check the time. Nine o'clock.

I sent a quick text to my mom and dad, knowing they'd hear the news by morning. There'd be hell to pay if I didn't tell them first.

I assured them I was okay, the store was okay, and I was handling the repairs. Too bad I had no idea how to handle any of this. I'd figure it out.

My parents were getting closer to retirement, something they'd never do if they thought running the store was too much for me. Not because they didn't trust me with the store but because they loved me too much to put that burden on me. I didn't tell them how personal the threat had been or how it was obviously connected to Justin's murder. The less they knew about that the better.

I pressed *Send* and said a little prayer they were already asleep and wouldn't see it until morning. Next, I texted the girls from book club, letting them know I was home. I didn't mention the break-in. They'd only feel bad for not staying. News of the break-in would be all over town by tomorrow anyway.

I rested my head against the seat and closed my eyes. I imagined trudging up my narrow staircase. I'd strip off my clothes, put on my fuzziest pajamas, and pull the covers up over my head.

A tap at the window startled me. I looked up to see Finn waiting, his breath puffing into the night air. He backed up, and I opened the door, climbing out with my purse clutched in my hand.

"Waking you up in cars is becoming a habit," he said warmly. If it was possible to hear a smile in someone's voice, this moment was it. The small smile slipped off his face, replaced with concern as he added, "I checked the house. Doors and windows appear to be intact. Nothing looks suspicious. I'd like to check inside if that's okay with you."

"If you think it's necessary," I said, sounding exhausted.

"I do," he said simply.

I sighed and led the way up the path. I used my key to open the pale-blue door and walked inside, flicking the switch that controlled the recessed light over the fireplace. "Do you mind if I change while you look around?" I asked.

"You going to a part of the house I haven't checked kind of defeats the purpose of me checking," he explained with a gentle smile.

I tossed my purse on the mid-century modern armchair in pale yellow that I'd found at a flea market last summer and sank down on the couch. "Check away," I said. "I'll be here when you're done."

Finn headed toward the kitchen, and I pulled a fuzzy blanket off the back of the gray couch, wrapping it around my body. Finn reappeared a few minutes later and declared the house free of intruders. I untangled myself from the blanket and threw it over the arm of the couch.

I met him by the stairs and laid a hand on his arm. "Thanks for coming tonight. Judging from the lack of a fancy suit, I'm guessing it's your night off," I said as I scanned his dark jeans and light-blue hoodie. "It really means a lot."

"I had to see what kind of trouble Gwen Stevens had gotten herself into this time," he said. His mouth twitched with a barely concealed smile.

"Watch it," I said as I swatted his chest.

Finn gazed down at me, his whiskey-brown eyes glowing in the dim light above the fireplace. "Believe me, I am," he whispered.

We held each other's gaze for a moment saturated with possibility. Despite my exhaustion, Finn's words both soothed and excited me. All these feelings could only mean one thing—it was time to walk away. "I better get to bed. Do you mind locking the door behind you? All you do is turn the latch on the knob and pull it shut," I explained.

Finn looked at my front door. "You don't have a deadbolt?" His tone left no question as to what he thought about this news.

"No?" I said, my voice rising high at the end.

"I'll come over tomorrow and install one," Finn said as if it was decided. "You can't trust these flimsy door handle locks."

I stepped onto the first stair, bringing my face level with his. I was too tired to argue with him about this. I patted his chest. "Okay, Finlay. If you think I need one, you're more than welcome to install it," I said.

Finn smirked, amusement flickering in his brown eyes. "Finlay?"

"Not it?" I asked flirtatiously.

He leaned in, his breath brushing warm against my lips and whispered, "Not even close."

Before I could respond, before I could get my brain to form a coherent thought, he turned and walked out the door, pulling it firmly shut behind him.

CHAPTER FIFTEEN

———

The next morning, I opened the front door to see my empty driveway and groaned. How could I have forgotten I didn't have my car? I needed to open Camelot Flowers in twenty minutes. Walking would take at least thirty. Plus, it was eight degrees out. Not ideal walking weather.

I needed a ride. I pulled my phone from my pocket and opened my Favorites tab. My parents weren't an option. Penny was already at work. My finger hovered over Chris's name. He had so much going on, and I was supposed to be relying on him less. On the other hand, it seemed ridiculous to invest too much effort in getting over my crush on him in light of the murder. Maybe I could try next month.

I was set to call Chris when a black truck pulled up to the curb. My stomach flipped at the sight, knowing exactly who was behind the wheel. The passenger window slid down, revealing a smiling Finn. "Need a ride?" he asked.

I laughed in disbelief as I headed for the truck. "Your timing couldn't be more perfect," I said as I reached the truck and rested my hands through the open window.

"I aim to please." Finn pretended to tip an imaginary cowboy hat. "I came by with a deadbolt. I have to be back at work in an hour, so I was hoping to catch you before you left."

I looked down to see a bag from Henry's Hardware store sitting on the floor. "You didn't have to do that," I said, feeling slightly embarrassed that this man I just met was going out of his way to do something nice for me. Embarrassed and maybe a little excited.

"I'll feel better knowing your house is more secure," Finn explained. "My dad was a contractor, and I worked for him in high school. It'll take me no time at all. Do you want a ride to work first?" he asked again.

My mouth curved into a wide smile as I said, "Absolutely."

"Climb in," Finn said.

I got into the truck and buckled my seat belt as Finn pulled away from the curb.

"This feels like a good time to lecture you about having inadequate locks on your door," he said in a teasing tone.

I leaned back against the leather seat and held my hands in front of the heating vent. "This is Star Junction. Most people don't lock their doors at all during the day," I said.

Finn shook his head. "I'll never understand that." He glanced at me before turning his attention back to the road. "I can drop you off and run back to your house to install the lock," he said, running through the plan. "If you're okay with that, I'll need a key."

"But you said you had to be at work soon," I pointed out. "You're not even dressed for work." I noticed for the first time he was wearing the same jeans and hoodie he'd been wearing last night. "Wait a minute. Have you been working all night?" I asked with concern. I looked at him more closely. His golden-brown eyes sported dark circles that rivaled the ones under my blue eyes. The only difference was the copious amount of concealer currently covering mine.

Finn waved away my concern and said, "I'm fine. It was a busy night. I'll sleep later."

"You don't have to put this deadbolt in right now," I insisted.

Finn's jaw tensed, although he kept his gaze focused ahead. "I'll feel better if it's in now," he said with determination.

I sensed arguing wasn't going to get me anywhere. "Okay, I'll give you my key, and maybe you can drop it off at the store later," I said, relenting.

"That works," Finn agreed. "And we're done processing your car. You can get the tire replaced and take it anytime."

His statement stirred up the anxiety that had been simmering beneath the surface since I'd found Justin's body, but I worked hard to ignore it. One problem at a time. Fixing the tire was something I could handle. "Roadside assistance is certainly coming in handy this week," I deadpanned.

We arrived at the store, and Finn pulled into a parking spot near the door. "I'll text you when I'm done at your house," he said.

"I'll be here," I said as I climbed out of the truck.

At least until three when Hailey arrives and I can hunt down some more answers about Justin's murder.

I said that last part to myself, knowing I'd get more than a lecture about having adequate locks on my doors if he knew what I was planning.

I slid the house key off my key ring. "Shoot me a text when you're on your way back," I said. "Sometimes I'm out on deliveries during the day." I started to close the door but paused. "Oh, and Finbar? Thanks for doing this," I said sincerely.

He barked out a laugh. "Finbar?" he asked incredulously.

"I'm just going with what Google suggests," I said, defending myself with a wide grin.

The look on Finn's face shifted. The amusement he showed at our little game faded, and his eyes gleamed with a desire that made that butterfly take up its dance in my stomach once again. He leaned forward. "You've been putting some thought into this." His voice, low and rough, teased a shiver up my spine.

"I've had to resort to extreme measures since you won't tell me what it is," I said breathlessly. Breathlessly? What a cliché I'd turned into. I thought of my crush on Chris. Maybe being a cliché around handsome men wasn't a new thing in my life.

"Maybe I enjoy this game too much to end it," he countered.

I stood in the open doorway, my back cold in the winter air but my face flushed from the heat in Finn's words.

"Hey, Gwen!" a woman's voice called from down the street.

I whipped around to see Emma from the book club pushing a stroller with her two-year-old daughter bundled in so many layers she resembled a pink potato. Emma's coat was a matching pink, and her white-blonde hair was tucked under a purple hat with a giant pompom on top.

The cold air on my face snapped me out of the flirtatious haze Finn had created. I waved to Emma before turning back to see Finn still watching me intently. "I better open the store," I said reluctantly.

"See you later?" Finn asked.

"Definitely," I said with a smile.

The truck pulled away as Emma pushed the stroller across the street toward me. Before she'd even reached my side, she called out, "I heard what happened last night after we left. Oh my gosh, Gwen, you could have been killed."

I didn't need a reminder of how scary the sound of the shattering glass had been. "I know," I said. "But thankfully no one wanted to hurt me."

"Well, I'm never leaving you alone after book club again. Us girls need to stick together," she said.

I found myself liking the idea. Book club was the only time I was at the store alone long after dark. "I won't argue again. There's safety in numbers."

Emma pulled me into a tight hug. "I've got to get going, but I wanted to make sure you're okay."

I smiled. "I'm totally okay."

Emma hesitated a moment longer, her gaze flicking to the boarded-up windows on the front of Camelot Flowers, but her daughter let out a little squawk. "I'll check in with you later," Emma promised.

"Sounds good," I said.

Emma hurried off, and my attention drifted to my car parked just down the street. It listed to one side. Back to reality.

I pulled the keys to Camelot Flowers from my purse and walked to the door. While I was glad the store was secure, the plywood covering the door and windows looked like ugly wounds on my normally beautiful storefront.

I needed to contact the insurance company, find someone to replace the glass, and get roadside assistance over to replace my tire, but one thing at a time. I unlocked the door and flipped on the lights.

The honey-colored wood floors normally glowed in the morning sunlight that streamed through the front windows. Today, they looked muted and dull. At least they were clean. It seemed Finn had done more than cover the windows. The floor had been covered with glittering shards of glass when I'd left the night before. In fact, besides the broken windows, there was no sign anything violent had happened at all.

I went through my normal opening routine, including brewing a pot of coffee in the back, scanning through any deliveries for the day, and watering the selection of plants that lived on a set of shelves near the window.

While not thinking about the threat from the night before would've been nice, I didn't have that luxury. Time was ticking, and everything I'd learned from TV and movies told me that solving this murder soon was key to solving it at all.

As I'd gotten to know Finn better, it became easier to trust his work on the investigation, but I wasn't a fool. With no other clear suspects, Chris became the easy answer. The vandalism and threat last night could only mean one thing, I'd talked to someone who knew something.

If I was failing in my investigation, there'd be no reason to threaten me. Why not just let me keep flailing about? It could only mean one thing—I'd talked to someone or learned something the killer didn't want me to know.

I needed to retrace my steps, so to speak, talk again to the people I'd already talked to. Someone knew something, and I knew just who to start with. The deliveries today would be the perfect excuse to pop into Derek Thompson's insurance agency. To be more accurate, his dad's insurance agency. I wasn't the only one from our high school graduating class going into the family business.

Derek, despite his smarminess and self-obsession, knew something about Justin's supposed girlfriend in Rose Lake. Ashley Kowalski's husband had ordered a bouquet of daisies, apparently Ashley's favorite flower, to be delivered to the dental office where she worked for her birthday today. The dentist happened to be next door to Thompson Insurance.

As the plan came together in my mind, my decision to find Justin's murderer galvanized, despite the threats. I wasn't scheduled to deliver the flowers until her lunch break, which gave me just enough time to deal with the shattered windows.

I skipped to the back and poured myself a cup of coffee before returning to the front desk in case a customer came in. Opening my notes app, I ran through my murder list. Derek first. If he gave me some information, once Hailey could watch the store later today, I'd make the drive to Rose Lake and find the mystery woman Justin had been seeing. If not… Well, I didn't really have a plan for *if not*, which worried me.

I took a bracing drink of the rich coffee. I might be stumbling around in the dark trying to solve this murder, but the killer was clearly worried. Even in the dark, if you stumbled around long enough, you were bound to bump into something useful.

* * *

A few hours later, I pushed through the door to Thompson Insurance. The office was small. Two desks sat facing each other over industrial-looking gray carpet. The walls were a crisp white, and despite the utilitarian look of the place, it was clean.

Derek glanced up as I walked in, looking momentarily stunned before recovering with that smarmy smile I'd come to hate over the years of him asking me out.

He stood, buttoning the jacket of this blue suit. "Gwen," he said smoothly. "To what do I owe the pleasure?"

I gave him a tight smile and reminded myself that it had been my idea to come here. If I wanted information, I needed to be nice. Or at least less disgusted by him than I normally was. "I was making a delivery next door and thought I'd pop in to see if you'd been able to remember the name of the woman Justin had been seeing in Rose Lake," I said, getting right to the point.

Maybe my wording was a bit leading. Derek hadn't had trouble remembering a name. He'd flat-out refused to tell me anything. I was hoping he wouldn't remember that.

"I don't know what you're talking about," he said casually before transitioning away from the topic with: "I've got tickets to a concert over in Abbottsville tomorrow night. Come with me."

"I can't," I said, trying to feign reluctance but failing miserably. "I've got plans." I didn't have plans, but if my conscience got the best of me over lying, I'd make plans. "You know something about Justin that could help Chris. Maybe not the identity of the other woman, but something," I pressed.

"What about tonight? We could grab a bite to eat? My place?" Derek asked. He was a pro at dodging my questions.

There was no way I was going to his place. Derek was persistent to the point of intrusive. Being alone with him didn't seem like the wisest choice. "Stop changing the subject," I said through clenched teeth. The longer I was with him, the harder it was to play nice.

That smarmy smile somehow grew. "We'd have fun. I promise," he said. His tone wasn't just laced with innuendo, it was drowning in it.

"I have no doubt *you'd* have fun," I challenged.

Then a new tactic occurred to me. Derek wasn't used to hearing no, but he also wasn't used to losing. "Unless," I said slowly, attempting to build some kind of tension. I leaned against the counter that separated the rest of the room from the small entryway. "Unless, you don't want to give me any information because you're protecting someone, like maybe yourself."

It took a moment for my words to sink in, but once they did, the smarmy smile vanished, replaced with just the kind of indignation I could use to my advantage.

"What are you implying," he snapped.

"I'm implying," I said, my voice as sharp as rose thorns, "that you could've murdered Justin, and now you're trying to throw me off the scent by hiding the identity of the person who he was cheating with."

Derek crossed his arms over his impressive chest, his gaze thundering with anger. I was suddenly very glad there was a counter between us. I'd been baiting him with my accusation, but what if it was true? What if I'd just taunted a murderer?

"That's the dumbest logic I've ever heard. If I was the killer, I'd want you to talk to another suspect," he said. He took a step forward, and I took a step back as he continued, "If I was the killer, I'd tell you to talk to Heidi Fischer about her little affair with Justin."

I bit back a squeal of triumph and forced myself to remain still, despite the happy dance I was doing in my head. No need to gloat in the face of besting Derek. "Heidi Fischer, you say?" I asked calmly. I tapped her name into the note in my phone.

"That's what I said," he replied, sounding triumphant, as if he'd won this little battle of the minds by proving to me that he wasn't the killer. All he'd proven was that he was easily baited, a fact I mentally tucked away for future use.

"I better get back to work," I said. Best to leave while I was ahead. I started to walk toward the door but turned back to see him watching me, his eyes traveling lower than was appropriate. Maybe he knew something else that could help.

Against my better judgment, I stopped. Derek was as connected with our former classmates as I was. If he could add some insight that would help Chris, I had to sacrifice a few more minutes in his presence. "Are you still in touch with Tony Reagan?" I asked.

"Sure, I see him when he comes home to visit his folks. Why do you ask?"

"It's probably nothing," I said quickly. Better to make Derek think I didn't care about the answer in case he suddenly got smart enough to try to leverage a date from me. "I ran into him at Bucky's last weekend. Then he posted something on Facebook about Justin finally getting what he deserved."

I considered telling Derek what Tommy had told me about the messages Tony had left on Justin's voicemail blaming Justin for ruining his life, but I held back. Tommy had gone out on a limb to tell me. If I wanted access to information from the police in the future, I needed to be careful what I shared with others now.

Derek leaned forward, a sly smile spreading across his face. "Are you investigating this murder?" His reaction couldn't have been more different from Finn's.

"I'm just talking to some people," I said pointedly. "Not investigating."

Derek's gaze raked my body. He walked up to the counter until we were just a foot apart. The scent of his musky cologne tickled my nose, and I held back a sneeze. "I'll keep my ears open," Derek said, remarkably more compliant with questions about Tony than about the woman Justin had been seeing on the side.

Maybe I'd stumbled onto some kind of bro-code with the affair. Maybe Derek hadn't wanted to tell Justin's romantic secrets, but he seemed to have no problem talking about Tony. "That Facebook post was probably about what happened between them senior year," Derek said.

I took a tiny step back. It did nothing to save me from Derek's cologne. "I thought they were friends," I said.

"They were, but after they got caught cheating off each other and failed two classes senior year, Tony never forgave Justin," Derek explained. "Tony had big plans after graduation, and his GPA tanked enough to derail those. He always blamed Justin, claiming it was Justin's idea to cheat."

"What kind of big plans?" I asked. Now we were getting somewhere.

"Tony was determined to become a sports agent," Derek said, scoffing. "Like someone from Star Junction was ever going to be hobnobbing with star athletes. Northwestern had a program in sports management. He was set on going there. He said he'd not only get the degree but have the connections after graduating to really make it. He didn't get in. His GPA was too low after Tony got caught helping Justin cheat during finals," he explained.

Derek didn't strike me as someone who took a lot of interest in other people's problems. "How do you know all this?" I asked suspiciously. Maybe Derek had been in on the cheating scandal too, although I never got the sense he was unhappy with his life, like he claimed Tony was.

Derek scowled and said, "Tony and I worked together stripping paint off old highway signs the summer after graduation. I had to listen to him rant about it every day."

"Thanks. That was helpful." *Surprisingly helpful*, I added in my head. Never in a million years did I imagine I'd be thanking Derek for anything. I turned and headed toward the door.

"Offer still stands," Derek called after me. "You and me. Anytime."

I hurried away, not dignifying his statement with a response. My mind worked to incorporate this new information about Tony. Star Junction residents were mostly solid middle-class families. A salary as an investment banker would be well beyond the reach of most people in town, but money wasn't everything. Having a dream shattered. Was that enough motive for murder? Even after all these years?

I was no expert, as Finn had reminded me countless times, but it seemed like this was a crime of passion. The screwdriver had been a weapon of convenience. If Tony was going to come back home to settle a decade old vendetta, wouldn't he come prepared?

I had just enough time to do some digging before I was scheduled to meet Penny at Just Beans. She'd texted early this morning, expressing horror about the vandalism at the store. She'd insisted we meet up after school let out, which was perfect timing since Hailey would be at the store.

I made it back to the store and flipped the sign from *Out on Deliveries* to *Open*. Sitting behind the counter, I pulled out my phone. I opened Facebook and typed out a message to Tony. *Hey, I saw what you posted on Facebook about Justin. You know Chris and I are close. I was wondering why you thought he killed Justin.*

I hit *Send* before I could second guess my decision to contact him. I picked up a pen and doodled flowers around the edge of an order slip. My mind sorted through the information I'd gathered over the last week, but no matter how I arranged it, a solid picture wouldn't form. Chris used his charm to get out of difficult situations. He wasn't going to murder someone just because they were upset with him.

Unless Justin came at him.

The thought flitted through my mind before I could stop it.

No! Even if Justin intended to hurt Chris, Chris would've been able to talk his way out of it.

I flipped the order slip over. I put Justin's name in the center and drew a circle around it. I drew a line coming off the circle and wrote *Samantha—cheated on, angry*. I added the mystery woman from Rose Lake, who now had a name and was supposedly pregnant with Justin's baby—Heidi Fischer. Off that circle, I added *Jealous Boyfriend?* Maybe Justin wasn't the only one who'd been cheating.

I tapped the pen against my chin as I stared at the refrigerated case filled with cut flowers. I needed to add a line for whatever was happening with Tom's truck. I didn't know anyone who chose a dump truck for joy riding.

While the rock that had been thrown through my window last night could've come from anywhere, I couldn't deny I'd seen a pile of rocks just like it when I'd visited the rock yard.

Maybe Justin hadn't been the one using Tom's trucks. Maybe someone else was and my poking around threatened their secret. Maybe it was that guy who shot me that death stare for no apparent reason. I made a note to find out who that guy was.

I added a line for Tony Reagan. He'd been in town and seemed to have a motive. I'd have to ask Finn about that. He'd said I should share anything I learned with him. Off to the side, I made a list—*Ask Finn about Tom, ask Finn about the box under Justin's bed, check in with Chris.*

Chris. Reluctantly, I added another line to my little diagram and wrote Chris's name. I hated doing it, but I had to admit Finn was right to suspect him. Even if the evidence was circumstantial, it wasn't nothing.

What was I missing? I wrote *Who threw the rock through the window last night?* next to the line about Palmer's rock yard. Rose Lake was only fifteen minutes away. It didn't have to be someone from Star Junction. I connected the question with a line to *Heidi Fischer.*

I needed to figure out where to find her. Maybe she'd be willing to talk to me. Adding names to this list, or eliminating them, was the priority before the police decided Chris was the only option.

I shot off a message to Chris, having failed to respond to him the night before. *What are you up to today? I'm having coffee with Penny after school gets out. I'm so glad the center isn't a crime scene anymore. That has to be a good sign, right? If the police really thought you did it, they probably wouldn't let you back in there. Heard anything from the police or your lawyer?*

I had a few hours to kill before I could talk all this over with Penny. I looked around the store. A few hours to kill and plenty of work to do. As much as I wanted finding Justin's killer to be the focus of my day, I had a business to run and today was ordering day.

I pulled up the website we ordered our wholesale flowers from and opened the program showing our current inventory. Ordering was mind numbing and tedious. Nothing like the creativity of putting together arrangements. If the saying *Time flies when you're having fun* was true, the next few hours were going to feel like years.

CHAPTER SIXTEEN

———

Just Beans sat tucked between Fresh and Clean—the laundromat in town—and Fairytale Sweets. My phone buzzed as I approached the door. Why was Uncle Stan calling me? I answered cheerfully, "Hey, Uncle Stan. How's your week going?"

"Guinevere," he said, his tone warning, "Why did I have to come into work this morning and see on the call sheet that Camelot Flowers had been vandalized, and more importantly, you'd been threatened?"

I mentally slapped myself on the forehead. With the thick mittens I was wearing, a real head slap would have felt more like a tickle. "I'm sorry I didn't call you. Finn was handling it, and I was so worn out by the time I got home, I went right to bed."

Uncle Stan's tone softened as he said, "I guess I can understand that, but I 'bout had a heart attack when I saw the report. Finn should have called me."

"Don't be upset with Finn. He handled the situation perfectly. Isn't that why you hired him? So you wouldn't have to take calls at all hours anymore?" I asked.

"You know that doesn't apply to you, Guinevere," he said brusquely. He cleared his throat before adding, "I also had a voicemail from Tom Palmer. He said you've been asking around about Justin's murder. I was set to call him back and tell him he must be mistaken, but I took a moment to think about it and it wasn't out of the realm of possibility. What do you have to say for yourself?"

I swallowed hard. A lecture from Uncle Stan was almost as potent as if it had come from my dad himself. I'd successfully downplayed what was happening in town to my parents. Maybe I should've focused my efforts closer to home. "I haven't exactly been asking around…" I said slowly.

"What would you call it, then?" he asked.

"I can't help it, Uncle Stan," I started, hoping throwing both his name and personal title into the mix would remind him how much he loved me. Scratch that idea. That's likely why he was so upset. "People keep talking to me. I'm not getting into any trouble on purpose."

It wasn't exactly true. The diagram in my pocket of all the leads I was planning to chase down burned like my lie had set my pants on fire.

"That's what you call what happened at Camelot Flowers last night? Not getting into any trouble?" Uncle Stan challenged.

I'd been foolish to not get ahead of this. I should've been stopping by the station more, assuring him I was safe. I was pacing in front of the window of Just Beans by now, Penny watching me with a confused expression on her face. I held up a finger, indicating I needed a moment.

"What happened at Camelot Flowers last night was scary, but no one actually tried to hurt me," I argued.

"Yet," Uncle Stan pointed out. "No one has hurt you yet."

"The sooner we catch the murderer, the sooner all of this will be over. I'm being extra safe in the meantime. I promise," I reassured.

"Well," Uncle Stan said, his voice growing gruff with emotion, "I wanted to check on you and see how you're holding up."

"I'm fine." It was another lie but a necessary one. "I'm just about to meet Penny for coffee."

"I heard Finn Butler installed a deadbolt on your front door. Don't know why I didn't think of that sooner," Uncle Stan said, sounding exhausted. The case was likely taking a toll on him as much as anyone else. I should've checked on him just like he was checking on me.

"You didn't think of it because I didn't need it. I'm not even sure I need it now," I said.

"He's a good man, that Finn. A good detective too," Uncle Stan added.

The more I interacted with Finn, the more I agreed with those statements. "I've gotta go. Penny's waiting on me," I said.

"You be careful," he warned again.

"I'll be the most careful citizen in Star Junction," I promised.

Uncle Stan chuckled. "Somehow I doubt that. Love you, Guinevere."

"Love you, too," I replied warmly.

I walked into the coffee shop, setting off a string of jingle bells. Penny sat at a small table tucked into the corner, and I gave her a little wave before stopping to place my order. After ordering a chai latte with almond milk, I leaned against the counter to wait. My phone buzzed in my pocket. It was a text from Finn. *The lock is installed. Can I drop off your key?*

I replied, *I'm at Just Beans across the street from my shop.*

The thought of seeing Finn sent a little thrill through my stomach. Although Penny had pushed the idea of dating the new police detective before either of us had met him, I wasn't sure what to do with these unexpected feelings.

The barista handed me my drink, and another text from Finn popped up. *Great. I've got to finish one more thing at work. Then I'll run over. See you soon.*

I sent back a thumbs-up and smiled like a fool all the way to the table where Penny was waiting.

"What's that smile for?" Penny asked with a sly smile. "You look like you found out you were nominated for an Academy Award. Or, you know, whatever type of award a florist would get."

"It's nothing," I said. I settled my coat across the back of the chair and hooked my purse over it. "Finn's stopping by to drop off my house key."

Penny choked on her coffee. "He has your house key?" she finally coughed out.

"He wanted to install a deadbolt on my front door after what happened last night. It's no big deal," I said dismissively, although inside, I was feeling more like Penny than I'd like to admit.

Penny's hazel eyes danced with delight. "A good-looking man cares about you enough to install a better lock on your house? It's not nothing."

I finally grinned. "I know," I admitted.

Penny collapsed back into her seat dramatically and declared, "It's straight out of a Hallmark movie."

If either of us was going to ever be nominated for an Academy Award, it would be Penny, but before I could comment on that, her eyes tightened and the smile slid off her face. I looked behind me to see Chris walk in. He headed in our direction.

"I swear that man has the worst timing," Penny muttered before pasting a smile on her face. "Hey, Chris." I could hear the falseness in Penny's voice, but I knew from experience Chris wouldn't pick up on it.

He shoved his hands into the pockets of his jeans. "Hey, Penny." He turned his attention to me, his normal million-watt grin dimmed. "Hey, Gwen. I hope it's okay I dropped by."

"What are you doing here?" Penny said, her passive-aggressive tone growing a little more aggressive.

I shot Penny a look that could've boiled the cooling coffee in her cup.

Chris put his hands on the back of the extra chair at the table but didn't sit. "I've been thinking a lot since I got out of jail," he said to me. His voice grew thick, and he cleared his throat. "I was wondering if we could talk sometime soon."

I glanced at Penny, who raised her eyebrows but stayed silent. "About the case?" I asked. "I could do it tonight."

Chris's eyes filled with disappointment. "I can't do tonight. My parents are coming into town," he said. Chris moved as if he were going to sit in the empty seat but then stopped. "And it's not about the case," he added.

His last words barely registered as I processed the fact that his parents were coming to town. "Your parents are coming here?" I asked in shock.

"I'm not allowed to leave town, and my dad wants to check on his investment. You know, the lawyer and everything," Chris explained.

"Do you need—" I started to offer my help, but Penny kicked me under the table. She was right. I was falling back into my old pattern of rescuing Chris. I took a deep breath and changed tactics. "I hope it goes okay," I said.

"Thanks," Chris said, clearly not looking forward to seeing his dad. "What about tomorrow night? We could get dinner?" he asked. I'd never seen him sound so uncertain.

"She has plans," Penny cut in.

"I do?" I asked in confusion.

"Yeah," Penny said, shooting me a look that said *play along*. "We're going bowling. It's a whole thing," she said to Chris.

I understood Penny's dedication to *rescue* me from my crush on Chris, but this was taking it a little too far. "I guess I have plans tomorrow," I said to Chris by way of apology for needing to say no. "Text me when you're done with dinner tonight. If it's not too late, we could talk then."

"I will," he said. He absently tapped the table and looked at me one more time. He opened his mouth as if to add something more but turned and walked up to the counter instead.

"What was that about?" I demanded in a tight whisper.

"What?" Penny asked, the picture of innocence as she swiped her finger through the whipped cream on top of her drink and licked it off.

"You know exactly what I'm talking about," I challenged. "We're going *bowling*?" My gaze cut to where Chris was chatting with the barista, making sure he couldn't overhear our conversation.

"Did I fail to mention that?" Her innocence routine wasn't going to work on me.

"Explain," I demanded.

"A bunch of the firefighters and police officers are going out. I don't want to be the only girl. I was going to invite you even before Chris showed up," she said.

"You didn't have to be so rude to Chris," I said.

"Yes, I did. It's part of my five-step plan to remove you from the clutches of Chris Crawford," she argued.

"Five steps?" I asked incredulously. "You actually created steps?"

"Not formally," Penny said, as if my very question was ridiculous. "It's more of a saying."

"That's not a saying," I deadpanned.

"Whatever," Penny said, sounding exasperated. "It's part of a plan. And the plan will have as many steps as it needs."

I found it best to ignore Penny when she got like this. "What do you think Chris wanted to talk about?" I asked. "He seemed so serious."

"Maybe he figured out who killed Justin and is devastated by who it is," Penny offered. "Maybe he's going to confess that he did it. The guilt's eating at him, and he can't take it anymore."

"You don't really believe that," I said.

Instead of answering me, her nose crinkled in concern. "Uh-oh," she whispered.

"What?" I asked.

Penny jerked her head in the direction of the door. I turned to see Chris leaving as Finn walked in. They stopped in the doorway, each man blocking the other's way. Chris's back was to me, but I could see Finn's jaw set and his eyes narrow. Finn said something I couldn't hear then stepped back and let Chris pass. Chris marched down the street, not looking back.

The breath I'd been holding rushed out all at once, and I looked at Penny in panic.

"Standoff at high noon," she said grimly.

Finn stood at the window, watching Chris until he disappeared around the corner. Suspicion burned in his eyes until his gaze landed on me. His face brightened as he walked over, his long legs covering the distance in a few steps.

"Hey, Gwen. Penny," he greeted.

Penny batted her eyelashes as she said, "It's so nice to see you again."

This wasn't going to go well. The less exposure Finn had to Penny, the better. "Thanks for dropping off my key," I said, trying to hurry Finn along. "I'm sure you need to get back to work."

"I'm sure he has a few minutes," Penny said as she nudged the chair across from her with her foot, inviting Finn to sit.

Finn took her up on the invitation and sat. "Just for a minute," he said. "I've got a phone call scheduled at four."

If he was going to stay, we needed to keep things about business. "About Justin?" I asked.

Finn lifted an eyebrow but said nothing.

"Okay, okay," I said, raising my hands in surrender. "I know you can't tell me."

Finn's knee brushed against mine in the confined space under the table. "I saw your car hasn't been repaired. Do you need a ride home from work?" he asked.

I purposefully avoided meeting Penny's gaze. She was going to have a field day with this. "Someone is supposed to come in the next hour to put on the spare. Thanks, though," I said sincerely.

While he hadn't been willing to answer my question about Justin, it could've been because of Penny's presence. "I was hoping to chat with you about a few things related to the case. Could I give you a call later today?" I asked.

"Details about the case?" Finn glanced in Penny's direction, confirming my suspicion that he wasn't willing to discuss this in front of her.

"Just doing my duty as a concerned citizen," I said. The explanation sounded laughable, even to me.

Finn rubbed his hand over his beard. "The danger of you asking around about the murder was already high, but after last night…" he hedged.

I couldn't lose my access to him. Not when the rock through the store window and the screwdriver in my tire told me I was getting close. "I promise. I'm not doing anything dangerous," I said.

Finn glanced at his watch and said, "I'll call you when I'm done with my phone call at four." He stood and handed me my house key along with the key to the new deadbolt. Our fingers brushed, and a spark jumped between us. A literal one. Static electricity was a constant problem in the winter.

"Sorry about that," I said, laughing.

Finn's gaze locked on mine, just as it had in his truck earlier today. "A little electricity is never a bad thing," he said, his gaze heating. He hesitated a moment before turning and walking out the door.

"Whoo," Penny said, collapsing back into her seat and fanning herself with her hand. "Detective Hottie is living up to his name."

"I thought we agreed to stop calling him that," I said, groaning.

"I didn't agree to anything," Penny teased as she leaned forward. "What's this new information you need to share with Detective Hottie?"

I looked around to make sure no one else was listening. Fortunately, the place wasn't very full. A couple sat near the fireplace at the back of the store, and a man waited for a drink at the counter. Other than that, we were alone.

"I found out the name of the woman Justin was having an affair with," I said, not even bothering to contain my excitement. I might be new at this whole murder thing, but besides discovering the shoebox under Justin's bed, discovering Heidi's identity felt like the biggest win of the case.

"No way," Penny exclaimed. "Who is it?"

"Her name is Heidi Fischer." I grimaced. "It's not a lot to go on, but it's more than I knew before."

"Leave it to me," Penny said confidently. "I'll find out where she works or something."

"How are you going to do that?" I asked incredulously.

"Through the power of social media," she replied, as if I were ridiculous for thinking it would be anything but simple.

I had to admit, I should've thought of that. I was too busy feeling triumphant at just learning her name. "You have to let me know as soon as you find her," I said.

"Pinky promise," Penny said. At least she didn't make me really hook my pinky with hers. "What else do you know?" she asked.

I filled her in on what I'd learned about Tony, the current investment banker who wished he was a sports agent, and the high school cheating scandal with Justin. I added how I thought the rock that had been thrown through the store window came from Palmer's Gravel and Rock where Justin used to work.

"You think the murderer could be Tom Palmer?" Penny exclaimed a little too loudly.

"Quiet," I practically hissed as I glanced around to see who might have overheard. The barista had glanced up at us but just as quickly returned to the set of drinks she was making.

Penny lowered her voice and said, "Like maybe Justin was doing something super bad with those trucks and Tom snapped?"

"No way," I said, shaking my head in disbelief. My gut twisted at the thought of Tom being a suspect in Justin's murder. "Tom is like Santa Claus. Santa doesn't murder people."

"You can't just keep eliminating suspects because they're nice," Penny argued. "Nice people murder other people all the time."

"Who else am I eliminating because they're nice?" I asked warily.

Penny picked at the sticker on her paper coffee cup.

Her silence was more chilling than her theory about Tom. "Penny," I said, my voice low. "Who else am I eliminating because I think they're nice?"

Penny didn't meet my gaze as she answered, "Chris."

"You can't be serious," I shot back.

Penny finally met my gaze, her expression filled with anguish. "There just seems to be a lot of evidence pointing at Chris. Jack was saying one of the officers told him they found Chris's fingerprints on the murder weapon."

As a firefighter, Penny's husband, Jack, worked in the same building as the police officers. The two groups even shared a common break room. "That can't be true," I said, feeling desperate. "Tommy told me they don't have those results back."

Penny shrugged and simply said, "That's what Jack told me."

Had the results really come back since I'd talked to Tommy on the street this morning? He'd been so sure it would take weeks.

"Of course Chris's fingerprints were on it. It was his

screwdriver," I argued.

"They were the only prints on it," Penny said with a grimace.

My blood chilled. "Maybe the murderer wore gloves," I said, grasping at straws.

"That's totally possible," Penny conceded. "I just want you to keep an open mind that Chris could be lying to you."

I shook my head so hard it hurt. "I know Chris better than anyone. I'd know if he was lying," I said.

"That's probably true," Penny said quietly.

Tears burned at the back of my eyes. I knew she was just trying to help, but her statements felt like a betrayal of Chris, which in turn felt like a betrayal of me. "I better get back to the store. The tow truck driver is supposed to arrive soon to put on my spare tire," I said, trying to hold back the tears.

Penny laid her hand over mine and begged, "Please don't be mad. I'm not saying Chris did it. I'm just saying you need to consider the possibility. I'm trying to protect you."

I gave her a weak smile. "I know, but I'm telling you he didn't do this," I insisted.

"I'm sure you're right," Penny said kindly, as if trying to soothe my impending tears more than believing her own words.

We gathered our trash, the mood very different from the teasing of earlier.

Penny wrapped me in a hug and said, "Love you much."

I returned the hug. As much as her words about Chris hurt, I believed her when she said she was only worried about me. "Love you much, too," I replied.

I made it back to Camelot Flowers in time to see a tow truck pull up behind my car. Every year when my dad bought me the highest-level roadside assistance as a Christmas present, I silently wondered why it couldn't be a Sephora gift card. This week, it had proven more than useful.

I walked up to the tow truck as the driver climbed out of the cab.

He looked down at the clipboard in his hand. "You Guinevere Stevens?"

"Yep," I said.

"Name's Kevin," he said, pointing to himself. "Pop your trunk. I'll get the spare on, and you'll be good to go, but don't drive it on the highway without getting a new tire."

Pulling the keys from my coat pocket, I hit the button to

unlock the trunk as Kevin walked to the back of his truck to grab his tools. I stared at the jagged hole in my tire, the offending screwdriver now in an evidence bag somewhere.

The hole was about an inch in diameter. I shuddered as I pictured a similar hole in Justin's chest. I hugged my arms across my body, not just against the cold but against the memories haunting me.

"All set," Kevin said, his statement shaking me from my musings about murder. He'd already put on the spare? How long had I been standing there lost in my troubled thoughts? I signed the paperwork, thanked Kevin, and checked in with Hailey to ensure she was okay with locking up. We closed early on Thursdays.

The window repair people were supposed to arrive tomorrow, and my car was drivable again. Two problems solved. Now I just needed to kill some time before Finn called me and I could tell him all the new information I'd collected pointing to suspects other than Chris.

CHAPTER SEVENTEEN

———

Waiting for Finn's phone call dominated my afternoon. I deep-cleaned my bathroom. I did a load of laundry. I even spent thirty minutes chipping the ice off the edges of my driveway.

I checked my phone every five minutes, making sure I hadn't missed Finn's call. My desire to see Finn again was purely motivated by my need to find Justin's killer and clear Chris's name. It had nothing to do with how fun it was to tease him about his name, or the way my stomach fluttered at the memory of the way he'd rushed in like a knight in shining armor at Camelot Flowers. At least that's what I tried to tell myself.

Instead of a phone call, at exactly five o'clock, Finn's truck rumbled around the corner and pulled up in front of my house. I brushed a strand of my honey-brown hair out of my eyes and leaned on the ice chipper my dad had bought me as a housewarming gift two years ago.

Finn climbed out of the truck and headed toward me.

"I wasn't expecting a house call," I said cheerfully.

Finn ran his hand through his dark-brown hair, which was mussed like he'd done the motion a hundred times already. "I needed to get out of the office," he said. "Your place is on my way home, so I thought I'd stop in and see what you wanted to talk about."

I leaned the ice chipper against the side of the house and motioned for Finn to follow me. "Come on in. I've got coffee, tea, something a little stronger if you're interested," I said as I climbed the small set of stairs to the front door.

Finn followed me into the house. It didn't escape my notice that he locked the deadbolt behind him. "I'm good, but thanks," he said. He shrugged out of his coat and looked around as if lost as to what to do with it.

"Let me take that for you," I said. I took his coat and hung it in the coat closet by the door.

Finn stepped out of his shoes and followed me to the couch. "What was it you wanted to talk to me about?" he asked.

Now that he was here, in my living room, I found myself nervous. I didn't want to go back to the days when all we'd done was fight about the murder investigation and Chris's alleged involvement.

"We haven't had a chance to really talk since the pie social," I said. "I wanted to fill you in on some things I found out," I said as I pulled my sweater sleeves down over my hands. "I also wanted to know if you've made any headway in the investigation."

Finn stared wearily at the fireplace. It was dark, unlit at the moment. I reached over and flipped the switch to start the flames.

"This is different than the investigations in Chicago," he said. The fire danced in shades of orange across his face.

"How so?" I asked.

Finn leaned his head back against the couch and closed his eyes. I had a feeling I was seeing a side of him few got to see. "In Chicago, we struggled through investigations with too little evidence, too few suspects. Here, it's like there are too many." He rubbed his hands across his eyes. "I was scheduled to go over what I have so far with my old partner from back in Chicago. It helps to talk things out, but he got called to a crime scene, and we had to cut our phone call short," Finn said.

I'd never considered that Finn was used to solving crimes with the help of a partner. Here, he was the boss. Giving orders, not taking them. It must be lonely. "I'm happy to talk things out with you," I offered.

A ghost of a smile graced his lips. "A few days ago, I would've shut that down…" he said before trailing off.

I held my breath, waiting for him to finish his sentence. When he didn't, I asked, "And now?"

"I may live to regret this, but I'd love to hear everything you know," he said.

I was tempted to pinch myself to make sure I wasn't dreaming. "What if you hear something you don't like?" I asked hesitantly.

"Like what?" Finn said, immediately sounding suspicious.

"Like information that doesn't line up with the evidence against Chris," I started with, although I was just as concerned Finn would be upset that I'd learned anything at all after his insistence before the pie social that me asking questions was dangerous.

"Despite what you may believe, I'm not convinced Chris is the killer," Finn said.

I wanted to pinch myself again. If I followed through on all these urges, I was going to have bruises up and down my arm at the rate these pinch-me moments were coming.

"There's something not right about all of this," Finn continued. "Something I'm missing. I can feel it in my gut." He ticked off his points on his fingers. "Chris's fingerprints were found on the murder weapon, but it was his tool in his building. I'd be suspicious if his prints weren't on it. Then we have Justin, who seems to have angered plenty of people. The girlfriend, Samantha, the woman he was allegedly having an affair with from Rose Lake, although no one seems to know her identity.

"There's the drugs you found under Justin's bed, along with the stack of cash," Finn continued, building up steam as he went. "A guy Justin went to high school with named Tony left him angry voicemails the night he was murdered, and Justin was recently fired from his job."

Okay, so Finn wasn't only focused on Chris as Justin's killer. It should've made me feel better, but instead, it highlighted how far away we were from finding the real murderer.

It was time for me to share the information I'd learned today. "I found out the identity of the woman Justin was having an affair with," I said, hoping against all hope that this might be the piece of information that broke the case wide open.

Finn sat up, looking much more awake. "How did you find that out?" he asked. He didn't sound upset. Simply curious. And a little shocked.

The answer to his question was going to reveal the truth that I hadn't simply been waiting around for information to fall into my lap. "I asked Derek Thompson," I said. "He and Justin were close. Even closer than Justin and Chris. If Justin was fooling around on Samantha, Derek would know about it."

"And he just told you?" Finn asked in disbelief. He ran his hand over his beard. "I interviewed Derek, and he swore he didn't know anything about it."

While earlier this week, I'd reveled in the idea that Finn might flounder in his attempts to navigate the small-town politics of Star Junction, now I simply felt bad for him. He was trying to do his job, and the loyalties of lifelong friendships were getting in his way.

"I may have accused Derek of murdering Justin to get a rise

out of him." I gave Finn a pained smile, unsure how he was going to like my strategy with Derek. "It worked. He was insulted and blurted out the name of the woman. Heidi Fischer, by the way," I said in conclusion.

Finn pulled out his phone and tapped something into it. A text message? A note to himself? Did he have a list of suspects on his phone like I did on mine?

"Are you sure I can't get you any coffee?" I asked.

Finn had looked exhausted this morning when he gave me a ride to work, but he looked downright haggard now.

"No, I'll never sleep tonight if I have coffee now, and I promised myself I was going to take a break. I'm no good to anyone if I'm falling asleep on the job," he replied. "In fact, I should probably get going. Learning the name of the woman from Rose Lake is helpful. I want to run it down and see what I can find."

"Need any help with that?" I asked hopefully. I'd trusted Penny to find out what she could about Heidi, but I had a feeling Finn's investigative resources would beat Penny's any day.

Finn chuckled softly, which was a good sign, but then he said, "No help needed. Believe me, just learning the name is help enough."

Shoot. Well, I couldn't expect him to say yes all the time, but since I never knew when he'd be in the mood to share, I had to take my chances when I got them. "Can I ask a question about the case?" I asked.

"Ask away," Finn said. "I can't promise I can answer it, but if I can, I will."

"What can you tell me about the box under Justin's bed?" I asked.

Finn stared at the ceiling. I could almost hear the mental processing he was going through to decide whether or not to answer my question. "I went back to the Hunt house the next morning and collected the box. I had to move the bed to get to it. You're right, I probably wouldn't have found it without you," he said.

It seemed like an inappropriate time to celebrate or gloat, so I said, "What was that white powder?"

Finn sat up and angled to face me. The look on his face sent nervous energy fluttering through my rib cage. "It was meth," he said, his tone grim. "And what's worse, it was cut with Fentanyl. If that's circulating around town, I'm surprised we haven't had an overdose yet."

I'd heard on the news a few months ago about the dangers of drug dealers mixing Fentanyl into their product. It made the drugs more addictive, but it was also easy to overdose. "Meth? In Star Junction?" I said incredulously.

"Wherever Justin got it, it just made this case more urgent. We need to find his killer, but we also need to find the source of this product and shut it down before someone dies. The thing is, the drugs could have nothing to do with his murder. I've got a lot of leads but not a lot of evidence," Finn said.

The words *except pointing to Chris* hung in the air between us.

"You can't think Chris had anything to do with those drugs," I said, feeling defensive of my friend.

Finn shook his head and said, "I don't have any evidence suggesting that."

I blew out a sigh of relief.

My phone buzzed, and I glanced at it to see a text from Penny. *You're coming to the mall with me. I'll be there in ten. You can't say no. I found her.*

"Do you need to take that?" Finn asked, watching as I read the text.

Penny had found Heidi? Already? I struggled with whether or not to tell Finn. I wasn't worried about my own safety. Penny and I would be surrounded by people at the mall, totally safe. Even if Penny was right about Heidi working there, I'd tell Finn when I was sure. I didn't want to send him on a wild-goose chase in case Penny had stumbled on the wrong Heidi Fischer. "Penny needs me to go to the mall with her," I said, answering his question vaguely.

"Don't say no on my account. I need to be getting home anyway, unless you want me crashing on your couch. Five more minutes in front of the fireplace, and I'm going to be a goner," Finn said.

I had to admit the thought of Finn asleep on my couch wasn't altogether horrible. "Let me at least tell you what I know and the questions I have. I can summarize it in five minutes, tops," I said.

"Go for it. Maybe it'll spark something I haven't connected yet," Finn said.

I shot off a quick text to Penny telling her I'd be ready. I also sent a text to Chris letting him know I'd be home later and would check in with him then. He meant well, but there was no way he was going to be done with his parents anytime soon. His mom would want to linger, not getting to see him as often as she'd like.

By the time I was finished with my texts, Finn looked about ready to fall asleep.

"Just a few more minutes, sleepyhead." I nudged his foot with my own.

Finn opened his eyes and turned his head, giving me a sleepy smile that only encouraged the swarm of butterflies in my stomach.

"Let me get my notes," I said as I jumped off the couch, giving myself some distance to lasso those butterflies into submission.

By the time I retrieved the paper with my notes from my purse, Finn was sitting up and looking more awake. He looked at the web diagram I'd drawn. "This is impressive," he said.

I couldn't tell if he was serious or making fun of my amateur attempts to sort my thoughts, but he sounded sincere. "It's like my own mini murder board," I replied.

"Certainly more portable than anything we have at the station," he said.

I smoothed out the paper. "Tom Palmer, Justin's old boss and the owner of Palmer's Gravel and Rock, is an old friend of my dad's," I explained to Finn. "I asked him why Justin got fired. He said someone had been taking one of his dump trucks out at night. He figured it out because he was spending more on gas even though he didn't have more orders."

"And Tom knew it was Justin?" Finn asked.

"He suspected. Justin denied it, but I guess he was the only one who could've been doing it," I said, still feeling confused why someone would want to ride around in a dump truck.

Finn stared out the window. It was already dark out. With the lights on in the living room, our own reflections were the only view out the window. He turned back to me and said, "What if Justin was using the trucks to transport drugs?"

"What?" I asked in shock. The thought had never occurred to me, but maybe it should have. "You think he was transporting a whole dump truck's worth of drugs?" I pictured the tiny bag I found under Justin's bed, but this time the back of a dump truck filled with them.

"I doubt a whole dump truck's worth, but a dump truck traveling back and forth between towns wouldn't raise a lot of suspicion. Any officers or state troopers would just assume the truck was hauling something from one town to another," Finn said slowly as if piecing things together. "No matter how many trips the truck made."

"But why not just use his own truck?" I asked. "People drive between Star Junction and the other small towns in the area all the time. You need to go to Walmart? Drive to Rose Lake. Want to see a movie? You drive to Kingston."

Finn rubbed his hand across the back of his neck. "I'm not sure, but there's something there. I can feel it," he said.

"I'm still voting for jealous lover," I said confidently. "Or jealous lover's lover."

My phone buzzed with a text from Penny. *Two minutes away. Be ready.*

I stood and said, "Penny's almost here."

Finn stood too and followed me to the door, where we both put our shoes on. I grabbed his coat from the closet and held it out for him before taking my own off the hanger.

Finn shrugged into his coat. "I'll make talking to Tom Palmer my first priority tomorrow." He yawned. "Right after I get some sleep."

"Are you going to be okay driving home?" I asked, concerned.

Finn opened the door for me, and we stepped outside in time to see Penny pull into my driveway.

"I'll be fine," Finn said. "I live over on Oak. It'll take me two minutes."

I hadn't taken the time to think about where Finn was living in town. Oak Street was lined with single family homes, small ranch houses with neat front yards. "Are you renting?" I asked.

"For now," Finn said as he looped his scarf around his neck and waited next to me on the steps as I locked the new deadbolt.

Finn's expression clouded. "Just a reminder… Don't tell anyone about the drugs or the fingerprints on the screwdriver. I can't risk people finding out I gave you confidential case information," he said.

I wanted to argue that he only had most of that information because I'd found the box under Justin's bed, but I didn't want to start a fight. Not when getting along with him was proving to be so nice. "I won't tell anyone," I promised.

"Including Chris," he said gravely.

The pang of guilt I felt at withholding this information from Chris was sharp, but I nodded my agreement. "Including Chris," I agreed.

Finn waved to Penny, who was waiting in her car. The shocked look on her face at seeing Finn leaving my house was enough to make me giggle. It felt good to laugh. Maybe a trip to the mall was exactly what I needed.

Penny took off toward the highway the moment I had my seat belt buckled. She didn't say hello. She didn't offer an explanation. She didn't even ask questions about what Finn was doing at my house. Instead, she said, "Take my phone and open Instagram."

"Instagram? Is that how you found her?" I asked, taking Penny's phone from her so she could put two hands back on the wheel.

"Will you just open Instagram?" she said impatiently.

I complied, mostly because it was clear she wasn't going to let this go. "It's open," I said.

"Search *Heidi Fischer*," Penny said. "Her account wasn't private, so it was pretty easy to find her. Thankfully there don't seem to be any other Heidi Fischers in the area, and she listed Rose Lake in her profile."

I searched the name. "There are a lot of Heidi Fischers."

We reached the edge of town, and Penny picked up speed on the highway. "Find the one from Rose Lake. It's in her account description. She's got red hair and is wearing a green dress in the profile picture."

I added the words *Rose Lake* to my search and found what Penny had described. "Got it. Ah, she's cute," I said.

"Don't let Samantha Weston hear you say that," Penny said with a grimace.

I thought back to my interaction with Justin's ex-girlfriend at the Piggly Wiggly earlier that week. She already wasn't a fan when she believed I was accusing her of Justin's murder. No way was I going to make it worse by letting her know I thought Heidi, Justin's other girlfriend, was cute.

CHAPTER EIGHTEEN

———

I scrolled through Heidi's Instagram feed and landed on a cozy picture of Heidi and Justin, proof Penny had found the right Heidi.

"And the mall?" I asked. "How do you know she works there?"

"Check her stories," Penny said.

I clicked on the little circle around her profile picture, and an image appeared of Heidi standing in front of Victoria's Secret. The words on the screen read *Another day, another dollar.* "She works at Victoria's Secret?" I asked.

"Apparently so," Penny replied.

The mall in Abbottsville was forty minutes from Star Junction. Rose Lake was between the two towns. Some residents from Star Junction commuted all the way to Abbottsville for work, but it was much more common in Rose Lake. With a population hovering around a hundred thousand, Abbottsville provided a source of employment often lacking in the small, rural towns around it.

"Let me get this straight," I said after scrolling through more photos, many of which were sprinkled with Justin's presence. "We're going to the mall to do what?" I asked. "Confront her about Justin? How do you know she's even still there?"

Penny reached over and tapped the phone screen. "Heidi posted the story about being at work twenty minutes ago. She's still there. I can feel it," Penny said with a confidence I wasn't sure I shared. "Plus, we're not going to *confront* her. We're going to innocently ask some questions, feel her out, get a sense about whether or not she's torn up about Justin's death, maybe confirm those pregnancy rumors once and for all."

"All without tipping her off or making her angry," I said doubtfully.

Penny shrugged. "If you want to tip her off and make her

upset, that's your prerogative. This is your investigation. Think of me as the Watson to your Sherlock," she said.

"So, I'm the genius who ends up causing a scene, and you're the calming influence who cleans up my messes?" I asked dryly.

"At least I called you a genius," Penny said with a smug grin.

"I'm not so sure I'd call you a calming influence—more of a pot-stirrer," I teased.

"I'm going to take that as a compliment," Penny said as she exited the highway near the mall.

We'd be there in minutes, and our plan was more an idea than any actual steps toward success, but I had to admit I was curious about Heidi. Had she known she was the other woman when she was dating Justin? Had she been okay with that? Was she angry like Samantha? Grieving Justin's death?

We parked near the food court entrance and hurried across the parking lot, our heads ducked against the bitter wind. Once inside, we cut through the food court toward Victoria's Secret. I looked longingly at the people enjoying their dinners. "I haven't eaten dinner yet. Have you?" I asked Penny.

"Case first, dinner second," Penny said, moving at a determined clip.

We turned to the right, and I had to resist the urge to go into Anthropologie and smell all the candles. "When did you go from 'This is a job for the police' to gung-ho private investigator?" I asked.

Penny's eyes lit up as she said, "We should do that."

"Do what?" I had a bad feeling about where this was going.

"Become private investigators," she said as if she couldn't believe I hadn't understood what she meant.

The Victoria's Secret storefront came into view.

"We're going to do that in all our free time?" I asked dryly. "Last I checked, we both had full-time jobs we loved."

"It could be our side hustle," Penny said, her hazel eyes dancing with delight.

"And what are we going to investigate? Donna Mayor's missing cat?" I deadpanned. Penny started to respond, but I hushed her, grabbing her arm. "There she is," I whispered. Heidi stood next to a rack of lacy underwear, her distinctive red hair giving her away immediately. "What's the plan?" I asked quietly.

Penny hooked her arm through mine and pulled me toward the store. "Don't worry. I've got a plan," she said confidently.

Just those words were enough to make me worried.

Penny approached Heidi and said, "I was wondering if you could help us."

Heidi turned to us with a smile. "Of course. What can I do for you?" she asked, her voice light and sweet.

"My friend here, she's got a big date this weekend, and she needs something spectacular, something out there." Penny leaned in and stage-whispered, "It's going to be her first time, and she's really nervous."

Heidi looked at me with a mixture of awe and pity. Heat rushed across my face. I was going to kill Penny.

"Something spectacular but also out there?" Heidi asked Penny as if I wasn't even there. "Are we talking elegant? Sexy?"

"Maybe something kind of scandalous," Penny said. "I haven't been in this store in years." Penny fingered a see-through teddy. "How risqué do you guys get?"

Heidi scanned my body. "Why don't I pull some things. I'd say you're a size small, but I'll also pull some mediums to be safe." She pointed toward the back of the store and added, "Meet me at the dressing rooms."

Heidi set off on her mission to find risqué lingerie for me while we headed toward the back of the store.

I waited until Heidi was out of earshot before turning on Penny. "What the heck?" I hissed. "I've got a hot date? It's my first time? Did you see the look she gave me?"

"Relax," Penny said, seemingly unfazed by my whispered outburst. "We've got her right where we want her. You try things on. I'll chat her up and get what we need."

I wanted to argue that we could've done that without the elaborate backstory, but Heidi returned with her arms filled with options for my big date before I could say anything else. She unlocked one of the dressing rooms and hung the slips of barely there fabric on the hooks.

"Let's start with these," Heidi said. "If you need any other sizes, let me know."

She closed the door, leaving me alone in the dressing room. What was I supposed to do now? I had no intention of trying any of these on.

Penny's voice reached my ears. "How long have you worked at the mall?" she asked Heidi.

If I'd had to guess from Heidi's Instagram and her

appearance, I'd say she was in her early twenties, several years younger than us, which also meant several years younger than Justin.

"Over a year," Heidi said, pride evident in her voice. "It's a good, steady job."

"We're from Star Junction," Penny said. "Driving over here is the only break we get from all that boredom."

Star Junction had certainly felt less boring in the last week.

"Tell me about it," Heidi said. "I'm from Rose Lake. Born and raised. It's sad when work is the most exciting part of your week." Someone tapped on the door, likely Heidi because she said, "You doing okay in there?"

"Just peachy," I called back, eternally grateful that the door went all the way to the floor. I reached over and rattled the hangers on the hook to sell the idea I was trying things on instead of what I was really doing—sitting on the bench prepared to take notes on my phone of anything useful Heidi might say.

"Don't forget to show me some of the options," Penny called back.

Now I was really going to kill her. Finn could investigate Penny's murder, and I could use my newfound sleuthing skills to get away with it. "Not going to happen," I called back.

"This new boyfriend of hers has her all distracted and nervous," Penny said in a patronizing tone. "Do you have a boyfriend?"

Penny's delivery was about as subtle as a sledgehammer, but I had to give it to her, it was working so far. Silence descended on our trio. What was happening out there? I heard sniffling, and then Penny said, "I'm sorry. I didn't mean to upset you."

That was it. Time to take over. I opened the door to see Heidi quietly crying with Penny awkwardly patting her back. "What's going on?" I asked.

"It's nothing," Heidi said, wiping away her tears. "I sort of had a boyfriend, but…"

"What is it?" Penny asked when it was clear Heidi wasn't going to continue on her own. "You can tell us anything."

A wave of guilt washed over me. We were pretending to care about this sweet girl, all the while caught up in our ulterior motives.

Heidi looked around, but thankfully we were the only customers in the store at the moment. She said, "You said you guys are from Star Junction?"

Penny nodded.

"I'm sure you heard about the guy who was murdered last weekend," Heidi said, wiping away the tears on her cheeks.

"Gwen here is the one who found his body. We were all friends from high school," Penny said.

I guess we were going the brutally honest route now. I put my hand on Heidi's shoulder. "Are you saying Justin was your boyfriend?" I asked.

Heidi pulled in a shaky breath. Her tears dried and her expression hardened as she said, "I thought he was, but apparently he was still seeing his ex-girlfriend."

If looks could kill…

"He lied to you?" I said, injecting just enough outrage into my voice to be believable, although the longer I thought about it, the angrier I was on Heidi's behalf. Justin lied to both Samantha and Heidi.

"Lied, cheated. Don't get me wrong, I'm upset he's dead, but…" Heidi trailed off but didn't finish, as if no further explanation was needed.

I'd assumed her tears were grief over Justin's death. If they were more about the fact that he'd dated her while also dating Samantha, that was a check in the jealous lovers column as far as I was concerned.

Penny picked up a pair of underwear from a table to our left, the first full-coverage pair I'd seen since we walked in. Cotton even. "I'm sure you can imagine all the rumors flying around Star Junction about who killed Justin. Is it the same in Rose Lake?" Penny asked, making it sound like it was an innocent question.

I had to admit, Penny had nailed it with that question.

Heidi glanced over her shoulder and said, "I'm going to need to get back to work before my manager notices how long we've been back here. I can't afford to lose my job." She looked at the untouched lingerie in the dressing room. Hopefully she thought I was just really good at rehanging the merchandise. "Did you find something that works?" she asked me.

"Nah, nothing today," I said.

Penny threw her arm around my shoulders. "That's okay. Sometimes wearing nothing at all is better." She turned back to Heidi. "Now about those rumors?"

Heidi fidgeted with the tape measure hanging around her neck. "I don't know about rumors, but Justin had a black eye a few weeks ago. He wouldn't tell me where he got it. Just kept telling me not to worry about it," she said.

A black eye? I hadn't noticed a black eye when I'd seen him at Chris's building or Bucky's. It had clearly happened long enough ago to have healed. "Do you have any guesses about how he got it?" I asked Heidi.

Heidi shrugged and said, "I didn't push."

"How'd you meet Justin?" Penny asked.

Heidi eyed us suspiciously. "You guys sure have a lot of questions about this."

"We're just a couple of curious gals," Penny said.

It was time to take control of this conversation before Penny turned this into a scene. Heidi didn't seem to know anything helpful. She seemed both broken up about Justin's death and angry with him for lying to her.

I wanted to either cross her off my list of suspects or nail her to the wall for Justin's murder, although standing in front of her, I couldn't imagine her killing someone in such a violent way. Too bad he wasn't strangled with a Victoria's Secret bra. That would've made things easier.

"Did you and Justin ever hang out in Star Junction?" I asked, trying to see if she'd admit to being in town around the time of his death.

Heidi wrinkled her perfect little nose. "No, which should've been my first clue something fishy was going on. He always had all these excuses as to why we needed to hang out at my apartment. I haven't been to Star Junction since the holiday market before Christmas." She blew out a breath as if the conversation was taking a toll on her. "That would've been about a month ago."

Penny leaned in and said boldly, "I'm going to cut right to the chase. We heard a rumor you were pregnant."

Heidi and I both sucked in a breath, me from shock, but from the way Heidi's face turned red and her brows snapped together, her gasp was from anger. "That's none of your business," she snapped.

"Is that a no?" Penny pressed.

"That's a *it's none of your business*," Heidi spat out.

"Did you kill Justin?" Penny asked, leaning in. "Find out he was cheating on you, or really cheating with you and decided he needed to pay with his life?"

I wasn't sure if I was mortified that Penny had been so blunt or thankful that she'd asked the question I hadn't had the guts to ask.

"No, I didn't kill him," Heidi said with a sneer.

"Although a killer wouldn't have any problem lying," Penny challenged.

Heidi's hands clenched at her side, but instead of responding, she flounced off toward the registers, leaving us standing alone in the back of the store.

I turned on Penny and said, "What was that, Watson? I think we switched parts."

"I told you the plan was loose. Let's get dinner. I'm starving," Penny said, seemingly unbothered by the scene she'd just created.

I followed Penny from the store, glancing over my shoulder to see Heidi shooting daggers at us from behind the registers. Maybe she hadn't killed Justin, but it didn't mean she wasn't hiding something.

We spent dinner debating whether or not we thought Heidi was lying about killing Justin. I'd been hopeful to find a solid suspect in Heidi but had my doubts that she was our murderer. I couldn't imagine she'd have any reason to be at Chris's building with Justin. Why Justin was there so late at night was still a mystery. I made a mental note to ask Chris if he had any theories about that.

I stirred the remnants of my soup and said, "Ready to head out? I'm exhausted."

"Yeah, I've got to get to school early tomorrow," Penny said. We stood to throw our trash away and headed toward the doors. "I just wish we'd found out something definitive," Penny said.

"If she's being honest, we can at least cross her off the list," I said optimistically.

"That's a big *if*," Penny said glumly. "It would've been perfect if she'd confessed."

"That would've been nice," I agreed. What kind of life did I live that I was hoping someone would confess a murder to me?

The temperature had dropped since we'd gotten to the mall, and the air crinkled inside my nose. Penny set off in the direction of her car, but I stopped short. "I need to use the bathroom."

"Want me to pull the car up?" Penny asked.

"That'd be great. I'll be fast," I promised.

I headed back inside, toward the long hallway off the food court, and turned the corner to see Heidi standing near the restrooms checking something on her phone. I debated whether or not to just hold it. We hadn't left things on the best of terms. Before I could decide, the door to the men's bathroom banged open. Heidi jammed her phone into her back pocket. A man walked up to her, and she threw her arms around his neck, kissing him with passion.

What?

The two parted, and they turned to walk down the hall, their gazes locked on each other. My mouth hung open. Heidi was kissing Derek Thompson. The same Derek Thompson who relentlessly asked me out. The same one who'd asked me out earlier today.

I ducked back into the food court before they could see me. What was Heidi doing making out with Derek?

They emerged from the hallway and headed straight toward Starbucks, Heidi's arm wrapped possessively around Derek's waist. Derek said something to Heidi. She threw her head back and laughed in response. Was this the same girl who had been crying about the death of her boyfriend an hour ago? Had she been faking her feelings about Justin for our benefit?

Finn's comment that a woman wouldn't have been strong enough to murder Justin flitted through my mind. What if he was wrong? Or maybe he was right. Maybe Derek wanted Heidi for himself and took out the competition. My stomach churned at the thought. Those guys were friends. *Had been* friends, at least.

My phone buzzed in my pocket, and I checked it to see a text from Penny letting me know she was out front. I took one last look at Derek and Heidi as they stood in line at Starbucks. Derek's hand wandered down Heidi's back. He slid his hand into her back pocket, and she leaned into him.

My phone buzzed again with the message *Where are you?*

Be right there. I took off down the hall toward the bathroom. Wait until Penny heard about this.

"What took you so long?" Penny asked as I slid into the front seat of her car a few minutes later. "The security guard was starting to give me some serious side-eye."

I buckled my seat belt as Penny steered away from the curb. "You're never going to believe what I just saw," I said breathlessly.

Penny glanced at me. "What?" she asked.

I paused for dramatic effect before saying, "Heidi making out with Derek Thompson."

The car swerved as Penny turned to look at me in shock.

The light in front of us turned red. "Watch it," I said, bracing my hand on the dashboard.

Penny slammed on the brakes, stopping just inches from the car in front of us. "You. Are. Kidding," she said, emphasizing each word.

"Full-on making out in the hallway by the bathrooms," I said, sharing in Penny's shock.

The light turned green, and Penny followed the white car in front of us through the intersection and onto the highway that would take us back to Star Junction. "What did they say when they saw you?" she asked.

"I ducked back into the food court before they could spot me," I said.

Penny tapped out a staccato beat on the steering wheel. "Let me get this straight… The same Heidi who was just crying about Justin was locking lips with Derek Sleazeball Thompson?"

The bare branches of the trees along the side of the highway whipped past in the light of the car's headlights. "I guess," I said as my mind struggled to understand the stark difference between the two Heidis I'd seen tonight.

"Maybe she's a sociopath," Penny said before gasping. "Maybe she killed Justin. What if she lied to us? What if she is pregnant? What if it's not Justin's baby at all? What if it's Derek's? What if it's Justin's, and she wants to convince Derek it's really his? What if—"

"Whoa! Someone has been watching too much true-crime TV," I interrupted with a laugh.

Penny shook her head and said, "Too much? Or just enough to keep us alive?" She rushed ahead without waiting for an answer. "Are you going to tell Finn about this?"

I pulled my hair over my shoulder and absently started braiding it. "I have to," I said definitively.

"Think he'll be mad you talked to Heidi?" Penny asked. She didn't sound worried. She sounded like she was gearing up to have a prime seat to some first-class drama. "What am I talking about?" she continued. "Now that he's got the hots for you, he'll probably be glad to have the information."

"He's got the hots for me?" I said with a disbelieving snort. "What kind of fantasy world do you live in?"

"The best kind, and he's definitely interested. I saw the way he was looking at you during the pie social." Penny shot me a glance before returning her attention to the road. "I also saw the way he looked when Chris walked into the church hall that night and you threw yourself into his arms."

"I didn't throw myself at anyone," I argued.

"Semantics. All I'm saying is he's interested," Penny said, tapping her forehead. "I have a sixth sense for these things."

I couldn't help but laugh, although I didn't want to encourage her wild ideas. "Does that mean you're going to open a PI business and a psychic business?" I teased.

"I probably could," Penny said with more confidence than my joke warranted. "Why am I wasting all this talent on teaching?"

"Because you love it," I said, trying to bring her back to some semblance of reality.

"You're right," Penny agreed. "I love the little buggers, and I love teaching them to love reading."

I stared out the window, pondering everything I'd learned, not the least of which was Penny's observation about Finn's supposed feelings for me. I'd felt a spark of attraction between us often enough, but I no longer trusted my ability to judge another person's interest. Chris was prime example number one of my failure in that area.

"Don't forget about bowling tomorrow night," Penny said, her words interrupting my scattered thoughts.

"I don't know," I hedged. After the week I'd had, I was looking forward to a quiet night at home with no intrigue, no drama and, most importantly, no threatening notes scribbled on rocks and thrown through my windows.

"It'll be fun. I promise. Just take one night off from murder. Justin's killer's not going anywhere," Penny pointed out.

That's what I was afraid of.

CHAPTER NINETEEN

———

I stared at my reflection in the bathroom mirror. The pale, early morning light filtering through the frosted window over my claw foot tub highlighted my bloodshot eyes. Dark circles seemed to have taken up permanent residence on my face.

I'd woken at two in the morning, fear flooding my body. My dreams were intensifying as the week went on. It had taken an hour of reading to be able to fall back asleep. I released my hair from its clip and ran a brush through it before twisting it back up on my head to keep it out of my way at work.

I headed to the kitchen and sent a text to Finn. *Penny and I...*

Tapping my finger against my lips, I considered how best to proceed. While we'd reached what felt like an understanding the night before, I didn't think for one minute Finn would approve of me hunting Heidi Fischer down instead of simply telling him where to find her.

I flipped the switch on my electric tea kettle and pulled a mug from the cabinet next to the sink. It was bright pink with black script that read *I got my kicks on Route 66,* a gift from my parents when they drove out to Arizona last fall. It wasn't that I was trying to do Finn's job. It was that I hadn't wanted to send him on a wild-goose chase.

The water in the kettle boiled, and I filled the mug, adding a peppermint tea bag. That was the perfect excuse. What if Penny had been wrong about Heidi's work? Heck, what if she'd been wrong about it being the right Heidi Fischer altogether? Okay, even I could admit that last one was a not just a shaky argument, but a ridiculous one. Good thing my first justification had been so solid. I'd been saving Finn time by finding Heidi myself.

With renewed confidence, I finished the text to Finn. *Penny and I were at the mall last night in Abbottsville and found out Heidi Fischer works there. We talked to her. She hadn't known about*

Justin's girlfriend while they were dating and was really upset about it when she found out.

But when had she found out? Before he died? After? Why hadn't I thought to ask that? I grimaced as I dunked the tea bag in the steaming water. I hadn't asked because I'd been too busy spending mental energy trying to figure out how to convince Heidi I'd been a real customer without prancing out of the dressing room in next to nothing.

My grimace melted into a sly smile. Penny was going to pay for that. Maybe not today. Maybe not tomorrow, but soon. I'd find some way to get her back, and I'd make sure it was hilarious. I huffed out a breath and took a sip of tea. Penny didn't embarrass easily. This wasn't going to be an easy task.

My phone rang, and I nearly dropped the mug of scalding tea in my lap. It was Finn. My stomach flipped, and I had to admit to myself it was a strange mix of excitement at the thought of hearing his voice and dread at what that voice might say now that he knew we'd gone and talked to Heidi.

I answered on the fourth ring. "Good morning," I said, keeping my voice light and friendly.

"You had a busy night last night," Finn's low voice rumbled over the phone.

Shoot. I couldn't tell if he was just stating a fact or if it was some sort of condemnation. "Penny needed a new outfit, and we got lucky running into Heidi," I said.

"That's why Penny squealed into your driveway last night like a woman on a mission? Because she needed a new outfit? Or because she found out Heidi worked at the mall and the two of you decided to play detective?" Finn asked.

Caught. But it didn't mean I had to admit it. "Penny takes her fashion very seriously."

The line was silent for a beat before Finn's laugh boomed over the line, erasing the tension in my shoulders. "You win," he said. "Tell me what you learned."

"I win? Just like that?" I asked in astonishment.

"Let's just say I decided I could spend a lot of energy trying to contain you or unleash you to do some good. Doesn't mean I won't worry about your safety," he added.

"You're worried about me, Thorfinn?" Those old-fashioned vapors were back, and I was close to swooning on the spot.

Finn barked out a laugh and said, "Thorfinn? You're getting colder."

"Doesn't mean I'm giving up," I said.

"I would expect nothing else," he replied.

"What do you want to know about Heidi?" I asked, bringing us back to the task at hand.

"Everything," he said.

"I told you in my text that she found out about Justin's girlfriend and was upset, which tells me she wasn't a willing participant in any kind of cheating scandal. It's like he had two separate lives. One in Star Junction and one in Rose Lake."

"With a dump truck for a ride between them," Finn muttered.

"You found out for sure he was the one taking out the trucks?" I asked.

"It's the most likely scenario," Finn said. "What else did you learn?"

I rattled off the short list of what we'd learned from Heidi. "Justin had a black eye a few weeks before he died, but he wouldn't tell her where he got it, which seems suspicious to me. He didn't have a black eye the day I saw him at the youth center or Bucky's. I have no idea how long it takes for a black eye to heal, but if you know, it could help you figure out who he might have gotten into a fight with. Maybe whoever punched him finished the job."

I continued, "Also, Heidi wouldn't confirm or deny if she's pregnant. She was super offended by the question and stalked off. Or maybe she stalked off when Penny asked her outright if she'd killed Justin. That seemed to make her really upset, which is understandable, but—"

"Wait," Finn interrupted. "Penny accused her of killing Justin?"

"Accused? Asked her about it? Who can really say?" I said innocently. The truth was, I couldn't remember how Penny had worded all of that. I was too busy mapping out an escape route through the store in case Heidi decided to add to the body count.

"There's a difference," Finn said dryly. "Have you two ever heard of tampering with a witness?"

"I'm pretty sure that's got to do with court and lawyers," I hedged. "And we're not quite there yet." I needed something to distract Finn from Penny's methods. "But I haven't told you the best part yet."

"You made a citizen's arrest and Heidi Fischer is tied up at

Penny's house as we speak?" he deadpanned.

"Don't be ridiculous," I said. "The best part happened after we talked to Heidi." I told him about seeing Heidi waiting by the restrooms and my shock at seeing her kissing Derek Thompson, who apparently didn't sit at home pining away that I wouldn't go on a date with him. "That has to mean something," I said after I'd painted what I thought was a pretty vivid scene. "Maybe they wanted to be together and took out the competition."

"Maybe…" Finn said slowly, sounding distracted, as if he were mentally sorting through all the information I'd just shared. "Thanks, Gwen," he said after a short pause. "While I'm not sure how I feel about your methods, the information was helpful."

"Glad to be of service," I said proudly.

"I've got to run," Finn said. "Keep me posted about anything else you may learn."

"Ditto," I said.

"Uh…that's not really how this works," he said.

"Can't blame a girl for trying," I said sweetly.

Finn's chuckle rolled over me like a warm blanket. "Talk to you later, Gwen."

"You too, Fionn," I said.

"Not it," he said simply before ending the call.

I found myself grinning like a fool as I grabbed a protein bar from my small pantry closet and sat down with the rest of my tea. Opening Facebook, I found an alert that I had a new message. It was from Tony Reagan.

I sat up a little straighter. In response to my question about why he'd written the Facebook post implying that Chris had killed Justin, he'd written *Everyone saw how mad Justin was Saturday at Bucky's. I talked to Mitch. He said Justin was killed in Chris's new building with one of his tools. Can't say I'm upset the guy's dead.*

At least he was honest about his feelings. If he'd murdered Justin, wouldn't he be working harder to seem cool with Justin now, no matter what had happened in their past?

His message continued. *I heard you're the one who found Justin's body. That had to have been rough. I can't imagine seeing a dead body.*

A chill ran up my spine as the image I'd tried to forget clouded my mind. I looked out the window at the row of evergreen trees lining the edge of my backyard and took a sip of my tea. He couldn't imagine seeing a dead body. Could I cross him off my list of suspects, or was he throwing me off the scent with a kind, innocent routine?

I popped the last bite of my protein bar into my mouth and typed, *Thanks. It was pretty awful.* I hesitated, trying to think of a way to get more information out of him, but I came up with nothing. Penny would probably just ask him if he did it, but that wasn't my style, and I didn't think a murderer was going to confess over Facebook messages. Instead, I finished with a bland: *See you around sometime.*

I was failing on every front. Besides the box I'd found under Justin's bed, had I really learned anything useful in all my sleuthing? I'd found Heidi's identity, but Finn would have found it eventually.

I set my mug in the sink and pulled my North Face fleece out of the front closet. The high today was going to be thirty-seven degrees. No need for a heavy winter coat in those mild temperatures. I needed to open the store. Then I'd take a minute to review my list again and figure out who else I could talk to. It had been almost a week since Justin's murder. Almost a week that a killer had been walking about Star Junction, or Rose Lake, like an innocent man. Or woman. See? I didn't even know the gender of Justin's killer.

I opened the front door and stepped onto the front stoop, my foot crunching down on something. A small paper bag lay in the center of the front step. Weird. I glanced around but didn't notice anything out of the ordinary.

I pulled the door closed behind me, taking care to lock the new deadbolt. I scooped up the little bag. It was from Henry's Hardware, the same place Finn and I had failed to find salt for the icy parking lot the night of the pie social. I peeked inside. A pile of mini screwdrivers covered the bottom of the bag, each one with a red handle.

A folded white piece of paper stood out among the red handles. I removed it from the bag, my hands shaking. In scrawling black ink, it read: *I told you to back off, but you didn't listen. I saw you with that police detective. Stop helping him. This is your last warning.*

My hands tightened around the package, and the bag let out a cracking sound. My gaze darted up and down the street. Was the killer watching me now? I crushed the bag and shoved it into my purse as I raced to my car, my eyes scanning the area for some unseen danger.

I unlocked the car and threw myself into the driver's seat, slamming and locking the door behind me. My breath came in shallow gasps, and I stared at the purse like it was going attack me. I yanked my phone out of my coat pocket and started a text to Finn. *Found a bag of screwdrivers on my front step. I'm scared.* My thumb hovered over the *Send* button, but I stopped.

I glanced over at my purse then back at the message. I was tired of feeling weak. I was tired of the fear from my nightmares leaking into my days. I didn't need to be rescued. No one had hurt me at Camelot Flowers, and no one was hurting me now.

While my stomach continued to churn, this was a lead I could follow. Someone had to have purchased these. Henry might remember someone buying a bag of mini screwdrivers. It couldn't be a typical purchase.

I set the phone in my cup holder and pulled out of the driveway. Five minutes later, I was parking in front of Camelot Flowers. I had a little time before I had to be at work. I tucked the bag of screwdrivers into my coat pocket and hurried down the street to the hardware store. "Henry?" I called out as the jingle bells tinkled over the door.

"I'm sorry. Henry's not here right now," a voice called from the back. A young woman with her long black hair pulled up into a high ponytail stepped out from the back room. "Can I help you with something?" she asked.

I looked around in confusion. "But Henry's always here."

"That's why his wife insisted he hire someone." The woman chuckled good-naturedly and approached, reaching out to shake my hand. "I'm Talia. Henry hired me a few days ago to help out around here," she explained.

"It's nice to meet you. I'm Gwen. My family owns Camelot Flowers just down the street." I shook her hand, debating asking her about the contents of the bag burning a hole in my pocket. She was new, but if the screwdrivers had been bought recently, she might know something.

"Camelot Flowers," she exclaimed with a smile. "I've been meaning to stop in one day before work. I see all the shelves of gifts through the windows. Your store is super cute."

"Thanks," I said, matching her smile.

Talia looked around at the packed aisles. "I'm still learning the ropes, but I'm happy to help you find anything you need," she said.

I fished the bag out of my pocket, thankful I'd thought to remove the threatening note and concoct a cover story on the way over. "Someone gave this to me as a gift but didn't leave a note. I was hoping Henry would remember who bought them so I can thank the person," I said earnestly.

Talia held out her hand, and I gave her the bag. I'd touched it. Now Talia. Finn wasn't going to be happy that the evidence was being contaminated. She looked in the bag, her face screwing up in confusion. "Someone gave you this as a gift?" she asked.

I forced out a laugh. It sounded as thin as it felt. "It's an inside joke," I said.

More like an inside threat.

"I definitely didn't sell a whole bag of mini screwdrivers. Do you want me to ask Henry when he comes back?" Talia asked, smiling. "He'll be in around lunchtime. I don't think he trusts me here all day by myself yet."

"That would be great." I fished a business card out of my purse and said, "My number's on here."

Talia took the card and scanned it. "Maybe I'll stop by when Henry gets back and deliver the news myself. I could pick up a plant for my apartment. I moved to town about a month ago."

I thought Talia must be new to Star Junction. I didn't remember seeing her around town. "Where'd you move from?" I asked.

"Rose Lake. One small town to another." She gave me a wry smile. "But I had an opportunity to move in with a friend and was ready to move out of my parents' house," she explained.

"Who's your friend? Maybe I know her," I said.

"Samantha Weston?" Talia said, phrasing it as a question instead of a statement.

Samantha Weston? I looked at Talia with new eyes. If she knew Samantha well enough to move in, she'd definitely known Justin. My gaze caught on the clock hanging above the cash register. I needed to have the store open in just a few minutes.

I wanted to use this opportunity to see if Talia knew anything about Justin that could be helpful, but I couldn't be late to work. "I know Samantha," I said. "Her sister was in my graduating class."

"Cool," Talia said. She held up my business card. "I'll see if Henry knows anything about your mysterious gift." Her face screwed up in confusion. "If it's an inside joke, wouldn't it be obvious who it was from?"

She had me there. "Thanks for checking with Henry. Gotta run," I said as I headed for the door.

I left the store to see a woman huddled in front of Camelot Flowers. Her back was to me, and she appeared to be looking down at something. Maybe her phone. "Sorry I'm running a little late," I said as I approached.

Margie, the police station receptionist and wannabe spy who'd snuck me in to visit Chris, turned and beamed up at me with a wide smile. "No worries, dear. I was just going to pick up a bouquet for Henry's wife, Rita, on my way to work. She's been sick with a nasty flu, and I thought some flowers would cheer her up."

Henry hadn't mentioned Rita was sick when Finn and I had gone to the hardware store looking for salt the night of the pie social. I unlocked the door and held it open for Margie. "That's a wonderful idea. Let me get the lights on and the heat turned up, and we'll figure out an arrangement she'll love."

Margie shrugged out of her knee-length puffy coat and draped it over her arm. "Don't hurry on my account. I'll just browse around while you get ready," she said.

Despite Margie's kind words to the contrary, I hurried to the back room and dropped my purse and coat on the floral couch. I snagged an apron from a hook near the door and looped it over my head before tying the green ribbons behind my back.

My parents had designed the aprons years ago. Camelot Flowers was written in emerald green, matching the ribbons. A gold crown, *to honor King Arthur,* my dad would explain to anyone who asked, was embroidered under the name of the store.

Margie was holding a small, crystal jewelry dish when I walked back into the front of the store.

"How're you doing after the break-in the other night?" Margie asked, gesturing with the jewelry dish toward the boarded-up windows in a way that had me worried she would drop it on the wood floors and break it. "I heard all about it," she continued. "I can't imagine how scary that must've been."

"It was awful, but all's well that ends well," I said brightly. I didn't need Margie telling my mom I wasn't sleeping. She'd feel the need to rush home from their trip. Getting out of the cold was good for my dad. There was no way I was going to be the reason they came back early. "Let's figure out what Rita would like for flowers."

"Finn mentioned he took you home the night of the break-in," Margie said, not taking my hint to change the subject. "He also mentioned he saw you last night. Finn's been mentioning you a lot." Her words dripped with extra meaning.

"Oh?" I feigned disinterest. It was like I could *feel* the rumor mill churning to life in Margie's mind.

"Yep, mentioning you quite a bit," she said with keen interest.

I turned toward the refrigerator case holding bouquets and cut flowers. "I told him I'd help him talk to some people about the murder investigation. You know how people are with outsiders. I'm just trying to help," I said.

"Interesting," Margie said, drawing the word out to an obnoxious length.

I turned back to Margie, my hand on the handle of the fridge door. "I just hope they catch this guy soon so Chris can stop worrying and I can get on with my life," I said.

Margie perched on the stool behind the counter as if she owned the place. I grinned, despite the difficult topic of Justin's murder. Margie tended to own any place she inhabited.

"Who's to say it was a guy?" Margie asked as she unwrapped a caramel from the little dish and popped it into her mouth. I made a mental note to add it to her bill. "What if a woman killed Justin?" she asked with a mouthful of sticky caramel. It came out more *Waff if a woban pilled Yustin?* but I was able to translate.

Finn's comment that a woman wouldn't have been strong enough to plunge the screwdriver into Justin's chest floated through my mind. I'd had my doubts about the accuracy of that statement before. Had Samantha murdered Justin in a fit of rage over his unfaithfulness? Had she been the one to leave that bag of screwdrivers on my front porch? Did Talia know? Was she covering for her friend?

What if it had been Heidi, enraged over Justin lying to her about having a girlfriend? She said she hadn't been to Star Junction since before Christmas a month ago, but that could have been a lie. It wasn't like there was a checkpoint coming into Star Junction, where visitors had to show ID.

"Everything okay, hon?" Margie's words snapped me back to reality.

"Oh, yeah," I said quickly before pulling three different

arrangements from the refrigerated case. "What do you think about one of these?" I'd chosen a more traditional bouquet of red roses, white carnations, and baby's breath, a bouquet with sprigs of dried lavender mixed with a variety of flowers in shades of purple and white, and a more modern bouquet featuring pink and orange ranunculus flowers, which looked like little bowls with their petals framing a dark center.

"Let me get a better look," Margie said as she tapped the counter in front of her.

I set the arrangements down and stuck my hands in the back pockets of my jeans. Maybe I'd run my concerns about Samantha past Finn. If only I didn't have this bowling thing tonight. I'd have to text him when I was done with work. Even if we couldn't get together, I could give him the information.

Margie studied the three bouquets before picking up the bouquet with the pink and orange ranunculus. "Rita will love this," Margie said. "A little sunshine on this dreary winter day."

"Excellent choice," I declared.

"You know, Finn is running himself ragged trying to find out who killed Justin. He's been all over town interviewing everyone he could find who was at Bucky's the night Justin was killed. Chasing down alibis. He even planned to drive to Chicago to interview Tony Reagan about some kind of beef he had with Justin. Stan talked him out of it. Said he could do the interview over the phone just as well."

"Do you want to include a card in the flowers?" I asked, pointing to the selection of tiny cards in a display stand on the counter.

Margie was taking no hints to change the subject this morning. She continued, "Especially after what happened here the other night. I can see it in his eyes. He's scared he won't find the killer in time and whoever hurt Justin will hurt someone else. Maybe even you." She unwrapped another caramel and smiled a grandmotherly smile at me. "I told him he needed to get more rest. Murders aren't solved in a day."

"This is a complicated case," I said, plucking a card from the display and setting in front of Margie with a pen.

Margie nodded her agreement and picked up the pen. She might not have been willing to change the subject, but at least she was willing to fill out the card. "A complicated case with a lot of evidence pointing to Chris," she said.

"The police are still focused on him?" I asked. The conversation with Finn at my house yesterday had given me new hope that he wasn't interested in railroading Chris, but he also wasn't going to take my word for it that Chris was innocent. He had to follow the evidence, even if it was circumstantial at the moment.

"They haven't found anything solid to point them in another direction," Margie said before bending her head over the card and scrawling a message to Rita wishing her good health.

I knew Finn was running down the drug angle. At least that didn't have anything to do with Chris. "Have you heard how Chris is doing?" I asked.

Margie looked at me with raised brows. "If anyone in this town knows how that boy is doing, it's you."

"Not this time," I said glumly.

By the time I'd gotten home from the mall, I'd been too exhausted to get together with Chris. I'd sent him a text telling him we'd need to catch up later and gone to bed. That, combined with my goal to create some healthy distance with Chris, left me more on the outside of how he was doing than I'd ever been before.

Movement through the one window in the front of the store that hadn't been shattered caught my attention, and I turned to see Derek walk past with a gym bag in his hand. In my opinion, selling insurance with his dad gave him entirely too much time to spend at the gym, but maybe that was just me.

A hastily put together plan formed in my mind, and I turned to Margie. "Do you want these flowers delivered, or do you want to take them to Rita yourself?" I asked.

"I'll take them, dear. I want to see how she's doing with my own eyes. Rita would say she's fine even if she was lying on her deathbed," Margie said, shaking her head.

"I'll wrap them up for you. We don't want the cold air killing the flowers before you even get there," I said.

"Wonderful," Margie said.

She put on her coat as I wrapped up the flowers and rung up the purchase, making sure to add the two caramels she'd eaten and the one she'd slipped into her coat pocket when she thought I wasn't paying attention.

Margie left with a promise to let me know how Rita enjoyed the flowers. I was out the door one minute later, flipping the sign to say *Out on delivery. Be back soon.* My hands empty of flowers, I was counting on a delivery of information that would help me find a killer.

Titan Fitness was two blocks down from Camelot Flowers past the coffee shop, Just Beans. I pushed through the doors and looked around. I'd never had much use for a gym membership, preferring to walk outside in the warmer months and huddle in front of my fireplace in the colder ones.

The gym was busier than I'd expected for midmorning. Two women and a man ran on treadmills to my left. Several people walked between weight machines and free weights across from me.

Over in the corner, a woman in hot-pink yoga tights and a matching sports bra kicked a hanging punching bag. She shifted and punched it repeatedly, the bag swaying on its chain.

I gasped as the woman grabbed a white hand towel and turned toward me as she mopped at the sweat on her face. Samantha Weston, Justin's ex-girlfriend and current member of my mini-murder board, had just been kicking that punching bag's butt.

Samantha's gaze snagged on mine, probably because I was standing there staring at her with my mouth hanging open. I snapped my mouth closed, forced a smile, and gave Samantha a little wave. Her eyes narrowed to slits before she whipped around and stalked to her water bottle by a wall of mirrors a few feet away.

Maybe Margie was right. Maybe Samantha was strong enough to murder Justin in a fit of rage. Chris used to have a punching bag like that hanging in his garage. I remember punching it once and yelping as pain shot through my hand. I'd been convinced it was broken. The bag hadn't moved at all. The bag had moved plenty with Samantha punching it.

"Gwen." Derek's voice invaded from behind me. "Thinking of joining the gym? Not that you need it. I mean, look at that tight—"

"I'm going to stop you right there," I said, turning toward Derek, whose gaze was nowhere near my face.

Despite my disgust at seeing Derek, I needed answers about what I'd seen at the mall the night before. I couldn't afford to be subtle or timid with a new threat hanging over my head. The note had said this was my final warning. What did that even mean? I needed to find out who killed Justin—*now*. I grabbed Derek's arm and dragged him toward a set of vending machines in the corner. "Come with me," I snapped.

There was a short hallway hidden by the vending machines that led to an emergency exit. I pulled Derek into the hallway and released his arm.

Before I could say anything, he tried to pull me into a hug. "I knew it was only a matter of time," he said.

"Eww, no." I pushed him away and took a step back, necessary insurance where Derek was concerned. "I need to ask you a question."

Derek folded his arms across his chest. He didn't mention my rejection of him. He didn't need to. I could see the anger in the tic of his jaw. "What kind of question?" he said with a sneer.

"What were you doing with Heidi Fischer at the mall last night?" I asked bluntly.

Derek dropped his arms to his side and took a step back, his expression stunned. "What do you mean?" he asked.

"Please. If this was some grand secret, you weren't working very hard to hide it. I saw you kissing by the bathrooms," I said.

Derek studied me for a moment, his eyes narrowing. "I don't know what business it is of yours. You and I aren't dating. You've made that very clear," he snapped.

"It's my business if it's a motive for murder," I argued.

Part of me was aware of the potential danger here. If Derek had murdered Justin to get to Heidi or to get back at Justin for going after Heidi, confronting him wasn't the safest move, especially not within lunging distance of an exit that likely led to the alley behind the gym. Had Derek been the one to leave the bag of screwdrivers on my doorstep? I'd have to rely on the fact that people were within screaming distance if he tried anything.

"A motive for murder?" Derek said, looking confused before the pieces seemed to click into place. "You think I killed Justin so I could date Heidi?" he said incredulously.

Now it was my turn to cross my arms over my chest. I waited, letting the silence answer his question.

Derek threw his head back and laughed. I had to admit, I hadn't been expecting that response. He patted my shoulder, his hand lingering a beat too long. "That's cute. I didn't need to murder Justin to have a chance with Heidi. She was always hopping from guy to guy," she said.

"Is she pregnant?" I said bluntly.

The color drained from Derek's face. "Where'd you hear that?"

"Around," I said. The truth was, I couldn't remember exactly where I'd heard it. Samantha? I'd talked to so many people, I'd started to lose track of the details.

"It's not true," he said, but his tone betrayed his doubts.

"If she is, are you worried it's your baby or worried it might not be?" I pressed.

That must have been a step too far, because Derek crowded into my space. "This is none of your business. You need to back off," he said menacingly.

I tried to take a step back but bumped into the emergency exit door. In for a penny—in for a pound. I doubled down on my quest to get something helpful out of Derek. "Where were you early this morning?" I asked.

My question seemed to throw him off balance for a moment. "We're done here," he snapped.

He turned to go, but I grabbed his arm. "If you had nothing to do with Justin's death, then it won't be a problem to tell me what you were doing this morning," I pressed.

If Derek had been the one to leave the package on my front steps, he'd be unlikely to admit it, but if he had a solid alibi, at least I could eliminate him as a suspect.

"I didn't get back into town until ten this morning," he said through gritted teeth.

"Didn't get back into town?" I asked.

"I spent the night in Rose Lake," he said. *With Heidi* was unspoken but clearly implied.

"Oh," I said.

I bit my lip, absorbing this information. If he was telling the truth, he probably wasn't Justin's killer. But even if he was telling the truth about spending the night in Rose Lake, he could be lying about what time he got back into town.

Derek started to walk away but turned before walking back into the main part of the gym. He grinned in the way that always made my skin crawl. "I'm going to forgive you these questions because I know you're all twisted up about your precious Chris being the main suspect in Justin's death. Remember, anytime. You and me," he said.

The fact that he thought I'd want to date him while he was clearly dating Heidi and possibly others turned my stomach. He walked away without waiting for a response. I couldn't linger over the results of our conversation. It hadn't taken long, but I didn't like to leave the store unattended in the middle of the day when I could help it.

Hailey wasn't scheduled to work today. We stayed open until six on Fridays in case people wanted to buy flowers on their way home from work for the weekend. I'd be stuck at the store most of the day before needing to rush home and get ready for bowling.

My head spun with keeping track of the people who had any kind of motive to kill Justin, even if it was a thin one. Two women, Samantha and Heidi, who'd been lied to and cheated on. Tony, who blamed Justin for ruining his life. Derek, although he denied it, who could have been angling to get Justin out of the way so he could be with Heidi.

Then there was the drug angle, the mystery surrounding the trucks at Palmer's Gravel and Rock, and whoever was threatening me. I pushed out into the cold winter air and headed back toward the sanctuary of Camelot Flowers, well aware that whoever murdered Justin might not even be on my mini-murder board yet. The stress of this was eating at me. Maybe Penny was right. Maybe I needed one night off from murder. I just wasn't sure I wanted to spend that night off bowling.

CHAPTER TWENTY

———

"Whose idea was bowling, anyway?" I said from the back seat of Jack and Penny's car. Why Penny had insisted on me riding with them was another mystery to add to the list, but I knew better than to try to fight her.

Jack passed Bucky's, which sat at the edge of town, and picked up speed as we entered the countryside. Ten Pins Down sat five miles out of town at the corner of two highways that led to a number of small towns like Star Junction, including Rose Lake.

Penny twisted in her seat. "The firefighters are thinking about joining a bowling league. I suggested they see if that's even a good idea before investing money in shirts, shoes, the whole shebang," she explained.

"Tonight'll be fun," Jack said as he slowed before turning into the gravel parking lot. "We invited everyone we know. They're going to have techno bowling later." He glanced at Penny with a wide grin on his face. "And the firefighters are going to be amazing at bowling."

Penny snorted out a laugh.

"Techno bowling?" I said, finally feeling excited about Penny dragging me out on a Friday night after a week of no sleep. "I love techno bowling." I managed a few disco moves despite being buckled in the back seat.

Jack pulled into a spot between two pickup trucks.

"I think we all remember what happened last time you went techno bowling," Penny said as we climbed out of the car.

"My foot slipped," I said, defending myself. "It's not my fault the ball flew into the other lane."

"We should have warned Dan she was coming," Penny said to Jack.

Dan was the owner, bartender, and de facto bouncer of Ten Pins Down. I didn't know what Penny was talking about. Dan loved me.

"Be nice, or I'm going home," I said to Penny.

"In what car?" she shot back with a sly grin.

I knew there'd been an ulterior motive for her offering me a ride.

The parking lot was packed, which wasn't unusual on a Friday night, especially in the winter when evenings at the lake or around the fire pit weren't comfortable options. "Are we going to even be able to get a lane?" I asked.

Jack held the door open for us and said, "We reserved a few lanes for tonight."

"A reservation. Ten Pins Down is going fancy on us," I joked.

We stepped into the chaos of families, couples, and groups like ours—laughing, joking, drinking, and blowing off steam after a long week of work. I knew from experience that in another hour, the families would head home to put kids to bed, changing the vibe of the bowling alley with the adults-only crowd.

Although smoking indoors had been outlawed years ago, the place still held a whiff of cigarette smoke from years of people bowling with a ball in one hand and a cigarette in another.

"There's our group," Penny said, waving to someone across the room.

I scanned down the lanes to see a bunch of guys from the fire department and police station standing around chatting at the end of three lanes currently occupied with other people.

"Our reservation is for six thirty, so those lanes should open up soon," Jack said as we headed over.

"I hope there's not an emergency in town tonight. Every first responder is already here," I said.

Karl, one of the firefighters, overheard me and laughed. He was as tall and skinny as Jack, Penny's husband, was broad and thick with muscles. Karl's brown hair was thinning on top and he wore wire-rim glasses. He looked more like an accountant than a firefighter. "Don't worry," Karl said. "We've got our walkies on. We're prepared to leave if necessary."

A man with a bushy dark-blond beard and large crooked nose laughed and said, "Plus, we left the probies back at the station."

205 | Marigolds, Mischief, and Murder | 205

"Now I'm even more nervous for the town," Penny said, earning laughs from the group.

I joined in the laughter, the stress and anxiety that had weighed on my shoulders over the last week sliding off like a ball speeding down a bowling lane. I turned to Penny and said, "Thanks for making me come."

"I think someone else is glad you're here too," Penny said with a gleam in her hazel eyes.

She nodded to our left, and I turned to see Finn watching us, his hands in the pockets of his jeans. Tonight, he was wearing a white T-shirt with an unbuttoned green and blue flannel shirt over it.

When I'd first met Finn, all I noticed was how out of place he looked in his fancy suits. Sure, he looked professional, but it made him look like the outsider that he was. After being trapped on the side of the road with him, I knew he wanted to fit in to Star Junction, make it his home. His wardrobe had taken a good turn as the week had gone by.

The man with the bushy beard and crooked nose that looked like it had been broken in a fight at some point and never set properly said something to make Karl and Jack roar with laughter. Penny leaned over and whispered in my ear, "That's Titus. New in town. Super hunky. If things don't work out with Finn…"

"You're incorrigible," I said, although I couldn't help the smile Penny's constant meddling caused. She meddled because she cared.

"You told me to help you find someone besides Chris. I'm just following directions," she said.

Titus was handsome in a mountain man kind of way, with a faded flannel shirt stretched across a thick chest that made it look like he chopped wood for a living. While his crooked nose hinted at some kind of altercation in his past, I could already tell he was good-natured by his joking around with the guys. Maybe he'd broken his nose saving someone from a fire instead of getting into a fight.

His bushy beard was at least five inches long, and a faded ball cap covered what I could tell was a mess of blond hair to match the beard. He was attractive in an unexpected way, but he wasn't my type. I caught Finn watching me and turned to Penny. "I'm going to go say hi to Finn," I said.

She was already talking to someone else and waved me onward in my task.

I weaved through the groups standing around chatting as we waited for our lanes, finally reaching Finn near the racks of bowling balls. "I didn't expect to see you here," I said.

Finn ran his hand through his dark-brown hair and grinned. "Tommy mentioned everyone was bowling. Didn't think it was something I should miss," he said.

I turned, and we stood shoulder to shoulder watching the bowlers for a moment, the silence feeling homey and comfortable instead of awkward. "How was your day?" I finally asked, breaking the silence.

Finn turned to face me. "Interesting," he said mysteriously.

I perked up. I was interested in interesting. Especially if it was about Justin's murder.

Finn nodded toward the bar and said, "I was just going to get a drink. Want to join me? It looks like we have at least six frames until that family of four is done over there."

"Will I get to hear more about your interesting day?" I asked.

"Is that a requirement for you to join me for a drink?" he teased.

I nodded, adopting a serious expression. "Unfortunately, it's a deal breaker."

Finn's smile widened, and he said, "Then I guess I'll have to tell you something about my day."

"About the case," I said, not eager to let Finn slide through on a technicality. "Not just about your day."

We moved to the bar and settled on two barstools covered in faded and cracked green leather. Dan, the bartender, slapped two cardboard coasters on the bar. Tonight, his Harley T-shirt was extra tight, showing off the muscles that made him an effective bouncer as well as bartender, not that he needed the skills often at Ten Pins Down. It was a family friendly establishment. For the most part.

"What can I get you?" Dan asked.

"Hey, Dan-the-man," I said. "I'd love a Lemon Drop."

He scowled at me before turning to Finn for his drink order. "And for you?" he asked.

"Just a club soda for me. With a twist of lime," Finn said.

I shot Finn a questioning look. Did he not drink?

"Technically still on duty," he said to my unvoiced question. "At least until this murder's over."

"And if you weren't on duty?" I asked.

Finn picked up the coaster and gave it a spin under his finger. "Whiskey. Neat."

"Huh," I said, attempting a spin of my own but only succeeding in flicking the coaster over the bar directly in the path of Dan, who was carrying our drinks. I stifled a laugh while Finn ducked his head, trying to hide his smile. "Sorry about that," I said to Dan.

Dan set a new coaster down in front of me with a little more force than he had the first one. Finn picked up his club soda and gave a questioning look to the bottle of beer in front of me. "What happened to the Lemon Drop?" Finn asked.

I picked up the beer and took a sip. "It's a fun little game Dan and I play. Isn't that right, Dan?" I shouted down the length of the bar.

Dan gave me another scowl. He might have even growled at me. I couldn't be sure with all the noise in the background.

I turned back to Finn and explained, "On my twenty-first birthday, some friends and I came in to have my first legal drink and do some bowling. I ordered a Cosmopolitan. I was very into *Sex and the City* at the time. Dan not so kindly told me he didn't serve frilly drinks and plopped a bottle of beer in front of me. I've been ordering all the frilly drinks I can think of ever since." I raised my bottle to Dan in salute. "I get a beer every time."

Finn chuckled and said, "And is Dan as delighted by this little game as you are?"

"I like to think so, deep inside," I said.

"So, what was that 'huh' response to my whiskey drinking?" Finn asked, switching topics.

Finn's question caught me off guard. I hadn't even realized I'd said it out loud. "Did I say that?" I asked, hoping he'd let the question slide.

"You most certainly did," he said, clearly intrigued. "And now you're blushing."

That's it. I was going to die of embarrassment, which meant I might as well give up on finding Justin's killer. It was up to law enforcement now. "It's nothing," I hedged.

"You can't get away with dodging questions. I'm a detective. I'm curious by nature," Finn replied.

I'd insist it was nothing, but I was having fun, feeling bold, and Finn wasn't going to drop it. "I've often thought your eyes were the color of whiskey," I said, forcing myself to hold his gaze, even though I could feel the heat in my cheeks.

The music didn't fade into the background. The chattering of those around us didn't miraculously stop like in the movies. There was no camera to push in on the two of us, but for a moment Finn held my gaze with those whiskey-brown eyes in a way that stole my breath.

He cleared his throat and took another healthy sip of the club soda. "I followed up on your Heidi lead today," he said, back to business.

"And?" I mentally followed him back into the land of murder investigations. Funny how that felt safer than whatever unspoken moment had just passed between us.

"She claims to have an alibi for the night of the murder. We're running that down now." He gave me a sheepish grin. "She also had some choice words for the two Star Junction 'idiots' who'd pointed me in her direction," he added.

"You told her it was us who told you where to find her?" I asked, horrified. I was never going to be able to go back to the mall unless I wanted to risk running into Heidi. Going back to Victoria's Secret was out of the question, although Penny had ensured I'd steer clear after her humiliating cover story of why we were there in the first place.

"No, but she assumed, said the timing of my call couldn't be a coincidence with your visit to the mall," Finn said.

I grimaced and said, "I've never run into her before. Not in town. Not in Rose Lake, and not at the mall. I'll just have to make sure to protect that streak."

"What about you?" Finn asked. "Any updates?"

"I do have some actually, although they're more theories and observations than anything concrete," I said.

"Even small things can break a case wide open," Finn said.

The door opened, and I glanced over my shoulder to see Chris walk in. I hadn't been expecting to see him here, but I should have. Although not a firefighter or police officer, he was buddies with most of the people here. He scanned the room, his face lighting into a smile when he saw the group huddled around lanes nine through twelve.

Finn stiffened besides me, taking a slug of the club soda, probably wishing it was whiskey. I felt the tug to go greet Chris, but I was in the middle of talking to Finn, and Chris could wait.

"You already know about Heidi and Derek," I said to Finn. Chris hadn't seen us yet, and I was hoping he wouldn't. We hadn't discussed my growing friendship with Finn, but I was sure Chris would have an opinion about it. An unfavorable one.

"I stopped by Derek's office earlier today," Finn said. "But his dad said he wasn't in."

"Star Junction tip—if Derek's not at work, check the gym," I said. I couldn't keep the disgust out of my voice, but if Finn noticed, he didn't say anything.

"Good to know," he said.

"I actually tracked Derek down at the gym myself," I said.

"And?" Finn asked.

"And he told me that Heidi's not pregnant, and he got super upset that I asked about it."

Finn pulled out his phone and typed something into it. "Thanks. His personal relationship with Justin's ex could be something to lean on. People say all kinds of things they wouldn't when they're upset."

I shook my head. "I always thought of Derek and Justin as good friends, but dating each other's exes? Being more upset about being questioned than your friend's death? I don't get it."

"It's hard to know what's really going on between two people. Maybe they were more friends of convenience than anything else," Finn said.

"I guess." I chewed on my bottom lip. I'd be devastated if a friend treated me how Derek was treating Justin. "There is one more thing," I said, remembering seeing Samantha at the gym. "I know you think the killer isn't a woman, because it would take a lot of strength to kill Justin with that screwdriver."

"I do," Finn said.

"I saw Samantha Weston, Justin's other ex-girlfriend, at the gym today. She was working out on one of the heavy bags," I said. "I was impressed with how much she got that bag moving. She's got to be stronger than she looks. It feels like she has a motive. I wouldn't count her out."

"Guys," Penny called from near the bowling lanes. "We're up."

Finn dropped a tip on the bar for Dan, and we headed toward the lanes. "Thanks for that info," he said. "I'll follow up on those leads tomorrow."

"Anything you can tell me that I don't already know?" I asked quickly. I had a feeling our open talk about the investigation was going to end the moment we reached the group.

"I talked to Tom out at the rock yard. I wasn't able to gather any forensic evidence since Justin had been fired weeks before and the trucks were both out on deliveries. I'm going to go back tomorrow and see if I can find any evidence that they'd been used to haul drugs. Besides that, I'm stalled until I get the rest of the forensics back. That is, unless something pans out with this Derek and Heidi lead," he said.

"If only the real world was more like TV," I muttered.

Finn chuckled and said, "I wouldn't normally agree, but in this case…"

"Good," Penny said, clapping her hands together, "we're all here. We need to divide up by lanes." Penny scanned the group. "Let's have a friendly competition. Whoever loses buys drinks."

"Do we get to pick our own teams?" Jack asked.

"Not a chance," Penny said, clearly taking charge of the group of firefighters and police officers. It didn't matter that most of them towered over her five-foot-four-inch frame or that she would be no physical match for any of them. Not even Kurt with his wiry frame. Penny's bossy personality—she called it leadership skills—wasn't based on size. "I'll pick the teams to make sure they're fair," she declared.

A minute later, we were standing in three groups of four. Penny may have wanted to keep the groups fair for her little competition, but I couldn't help but think there was an ulterior motive to her madness.

I was on a team with Karl, who I'd mentally labeled the faux-accountant; Titus, the mountain man; and Finn, the man I was having entirely too much fun flirting with. Chris was on a team with three of the police officers. Penny's team was conveniently situated in the lane between us.

I shot her a look, but she simply plastered an innocent expression on her face and said, "What?"

"You know what," I said accusingly.

She actually batted her eyes at me. "I have no idea what you're talking about," she said lightly.

Karl rubbed his hands together and adjusted his wire-rim glasses. "Let's get this show on the road. I'm looking forward to a free round of drinks."

"I'm going to run to the restroom," I said to the group.

"Be back before it's your turn," Karl said as he hefted a ball in his hands.

I gave him a salute and headed to the bathrooms in the back of the building. A gust of cold air blew in through the doors as they opened to reveal Mitch, sporting his signature faded wranglers and beat-up Texaco baseball cap, and Derek, his blond buzz cut looking freshly buzzed, walking in with two women. Scratch that—walking in with Heidi Fischer and a woman I didn't recognize.

Finn mentioned he'd been trying to talk to Derek. I rushed back to our lanes and grabbed Finn's arm. "Come with me," I said.

Finn glanced around as if trying to determine if there was some kind of threat. Maybe I was verging on deranged in my excitement.

"It's nothing bad," I assured him. "It's like a gift."

"A gift?" But he didn't question me further, instead following me toward the bar, where I could see Mitch and Derek ordering drinks.

"Where're you going?" Karl shouted after us.

"One minute," I called over my shoulder. Titus was up, which meant Finn was next. I didn't want to keep them waiting, but murder trumped bowling. I pulled Finn to a stop several yards away from the bar. "Look," I said gesturing toward the crowded bar.

"What am I looking at?" Finn said slowly.

I smiled proudly and said, "Derek Thompson. You wanted to talk to him? There he is."

CHAPTER TWENTY-ONE

———

Finn's gaze cut to mine before returning to study Derek. "I'm not usually in the business of interviewing people in a bowling alley," he said, although I could see he wanted to talk to Derek.

"If you stay in Star Junction, I'm sure it won't be the last time," I encouraged. I grabbed his arm again and pulled him forward, stopping in front of Mitch and Derek, who had left their dates at a high-top table cross the room. "Derek? You remember Detective Butler," I said. "He was looking for you earlier today, but you'd already left work."

Derek paled, the smarmy self-confidence I associated with him draining away. "You wanted to talk to me again?" he asked incredulously.

"It's nothing," Finn said reassuringly. "Just double checking some things about the Justin Hunt murder. It'll just take a minute."

Derek glanced at Mitch, but Mitch said nothing in the way of helping Derek out. Finally, Derek looked back at Finn and said, "What do you want to know?"

"It's kind of loud right here. Why don't we step closer to the door?" Finn said, walking away without waiting for a response. It worked, because Derek followed.

I leaned back against the bar where Derek had been standing, desperately wishing Finn had asked me to come along.

"What do you think he wants to talk to Thompson about?" Mitch asked as he pulled his beat-up baseball cap off his head, ran his fingers through his thick dark hair, and resettled the hat into place.

"I have no clue," I said. It was a lie, but I wasn't going to give any details of the case away. At least not to Mitch. Penny didn't count. She was my best friend. Chris didn't count either. He was the prime suspect.

"Last I heard, they were still looking at Chris for the murder," Mitch said, still watching Finn and Derek, his fuzzy, caterpillar-esque eyebrows snapping together.

The rest of the forensics better hold some damning evidence clearing Chris and implicating someone else, or I was afraid Mitch was right. "I think they're following a bunch of different leads," I said blandly.

"That's good," Mitch said. He turned to look at me slowly, as if it took effort for him to look away from Finn and Derek. "You seem close with the new detective," Mitch added.

I shrugged. "I've been helping him figure out who to talk to," I said. "He doesn't know all the ins and outs of Star Junction yet."

Dan shot me a dirty look as he walked by, as if daring me to order another frilly drink.

I grinned back at him, continuing to believe he enjoyed our little repartee. "I saw Derek's here with Heidi," I said to Mitch.

"You know Heidi?" Mitch asked before taking a swig of his beer.

"I know she was dating Justin," I said.

Mitch nodded, as if appraising my statement, and said, "They weren't serious."

"Tell that to Samantha," I challenged. My gaze drifted toward the bowling lanes. Karl, the firefighter, stood with his arms crossed, staring daggers at me. I grimaced and held up one finger, asking for a little more time.

I couldn't hear his scoff, but I could see it.

Finn and Derek walked back to us, and my throat burned with every question I wanted to ask but couldn't in front of Mitch and Derek. Instead, I looped my arm through Finn's. "Looks like the boys are waiting for us. Ready to get back to bowling?" I asked cheerfully.

Finn slipped his phone in his back pocket. "Ready," he said before turning to Derek and Mitch. "Thanks for your time."

"Our pleasure," Mitch said, answering for both of them.

As we walked back toward the lanes, I couldn't hold the questions in any longer. "Learn anything helpful? Did Derek crack? Did he confess to killing Justin? No, I suppose not, or you'd have arrested him. Do you think he could have done it, because that would really solve a problem for me."

Finn pulled to a stop several feet away from where Karl continued to glare at us. "That's a lot of questions. And what kind of problem do you have that would be solved by Derek being arrested?"

Oops. I hadn't meant to mention that out loud. "That's nothing. Don't worry about it. What about the murder?" I asked.

"I think we already established that I don't let questions go with an answer of 'that's nothing,'" Finn pressed.

I really didn't want to get into it right now. I'd made the mistake of mentioning it to Chris last year. He'd gotten red in the face, pulled out his phone, and shot off a series of texts to Derek. Guess what? Those texts accomplished nothing. In fact, I think they encouraged Derek to double-down. I didn't need anyone riding to my rescue. I needed answers about Justin's murder. "I'll explain later," I lied. "What about the case?"

"I didn't learn anything actionable," Finn said in tacit agreement to let me tell him about my problem with Derek later. "Derek says he and Heidi are off and on," he continued. "He didn't seem to mind she was dating Justin. He definitely denied having any motive to murder the guy."

Derek could deny it all day long, but there was a small part of me that relished the thought of him behind bars and out of my hair.

We walked the rest of the short distance to the lane where Titus was sitting silently and peacefully as if our delay didn't faze him at all. Meanwhile, Karl seemed a little too interested in being the team to win the free drinks.

"There you are," Karl said, all business. "You're up, Butler."

"Sorry about the wait," Finn said as he picked up his ball.

Penny walked over to me and whispered, "Did I see Finn talking to Derek? Is he going to arrest him?"

"Yes and no," I said in answer to her questions. "Derek is a creep, but can you really see him murdering someone?"

"Can you see anyone you've talked to murdering someone?" she asked.

"No," I said dejectedly as I realized she was right. "Maybe Tony?" I offered.

Penny chuckled and said, "You just want it to be Tony, because you know him the least."

"You might be right," I said glumly.

Finn finished his frames with a total of nine pins down.

"My turn," I said to Penny.

"Good luck. Remember what happened last time," she said as she walked away.

I was never going to hear the end of throwing that ball into the next lane. If Penny had been trying to get into my head, she'd done a pretty good job. The last thing I wanted to do was embarrass myself in front of the guys.

I picked up my ball and pulled in a steadying breath. Launching the ball down the lane, I put every bit of effort into not stepping over the line, which had directly led to my feet flying out from under me and my ball bouncing into the other lane last time. Who knew the actual alley in a bowling alley was so slippery? I succeeded in staying on my feet this time, but my ball went directly into the gutter. That wasn't much better.

"That's okay," Finn said encouragingly. "You'll get the next one."

Karl looked less certain. Titus gave me a friendly grin but said nothing.

I held my hand over the air vent as I waited for my ball to return. I could feel the eyes of my team watching me. *Pull it together, Gwen.* I wasn't a champion bowler, but I was better than this.

The ball finally returned, and I grabbed it thankfully. I just needed to get this over with. I sent it down the lane without giving myself too much time to overthink it. Turning before I could see whatever disaster was about to strike, I caught Finn watching me, a warm smile on his face, which only drew my attention to his sexy beard that I was finding myself spending way too much time thinking about.

"That's better than nothing," Karl muttered as he approached to take his turn.

I looked behind me in time to see I'd managed to knock down four pins. That *was* better than nothing.

The next frames flew by in laughter. I managed to hold my own, even getting a strike on frame seven. By the time we were bowling our last frames, it was going to be up to Finn and me to bring it home. The other two teams had finished first. Apparently, talking to Derek and Mitch had set us back a few frames.

Everyone gathered at the end of our lane. If either Finn or I bowled a strike, we'd win. My stomach fluttered with nervous energy, but not like the nerves I'd carried all week. These nerves filled my body with warmth and light. "We can do this," I said to my team. I gave Finn an encouraging slap on the back.

Really, I needed Finn to do it. We couldn't count on me to pull out a strike. He'd managed to bowl four strikes to my one, so it wasn't outside the realm of possibility that we could win this.

He pretended to crack his knuckles. "All in a day's work," Finn said confidently.

Finn focused, taking three steps before releasing the ball. It sailed down the center of the lane. All ten pins exploded from their positions. The reaction to Finn's strike was mixed as groans and grumbles blended with the cheers from our team.

I turned to Penny and then Chris. "Ha!" I said. "Who's the winner now?"

Penny scowled at me, although I didn't know what she had to complain about. With her team coming in second, she wasn't paying for anyone's drinks. Finn sauntered over.

"I knew you had it in you," I said to him, raising my hand for another high-five. Our palms connected, and he caught my hand in his. He held my hand for a breath before releasing it.

Karl clapped Finn on his back. "Ever thought about joining a bowling league?" he asked. They set off toward the bar together. I glanced back at the screen showing our score. We didn't need me to bowl my frames, but I wasn't going to leave the game unfinished.

I grabbed my ball and sent it flying down the lane. Nine pins knocked over. Instead of waiting for my ball to return, I grabbed one of the other balls and rolled it down the lane, not even caring when it missed the last pin.

Penny was the only one who'd bothered to wait for me. She gave me a polite golf clap. "Much better than last time," she said, linking her arm through mine as we headed toward the group gathered at the bar. "See? Tonight was fun. Aren't you glad you came out?" she asked.

Penny was right. Justin's murder had given a single-minded sense of purpose to my days, but it had robbed me of my joy. It was good to see it wasn't gone completely. With this sense of happiness came a deep exhaustion. Not like the kind fueled by fear, but the kind that led to restful sleep. "Thanks for talking me into it," I said to Penny. "But I think I'm going to call it a night."

"What? But we're just getting started," Penny said.

This was the disadvantage of not having my own car here and why I'd first fought Penny's plan to pick me up. "Maybe Jack could run me home real quick?" I asked hopefully. The round trip would take him twenty minutes. He'd be back before the group was on their second round of drinks.

Finn stepped over, leaving his conversation with Karl. "I can drop you at home," he said.

"No," I said, waving away his offer. "I can't ask you to do that."

"Sure she can," Penny said, practically pushing me at him. "Thanks, Finn. See you later," she said to me before running off to join her husband, Jack.

"You've already given me plenty of rides this week," I said to Finn as I adjusted my purse on my shoulder.

"I'm heading out anyway," Finn said. "I'm going to go back to the precinct and go through the case file again."

Here I was, leaving with visions of my warm, cozy bed dancing through my head, and Finn was going back to work. I was half tempted to see if he'd let me come with him. I'd never seen the file. But before I could suggest it, a wide yawn split my face.

Finn's chuckle was just as warm and cozy as the bed I couldn't wait to crawl into. "Let's get you home," he said.

Chris looked up from a conversation he was having with Penny's husband, Jack. "You're leaving?" he asked me.

"I'm tired. Winning took a lot out of me," I said with a cheeky grin.

Chris smiled, but it was thin as he took in Finn by my side. "Do you need a ride? I don't mind," Chris said.

"Thanks, buddy," Finn said. "We've got it covered."

Chris's jaw ticked, but he didn't argue. He gave me a brief hug and said, "Let's hang out tomorrow. I've hardly seen you this week."

"Give me a call when you're up tomorrow," I said before turning to Finn. "You ready?"

Finn and Chris stared at each other for a moment, much like they had at the coffee shop. I glanced over to see Penny watching the three of us. Her eyes widened, and she mouthed *oh my gosh* as she pointed between the two men.

I gave her a look that I hoped communicated some mixture of *knock it off* and *grow up*. She just grinned. She'd gotten the message. She just didn't care.

"Ready to go?" I said to Finn again, pulling him out of whatever weird standoff was happening between the two men.

"Whenever you are," he replied.

Chris watched us walk out the door, his hands shoved in the pockets of his jeans.

The chilly walk to Finn's truck erased some of my exhaustion, but not all of it. The front bumper still held the evidence of our accident from Tuesday night. Ten minutes later, we were pulling up in front of my house. I half expected Finn to insist on checking my house again but then remembered he didn't know about the bag of screwdrivers.

"I'll walk you to the door. Make sure you get in okay," Finn said before jumping out of the car and opening my door for me.

"Thanks, but that's not necessary," I said as he helped me down from the truck. "Star Junction is a very safe town. At least normally."

"It'll make me feel better. Really, you'd be doing me a favor," he said.

I shot him a sideways glance, his words making me smile. "I guess if it'll make you feel better," I said wryly. Scanning the stoop, I breathed a sigh of relief. It was clear of threatening notes or packages.

I made it to the top step and turned, Finn one step below me, bringing us closer to eye level. "Thanks for the ride," I said, suddenly overwhelmed by his proximity and that weird urge to run my fingers over his beard.

Finn's breath puffed into the cold air, the glow from my porch light dancing in his eyes. "Tonight was fun," he said.

"Star Junction might not be as exciting as Chicago, but we manage to have a good time," I replied with a smile.

Finn shuffled his feet. He kicked at a chunk of dirty snow on the edge of the step before lifting his gaze to meet mine. "I'd like to take you out on a date," he said in a rush of words.

"A date?" I repeated, as if I was having a hard time making sense of his words.

"Yes, a date." He chuckled, but his eyes betrayed his uncertainty. "It'll have to wait until this murder is solved, but what do you say?"

Butterflies rioted in my chest, and I gave him what I hoped was a flirty grin. "On one condition," I said.

"Here we go with the conditions again," he complained, but his grin matched my own. "Name it."

"Tell me what Finn stands for," I said.

For a moment, I thought he wasn't going to answer me. We stood in the moonlight, gazes locked, just inches apart. Finn's voice dropped low. "So, if I tell you, you'll say yes?" he asked.

I nodded, finding myself at a loss for words under the intensity of his gaze.

Finn leaned in. For a brief moment, I wondered if he was going to kiss me, but instead, his mouth lingered near my ear, his breath sending tendrils of warmth through my body. "It's Griffin," he whispered before pulling back. "I'm going to solve this murder. Then I'm taking you out on a date." He turned and walked back to his truck, leaving me breathless on my doorstep.

CHAPTER TWENTY-TWO

———

Ding, ding, ding.

I jerked awake.

The dreamland hammock swaying in the gentle breeze, Finn's arms around me, dissolved into the reality of my cold, dark bedroom.

I collapsed back on the pillow. Why did my alarm always go off in the middle of the best dreams? I rubbed my eyes.

Wait a minute.

The room was dark.

It wasn't my alarm. I scrambled for the phone to check the time. Four in the morning. Who was texting me at four in the morning? I shook the last vestiges of sleep from my mind and opened the message.

It was from Chris.

Emergency! Come to the center.

I dropped the phone as if it had bitten me. Images from last weekend flashed through my mind. The same text. The same wording. A dead body.

I scooped up the phone, flung the covers to the floor, and raced down the stairs, no hesitation this time. I shoved my feet into boots and yanked my coat off the hook by the door.

As I cranked my car to life, I glanced down at the phone in the passenger seat. I should text Finn. I might be operating on instinct, but I wasn't stupid. I hesitated, my finger hovering over the screen.

What if this was nothing? How stupid would I feel if I pulled Finn out of bed, only to find Chris working away installing cabinets? I dropped the phone into the cup holder and put the car in reverse. I'd wait and see if Chris's car was at the center before sending the text to Finn.

If I found the parking lot empty again, I'd send the text and wait in the car. If Chris had thoughtlessly summoned me to ask advice on paint color, I wasn't going to bother waking Finn. It would be just like Chris. He spent most of his life wrapped up in his own little world, not thinking about the consequences of his actions on others.

I pulled into the parking lot to see Chris's old Jeep parked by the front door. I huffed out a breath. Everything was okay. Maybe not everything. I was going to kill Chris for scaring me, not to mention pulling me out of bed so early in the morning. I parked next to his car and cut the lights.

His car was here, but the building was dark. I glanced around. The rest of the parking lot sat empty. Why would he work in the dark?

Light from the full moon illuminated the parking lot and surrounding area, bouncing off the windows and making it impossible to see inside. I glanced down at my phone and back at the building.

With a sigh, I picked up the phone and typed out a message to Finn. *Chris texted me using the exact same words as last week. I'm at the center. His car is here, but the building is dark. Could be nothing. I'm going to check it out. I'll let you know what I find.*

There. Finn could do with that what he wanted.

Despite my best efforts to be careful, the sound of my car door closing echoed across the parking lot, sounding like gunfire. I hesitated. This was the moment. I could still go back to my car and wait for Finn to respond.

I rolled my shoulders and chastised my overactive imagination. Chris was waiting for me. I was being ridiculous. Finn had said to trust my instincts, but right now my instincts splintered in every direction, all possibilities playing through my mind.

I pushed against the door, and it swung open an inch. Just like last week. I shuddered but continued, sliding through the crack and letting the door close behind me.

I waited by the door, giving my eyes time to adjust. The moon filtered through the windows lining the front of the building, but a few feet in, the room disappeared into shadows.

"Chris?" My voice sounded thin in the empty space. "I got your text. What's going on? If this is a joke, it's not very funny." I took a few steps into the room. "Chris?"

A work light on a stand blazed on to my left, and I lifted my hand, shielding my eyes from the sudden brightness.

"Look, Chris," a voice jeered from the darkness. "She did come. I told you she would. Everyone knows she'd do anything for you."

I sucked in a sharp breath and turned back toward the door, but my feet wouldn't move as my mind worked to place the voice. Wherever I'd heard it before, it had never been filled with that kind of cold, hard malice.

As I turned, my eyes adjusted to the light. My hand flew to my mouth, muffling the scream that erupted from my lungs. Under the light of a construction lamp, Chris sat tied to a chair, duct tape across his mouth, his eyes wild with fear.

The fear coursing through my body screamed at me to run. Run out the door. Run to Chris. I stood frozen, caught in a war between saving myself and saving my friend. My eyes strained through the shadows trying to find the person responsible.

"What do you want?" My voice echoed into the darkness. I surprised myself with the question. My mind, a flood of adrenaline and terror, operated on its own.

"What do I want? I want Chris to go to prison for Justin's murder like he was supposed to. You just couldn't leave it alone. Heaven forbid anything happens to your precious little Chris. You're pathetic," the voice jeered.

The man's words slammed into me, clearing away some of the fear. "Fine," I shouted, my voice sounding stronger. "I'll stop. Just leave. I don't even know who you are."

"Nice try. You think I'm stupid?" Out of the darkness emerged Mitch, same faded wranglers and beat-up baseball cap he'd been wearing at the bowling alley earlier. The look of contempt on his face twisted through me until I choked on the fear.

"Mitch? I don't understand," I said, staring dumbfounded at the man I'd known since we were kids.

"Shut up! You don't need to understand. All you need to know is if you try to run, I'll kill your boyfriend here," he shouted.

Chris struggled against the duct tape holding his arms and legs to the chair. Panic blazed in his eyes, his muffled cries leaking through the duct tape covering his mouth.

"You shut up too," Mitch barked to Chris as the back of Mitch's hand connected with Chris's face.

"Stop it!" I shouted. "Stop hurting him."

Everything would be okay. Finn would get my text and show

up. I just needed to buy him some time. "This was your big plan?" I asked Mitch. "The police are never going to believe Chris killed Justin now that someone abducted him and beat him up."

Mitch curled his upper lip, grabbed a corner of the tape covering Chris's mouth, and yanked, ripping it off as Chris let out a grunt of pain. Mitch turned to Chris and grabbed him by the chin. "You stay quiet, and I'll let you say goodbye to your girlfriend here. Make a scene, and the tape's going back on. Understand?" he asked Chris.

Chris nodded, his gaze focused on me. "I'm so sorry," he croaked out.

"This is not your fault." My voice turned steely. "It's his." Anger at Mitch's betrayal—plus the fear of what was going to happen to me, to Chris—swirled together and pressed on my chest like a heavy weight.

"No," Mitch said, pointing his finger in my direction. "This is *your* fault. You poked around where you didn't belong. That new detective doesn't know anything about Star Junction. Left on his own, he would have been chasing his tail trying to figure out who killed Justin. Lucky for me," Mitch said, taking a step toward me, "Chris and Justin got into a fight at just the right time. What happened to Justin was a long time coming. I saw my opportunity and took it."

"Gwen, run! Get out of here," Chris said, struggling against his restraints.

"You run, and I'll kill him," Mitch said coldly.

My gaze cut between Mitch's cold, hard expression and Chris's desperate one. I had no doubt Mitch was telling the truth. I also had no doubt he planned to kill both of us anyway. At least with me here, we stood a chance. People always underestimated me. I prayed Mitch would do the same.

"I'm not leaving you," I said to Chris.

Chris dropped his head and moaned.

Mitch stopped a few feet from me and turned back to Chris and said, "I told you she'd never leave you here. You never saw how much she cared about you. Everyone else did, but you have this special talent for being blind to everything around you, Crawford."

I scanned the ground, frantically looking for a weapon as Mitch taunted Chris. I'd never been so grateful for the cluttered construction site. I eased to my right and traded the phone in my hand for a large wrench sitting on the folding table.

Mitch continued taunting Chris while I slid back into place and hid the wrench behind my back. "Mitch, none of this makes any sense. You weren't even on my list of suspects. How is killing me or Chris going to take the suspicion off you?" I asked.

Mitch whipped toward me, his face contorted in anger. "I didn't even make your precious suspect list?" he taunted. "It didn't matter that you were fumbling around in the dark. Even a blind dog finds the water bowl some of the time."

Anger flared through me. I couldn't believe someone I'd been friendly with, even if we hadn't been particularly close, would talk to me like that. "That's just rude," I snapped at him.

Mitch straightened, as if taken aback by my words, before he bellowed out a laugh. "I just told you that I'm going to kill you, and you're upset that I compared you to a dog?"

"A blind dog," I pointed out, fully aware that he was right. It was stupid to worry about an insult, but I couldn't seem to stop myself. Maybe this was what shock was like. Could shock make someone ignore the real threat and focus on something they could control? Was that why people in horror movies always walked toward the creepy sound coming from the basement instead of getting out of the house?

"So, you're the one who threw the rocks and broke the windows at Camelot Flowers," I said, remembering my plan to give Finn time to show up and save the day. Mitch seemed to be in the mood to talk. I was happy to give him the opportunity. "And left the bag of screwdrivers on my front porch?"

Mitch had stopped halfway between Chris and me, too far away for the wrench hidden behind my back to do any good, but too close to make running an option anymore. He'd be on me before I could reach the door.

Shaking his head, Mitch said, "I thought you'd be smart enough to drop it with the threat at Camelot Flowers. If you had, we wouldn't be here tonight. You'd just been out to talk to Palmer at the rock yard. That place was one of Justin's many stupid mistakes. Who forgets to refill the gas tank?"

"And the screwdrivers on my front steps?" I asked while listening for the rumble of Finn's truck in the parking lot. Unfortunately, it was silent save for Mitch's oral report on all the reasons he deserved to kill me.

"I drove past your house the night before and saw the new

detective leaving your house." He glanced over his shoulder at Chris and added, "Did you know how cozy they were getting? Looks like you had your chance with her and blew it."

Chris flinched as if Mitch's statement had been one more physical blow to his body. Chris looked at me, his eyes pleading with me as he said, "Gwen, leave now before Mitch can hurt you. I'll be fine." We all knew that was a lie.

"Shut up," Mitch shouted, the sound echoing around the cavernous space. He took a step toward Chris, but I couldn't let Mitch do any more damage, not when Chris was tied up and helpless.

"Hey!" I yelled, drawing Mitch's attention back to me. "You said I was a blind dog bumbling around with no clue what I was doing. That doesn't explain any of this. You killed Justin, which still makes no sense to me, proving your point that I was never going to figure out it was you."

Mitch glared at me as he spit out, "You talked to Tom at the rock yard, you were constantly talking to the detective like he's your new best friend, and then Heidi Fischer told Derek you were harassing her at the mall. Derek mentioned it to me at the bowling alley last night after you pointed the detective in Derek's direction."

Mitch continued, "Fortunately for me, Tommy came to the bowling alley last night after his shift was done. He was still in his police officer uniform and everything. I got a few drinks into him, acted all concerned, and he spilled that the detective was pursuing a motive tied to drugs that had been found under Justin's bed. Drugs," Mitch sneered at me, "that it turns out you were the one to find. This isn't just about covering my tracks. This is about payback."

Mitch lunged at me, and I screamed, swinging the wrench at his head. His hands flew up, and he jerked to the side, but not quickly enough. The wrench connected with his shoulder. He roared in pain and yanked the wrench out of my hands, knocking me to the floor.

"No!" Chris shouted.

"You just made a big mistake," Mitch said through clenched teeth.

I scrambled backward. A long piece of scrap wood lay on the ground a few feet away. I reached for it, but Mitch was faster and kicked it out of the way. Flipping over onto my knees, I lurched to my feet.

I whipped around in time to see Mitch coming at me like a linebacker going in for a tackle. I tried to run, but my foot slipped, and he slammed into me. My back smashed into the wall, knocking the air from my lungs. Mitch leaned into me with his good arm, pinning me in place.

"Mitch, stop! Please!" Chris yelled.

I gasped, each breath too small, too shallow. My hands pushed against his body, but he was unmovable.

"Why?" I wheezed. "What did Justin ever do to you?"

Mitch cocked his head. "Justin didn't do anything to me. It wasn't personal. It was business."

"Business?" I started to feel lightheaded. I needed Mitch distracted. I needed space to breathe.

"I wasn't Justin's friend. I was his boss. You know Justin… He couldn't keep himself out of trouble. The mistakes started adding up until I couldn't ignore them anymore. Something needed to be done."

Chris frantically pulled at the tape holding his wrists to the chair.

I needed to buy Chris some time. Maybe he could get free. I turned my attention back to Mitch. "You were his boss? But Justin worked at the rock yard."

Mitch grabbed me by the shoulders, the grip with his left hand weaker than his right. The wrench hadn't stopped him, but it had injured him. "Justin worked for Palmer because I told him to," Mitch said.

Where was Finn? How much time had passed since I'd texted him? He had to know something was wrong by now.

Mitch continued, "If Justin wasn't such a screw-up, I wouldn't have been forced to deal with him. It was him or me. I have bosses too."

My phone rang from across the room, the cheery ringtone in stark contrast to the violent scene.

Finn!

Mitch glanced behind him in the direction of the sound. I wedged both hands between our bodies and shoved. But he didn't move, and it only made him angrier. He dug his fingers into my shoulders.

"What do you mean, it was him or you?" I asked, frantic to keep Mitch talking.

A cruel smile spread across his face. "It's none of your

business," he said quietly, "but since you're about to die, I don't mind telling you."

My mind raced, flicking through the self-defense classes I'd taken over the years. My brain wouldn't focus. Pain. Fear. Chris. Mitch.

Mitch continued, "Justin's one and only job was to move the drugs. Simple. Pick it up when he's supposed to. Drop it off when he's supposed to. Keep the job at Palmer's so we had access to the trucks." Mitch shook his head. "Idiot never refilled the tanks and got himself fired. Hiring him was my biggest mistake."

"Why drugs?" The idyllic picture I had of Star Junction and its hardworking, churchgoing residents was fading faster than a bouquet of roses without water.

Mitch sneered. "You live your sheltered existence, but you have no idea what's happening in the privacy of people's homes. Where there's a demand, I'm more than happy to fill it."

I sucked in a breath, which only caused Mitch to laugh. He wrapped his hand around my arm and pulled me toward Chris. "Time to end this. It's going to get light soon, and I need to be out of town before someone finds you."

I stumbled behind Mitch, trying to stay on my feet. In the struggle, we'd moved out of Chris's eyeline. Mitch whipped Chris's chair around so it was facing us.

"When Justin loaned the money that was meant for the next shipment to Crawford here…" Mitch shook his head in disgust. "The guy had no sense. I go out of town one weekend, leave the bank with him, and he takes half of it to help out his buddy. When I got back, he was all like 'He's going to pay it back with interest. I thought you'd be happy.' I wasn't happy. What do I say to the guy above me? We invested your money in a community center designed to keep kids off drugs?"

"But I paid Justin back," Chris interjected.

"Don't you get it?" Mitch snarled. "Loaning you that money put both Justin and me in danger. All his talk about how you were going to pay him back with interest, which was going to double the money. That wasn't our money to give out. That money was to pay our suppliers for the next shipment." Mitch stalked a tight circle around Chris. "If you hadn't had some kind of crisis of conscience and paid Justin back when you did, he and I would both be dead. I couldn't risk something like that happening again. Justin had to go."

"Just let Gwen leave," Chris begged.

Mitch hit Chris with enough force to make the chair lean precariously to the side before jarring back to the ground. Chris grunted, but pain flashed across Mitch's face too. His shoulder. This was my last hope. I needed him to face me. I needed access to that shoulder.

I took a deep breath and taunted a murderer. "Justin was right, you know. You're the idiot."

Mitch whipped around. "What did you say?" he growled.

"I said he was right. You're the one who's an idiot." I had no idea what I was saying. Justin and I had never talked about Mitch, but it seemed to be working.

Mitch closed the distance between us and grabbed my arm, our faces inches apart, his nose lined up with my forehead. "You little b—"

I closed my hand around Mitch's injured shoulder, jerked my head back, and swung my forehead into his face as hard as I could.

Mitch roared in pain, and his grip on my arm loosened. I slid out of his reach and searched the area for anything I could use to stop him. My gaze landed on a metal pipe lying on the counter next to the sink, and I scooped it up. It wasn't very big, but it was heavy. Mitch bent over, holding his face.

"This is for hurting Chris," I said as I swung the pipe at his temple.

He jerked his head up in time to see the pipe coming, but this time he couldn't avoid my attack. The pipe connected, and Mitch's eyes widened in shock before rolling back in his head as he crumbled to the ground.

The pipe dropped from my hands with a clang, the sound echoing through the large space. I stared at Mitch, the childhood friend who'd turned out to be an enemy.

"Gwen!" Chris's strangled cry broke through my shock. "Gwen, I thought I was going to lose you."

I rushed to his side and pulled at the tape holding his arm to the chair.

"How did he get you tied up like this?" I glanced over at Mitch, who lay unmoving on the floor. "Do you think I killed him?" I asked, my voice shaking.

"Who cares? He deserved it. Watching him hurt you?" Chris stopped, his voice thick with emotion. "When I thought I was going to lose you forever?" His statements hung in the air, too horrific to finish.

"How did he get you into this chair?" I repeated.

Chris rolled his neck. "I was working late. Since I haven't had anything else to do, I've been pouring myself into finishing the remodel. I was bent over picking up a box of nails when something hit me over the head. I woke up tied to this chair, Mitch sitting across from me."

I freed the last piece of tape holding Chris's wrist. He reached up and cupped my face. "I can't lose you," he said as his eyes welled with unshed tears.

"You won't," I promised. I glanced at Mitch to make sure he wasn't waking up.

"I'm serious Gwen. I can't lose you," Chris said again.

"You work on your other wrist. I'll work on getting your feet free," I said as I bent over and pulled at the tape around Chris's ankles. I freed his left leg before he'd finished on his wrist. I started on his other ankle. "We need to call 9-1-1. Mitch might wake up," I said nervously.

"I hope he does," Chris said with venom in his voice.

"No, you don't," I chided gently.

Chris was finally in the clear. The last thing I needed was him getting into trouble with the law for attacking Mitch out of some need to avenge me. I pulled the last piece of tape from his ankle. "That's not who you are," I added.

"It's who I am when someone threatens you," he said. He finally freed his hand. Before I could respond, he stood, wrapped both arms around me, and crushed me against his chest. He winced with the pain but didn't let go.

"I'm so glad you're safe," I said into his chest.

Chris eased back from the hug, his gaze filled with emotion I rarely saw in him. There was no teasing glint and no flirty but empty gleam. What I was seeing was something real, and it was directed right at me.

"Gwen, I—" Chris started, but the door banged open, drawing our attention to where Finn stood, illuminated by the light of the moon.

Finn's eyes widened as he took in the scene of Chris and me standing next to Mitch's prone body, all three of us illuminated by the set of construction lights Mitch had turned on when I arrived.

Marching across the room, Finn's gaze darted between the

chair Chris had been tied to, Mitch's unmoving form, and me. Flashing red and blue lights bounced around the room as two police cruisers pulled to a stop outside the door. Finn reached my side, and his gaze swept across me. "Are you hurt? What happened here?" he asked.

I pointed to Mitch. "There's your murderer," I said as I shuddered at the realization of how close I'd come to being just like Justin. "I'm okay, but someone should check out Chris. Mitch hit him over the head before tying him to that chair."

Finn unclipped a radio from his belt and said, "I need an ambulance at 504 Lincoln." He listened to the response, which sounded like a garbled mess to me but must have made sense to him.

"I'm fine. I don't need an ambulance," Chris said, rubbing his jaw where Mitch had punched him.

"Looks like *he* does," Finn said, jerking his head in Mitch's direction. Mitch still hadn't woken up. "Someone care to explain to me what happened here?"

Two officers in uniform, Jefferies and Tommy, walked into the building. Tommy took in the scene, his gaze landing on me. "How do you keep landing yourself in the middle of trouble?" he asked, looking bewildered at the scene.

"I don't know," I admitted as I gingerly reached behind me and touched the back of my head. The dull ache from Mitch pushing my head into the wall had skipped right past throbbing to pounding.

Jefferies, who had also been at the scene the night of Justin's murder, flicked the master switch, flooding the room with light.

Tommy let out a low whistle as he took in the scene.

The reality of what I'd just survived slammed into me. My breath caught, the panic threatening to overwhelm my senses. I needed to stay focused on the facts. I could have a meltdown later. Alone.

"Mitch tried to kill us." My voice wobbled, and I swiped at the tears running down my face. "He killed Justin," I added.

Both Finn and Chris moved to comfort me, but Chris was closer. He pulled me into a hug, his hand moving in soothing circles on my back as he said, "It's okay. We're safe now. It's over. It's all over."

Finn cleared his throat, and I stepped away from Chris as an ambulance pulled into the parking lot. "We're going to let the paramedics take a look at you both. Adrenaline can mask injuries. Then we'll need to take your statements," Finn said.

I pulled the sleeves of my sweatshirt down over my hands and twisted them into a tight knot. "What about Mitch?" I asked.

"You let us worry about Mitch." Finn's words held all the strength and comfort I needed at the moment. I didn't have to worry about Mitch anymore. I didn't have to worry about Justin's murder or Chris being accused of something he didn't do. It was finally over.

Two paramedics came striding through the door and surveyed the scene. They headed across the room. One of them stopped in front of me, while the other knelt by Mitch.

The paramedic scanned my body and then glanced over at Chris, assessing him as well. She was a few inches taller than me, and her black, curly hair was tied in a ponytail at her neck. "My name is Shana," she said. "We're going to get you checked out. Tell me about any injuries."

The paramedic kneeling next to Mitch checked his pulse. "His pulse is strong and steady," he said to Shana. "Do you know what happened to him?" The last question was directed to me.

"Yeah," I said wearily. "I hit him with a pipe."

The paramedic raised one eyebrow.

"And a wrench. And I headbutted his face. He tried to kill me," I added as an afterthought.

Shana's eyes widened, but she simply said, "Are you hurt anywhere?"

I reached for the back of my head. "He hit my head into the wall a few times. I'm okay, really. You should check Chris," I said.

Shana rummaged through her bag and came out with a disposable ice pack. She broke it and gave it a few shakes before handing it to me. She flashed a pen light over my face, tracking my pupils. "Your cognitive skills seem intact. Put this on your head," she instructed.

I put the ice pack against the back of my head, hissing as the cold plastic came into contact with the tender bruise already forming. Shana moved over to Chris as I walked to a folding chair across the room and collapsed into it.

Finn was at my side within seconds. He crouched down next to me, his hand tracing down my arm, his gaze filled with concern. "I should've been here sooner," he said, his voice holding a note of self-recrimination.

While the terrifying moments with Mitch had felt like an eternity, I had a feeling not much time had passed. I settled my hand over his. "Thank you for coming," I said.

Finn looked like he wanted to say something else but hesitated. He glanced at the scene across the room where the paramedic had rolled Mitch onto his back. Shana was dabbing at the raw spots on Chris's wrists from where he'd been restrained.

By the time Finn looked back at me, he'd shifted from Finn to Detective Butler. Back to business. He stood and pulled a chair over next to mine. The last time we'd sat like this in this room, there'd been a table between us. Now, we sat knee to knee as Finn pulled his phone from his pocket. "I don't have my tape recorder," he said. "This will have to do." He opened the voice recorder app and pressed the record button. "Tell me what happened."

I shifted the ice pack. "I got here in the middle of everything, but I'll tell you what I know." I spent the next few minutes running through everything Mitch had done since I walked through the door and everything he'd told me.

"He told you all of that?" Finn asked incredulously.

I shrugged. "He didn't think I'd live to tell anyone. He underestimated me. People do it all the time."

Like last weekend, Finn asked the same questions over and over. Unlike last weekend, I wasn't irritated by those questions. He remained professional during the questioning until I described Mitch slamming me into the wall. His expression thundered with anger, and he took my hand in his, as if needing a physical reminder that I was safe.

"We need to get pictures of your injuries," Finn said. He turned and caught Tommy's gaze. "Grab the kit from the cruiser," Finn instructed. Tommy nodded and headed outside. "I'm going to need to oversee evidence collection," Finn explained. "If you're cleared by the paramedics, I'm assuming you're going to want to go home. I'd like to come by and check on you when I'm done."

"I'd like that," I said.

Chris headed toward us as Finn stood. "Sit tight," Finn said. "I'll be back with the camera, and we'll get you out of here."

Chris stopped Finn as they crossed paths, grasping Finn's hand in what looked like a firm handshake. "Thanks for everything you did to find Justin's killer. I know this was a difficult case. I'm sure we'll see a lot of each other around town. I hope we can put this past week behind us," Chris said.

Finn looked just as surprised as I felt at Chris's statement. Finn clapped Chris on the shoulder and said, "I'm glad we discovered the truth. What you're building here will be an asset to the community. Anything I can do to help, you let me know."

"Thanks," Chris said. "I appreciate that."

Finn walked across the room to Tommy, and they began conferring about something. Chris watched them for a second before turning back to me. He looked uncertain. It was a new look on him.

"Before we got interrupted," Chris said, dropping his gaze to the floor for a moment before raising it to meet mine again. He cleared his throat and straightened his spine. "Go out with me. Soon." He laughed but it was nervous. "As soon as possible," he added.

My breath hitched. "Like on a date?" Before he could answer, I shook my head and said, "You're in shock. You don't know what you're saying." Was it possible all my dreams were coming true just hours after saying yes to a date with Finn? Was being with Chris still my dream? Should I feel happier? Less confused?

"Say yes," Chris urged. "One date. Let me show you this is real."

"Yes," I whispered. Whether this was the shock talking or not, I owed it to myself to see if what Chris was saying was true.

*   *   *

I trudged across the parking lot twenty minutes later. Chris was heading to the hospital with possible broken ribs. Mitch had woken up handcuffed to a gurney. He'd refused to say anything without an attorney present. I wasn't sure what good an attorney was going to do him after everything he'd done, not to mention everything he'd told Chris and me.

The sun hovered over the trees in the distance, tingeing the clouds soft shades of pink and gold. Finn had finally given me permission to leave after taking pictures of me from every conceivable angle. He'd given me a crushing hug, whispering he'd see me soon, before joining Jefferies and Tommy, the other officers, in evidence collecting.

My head hurt. My heart grieved at the way Mitch's decisions had hurt so many in our community. Justin's parents, Samantha, Chris, me. Maybe even Heidi. Not to mention all the people who'd walked through the past week scared that a murderer was loose in Star Junction. I wanted to go home, take a shower, and crawl into bed.

The sound of squealing tires shook me from my stupor. I yelped and jumped, dropping my car keys as Penny's car skidded to a stop.

"Gwen! Oh, my God!" Penny burst out of the car with the kind of energy only she could muster this early in the morning.

"Penny?" My fuzzy brain tried to make sense of her presence. "What are you doing here?" I asked.

"Chris called. Said you might need someone to be with you," Penny said, looking me over.

"Chris called you?" I asked. I glanced over my shoulder at the building before turning back to Penny. "When did he—?"

"We can talk all about it later. Let's get you home," Penny said as she bustled about and loaded me into her car. If I hadn't beaten her to it, she might have tried to buckle me in. "We'll get your car later," she explained when she saw me looking at my car parked a few spots away.

The sky shifted from pink to blue as Penny prattled on. We were at my house within minutes. I climbed out of the car while Penny grabbed a plastic grocery bag from the back. "Ice cream," she said to my questioning gaze. "And stuff to make breakfast. I wasn't sure what you'd want."

"What I want is to take a shower, get some sleep, and forget this whole thing ever happened," I said.

"We can definitely do those first two," Penny said, taking my keys from me and unlocking the front door. "I'm not so sure about that last one." Penny opened the door and ushered me inside. "What do you want? Ice cream? Breakfast?"

"Both?" I said.

"Both it is," Penny declared. "Go take that shower, and I'll get everything ready."

I trudged upstairs and stripped off my clothes, tossing them in the corner. Moments later, I stood under the hot water, letting it soothe my battered body and soul until it ran lukewarm.

Walking into my bedroom, wrapped in a towel, I sniffed the air as the smell of bacon wafted in from downstairs. Exhaustion pressed heavy on me, but my stomach rumbled at the thought of food. I dressed in pajamas, prepared to crash as soon as possible.

Penny stood in front of the stove, setting the cooked bacon on a plate lined with paper towels, turning when she heard me enter. "You look better," she said with a smile.

"I feel better," I admitted as I collapsed onto a chair at the table.

Penny bustled around setting the bacon as well as cut up fruit in front of me. "One more thing," she said as she moved back to the counter. She removed a plate of pancakes from the oven where she'd been keeping them warm.

"You didn't have to do all this," I insisted.

"Yes, I did," Penny said, sitting across from me. "Now, tell me what happened, because Chris was vague to say the least."

I piled food onto my plate, tempted to make an excuse. Everything that had happened at the center floated around me like a dark cloud. Finding Justin's killer had been the focus of my life for a week. Now that the case was solved, the victory felt hollow. "It started with a text from Chris early this morning," I finally said.

As much as I wanted to pull the covers over my head and pretend the showdown with Mitch hadn't happened, I couldn't do that to Penny. She'd been by my side through all of this. She deserved to know the story.

Despite my reservations, I found telling Penny about Mitch cathartic. She gasped at all the right spots. When I finally finished, we sat across from our untouched breakfast. "Mitch Alcomb," Penny whispered. "I never would've thought it."

I picked up a slice of bacon and took a bite. "Me neither. That's the thing I can't get over. If he'd just left it alone, if he'd laid low, I can't imagine this ever tracing back to him," I said.

Penny shook her head and said, "Maybe he was nervous other people would rat him out. I'm sure it wasn't just him and Justin doing the drug thing."

"Still…" I said as I cut off a piece of pancake. With that first bite of bacon, hunger roared through my body. "I guess it all boiled down to the drug thing. Not a vendetta from the past. Not a jealous ex. Drugs."

"I'm not naïve that people in town use drugs, but meth?" Penny said, sounding as shocked as I felt.

"I know," I said. "It makes my chest tight just thinking about it."

"What about Derek and Heidi?" Penny asked.

"It sounds like that was incidental. Mitch didn't mention it at least," I said as I cut another piece of the delicious pancakes. "These are amazing, by the way."

Penny beamed and said, "Thanks. It's my grandmother's recipe. There's a secret ingredient."

"Please, don't tell me it's love," I cracked.

"Nope, beer," Penny said.

I barked out a laugh, nearly choking on the water I'd been attempting to drink. "Beer?" I finally managed to sputter out.

"What can I say? Grandma was a wild woman and an amazing cook," Penny said with a sly grin.

"There's something else I haven't told you," I said, setting my fork down. As my stomach filled, a pleasant sleepiness washed over me. I wasn't going to make it much longer.

"Is it worse than meth?" Penny said, looking wary.

I laughed lightly and said, "Better." I thought about both Chris and Finn, my smile slipping. "At least I hope so."

Penny leaned forward and rested her elbows on the table. "Now I'm intrigued," she said.

"Last night, after bowling…" I started before trailing off.

"Yes?" Penny said as she made as gesture as if hurrying me along.

"Finn asked me out on a date," I said in a rush of words.

Penny remained silent for a moment, looking stunned, before her eyes gleamed with delight. "I knew it. I knew it was only a matter of time," she declared with glee.

"That's not all," I added.

"That's not all?" she practically shrieked.

"Chris asked me out on a date too," I said.

If Penny had looked stunned before, it was nothing compared to now. "Chris… What do you mean a date?" she asked.

I grinned widely, allowing myself to enjoy the moment, a bright spot in so much recent darkness. "He insists it's a real date," I said.

"What did you say?" she asked.

"I said yes." The clock ticked on the wall. Somewhere outside, someone had started up a snowblower. Still Penny was silent. "Say something," I finally said.

"Let me get this straight," Penny said. If Penny leaned forward any more, she'd be practically in my lap. "You agreed to dates with both Finn and Chris."

My cheeks warmed as I thought of both men, one I'd known most of my life and one I'd just started to get to know. They couldn't be more different, but in ways that made each one appealing. "You're the one who said I needed to get out there and date," I said.

I could tell Penny was warming to the idea as her smile grew more enthusiastic by the second. "Is there no end to my talent? Teacher by day, private investigator and psychic by night. Now a matchmaker?" she said with delight.

I stood and collected our empty plates, depositing them in the sink. "I don't think you can claim credit for these dates," I teased.

"I'm sorry," Penny said. "Did you say something? I was too busy planning what you're going to wear on these *two* dates."

I turned and leaned back against the counter. A flutter of anticipation moved through my stomach. "What did I get myself into?" I asked, not even bothering to dim the wide smile on my face.

Penny's grin matched my own as she said, "Sounds like you got yourself into the potential for a whole lotta fun."

ABOUT THE AUTHOR

Erica Wynters may have lived most of her life in the frigid Midwest, but now she spends her time in the warmth and sunshine of Arizona. She loves hiking, hunting down waterfalls in the desert, reading (of course), and napping. Can napping be considered a hobby? When not weaving tales of mystery with plenty of quirky characters, laughs, and a dash of romance, Erica works as a Marriage and Family Therapist helping others find their Happily Ever Afters.

To learn more about Erica, visit her online at:
www.ericawynters.com

Made in United States
North Haven, CT
19 February 2024

48941336R00143